Frederic Henry Hedge

Martin Luther

And Other Essays

Frederic Henry Hedge

Martin Luther
And Other Essays

ISBN/EAN: 9783337127008

Printed in Europe, USA, Canada, Australia, Japan

Cover: Foto ©Raphael Reischuk / pixelio.de

More available books at **www.hansebooks.com**

MARTIN LUTHER

AND OTHER ESSAYS.

BY

F. H. HEDGE,

AUTHOR OF REASON IN RELIGION, PRIMEVAL WORLD OF HEBREW TRADITION, WAYS OF THE SPIRIT, ATHEISM IN PHILOSOPHY, HOURS WITH GERMAN CLASSICS, ETC.

BOSTON:

ROBERTS BROTHERS.

1888.

University Press:

JOHN WILSON AND SON, CAMBRIDGE.

CONTENTS.

ESSAYS.

MARTIN LUTHER.

[*From the Atlantic Monthly of December, 1883.*]

THE power which presides over human destiny and shapes the processes of history is wont to conceal its ulterior purpose from the agents it employs, who, while pursuing their special aims and fulfilling their appointed tasks, are, unknown to themselves, initiating a new era, founding a new world.

Such significance attaches to the name of Luther, one of that select band of providential men who stand conspicuous among their contemporaries as makers of history. For the Protestant Reformation which he inaugurated is very imperfectly apprehended if construed solely as a schism in the Church, a new departure in religion. In a larger view, it was our modern world, with its social developments, its liberties, its science, its new conditions of being, evolving itself from the old.

1

It would be claiming too much to assume that all of good which distinguishes these latter centuries from mediæval time is wholly due to that one event, that humanity would have made no progress in science and the arts of life but for Luther and his work. Other contemporary agencies, independent of the rupture with Rome,—the printing-press, the revival of letters, the discovery of a new continent, and other geographical and astronomical findings,—have had their share in the regeneration of secular life.

But this we may safely assert: that the dearest goods of our estate — civil independence, spiritual emancipation, individual scope, the large room, the unbound thought, the free pen, whatever is most characteristic of this New England of our inheritance — we owe to the Saxon reformer.

A compatriot of Luther, the critic-poet Lessing, has made us familiar with the idea of an Education of the Human Race. Vico had previously affirmed a law of historic development, and inferred from that law a progressive improvement of man's estate. Lessing supplemented the New Science of Vico with a more distinct recognition of divine agency and an educating purpose in the method of history. But Lessing confined his view of divine education to the truths of religion. For these the school is the Church. But religion is only one side of human nature. Man as a denizen of this earthly world has secular interests and a secular calling which may, in some future synthesis, be found to be the necessary complement of the spiritual, the other pole of the same social whole, but meanwhile require for their right development and full satisfaction another school, co-ordinate with but independent of the Church. That school is the nation.

Now, the nation, in the ages following the decline of Rome, had had no proper status in Christian history. There were peoples — Italian, French, English, German — distributed in territorial groups, but no nation, no polity conterminous with the territorial limits of each country, compacted and confined by those limits, having its own independent sovereign head. France, Germany, England, were mere geographical expressions. The peoples inhabiting these countries had a common head in the Bishop of Rome, whose power might be checked by the rival German Empire when the Emperor was a man of force, a veritable ruler of men, and the papal incumbent an imbecile, but who, on the whole, was acknowledged supreme. Europe was ecclesiastically one ; and the ecclesiastical overruled, absorbed, the civil.

But already, before the birth of Luther, from the dawn of the fourteenth century, the civil power had begun to disengage itself from the spiritual. The peoples here and there had consolidated into nations. Philip of France had defied the Pope of his day and hurled him from his throne. The Golden Bull had made the German Empire independent of papal dictation in the choice of its incumbents. Meanwhile the Babylonish Captivity and subsequent dyarchy in the pontificate had sapped the prestige of the Roman See. As we enter the fifteenth century we find the principle of nationality formally recognized by the Church. At the Council of Constance the assembly decided to vote by nations instead of dioceses, each nation having a distinct voice. Then it appeared that the nation had become a reality and a power in Christendom.

Another century was needed to break the chain which bound in ecclesiastical dependence on Rome the nations especially charged with the conduct of mankind. And a man was needed who had known from personal experience the stress of that chain, and whose moral convictions were too exigent to allow of compliance and complicity with manifest falsehood and deadly wrong. To ecclesiastical severance succeeded political. To Martin Luther, above all men, we Anglo-Americans are indebted for national independence and mental freedom.

It is from this point of view, and not as a teacher

of religious truth, that he claims our interest. As a theologian, as a thinker, he has taught us little. Men of inferior note have contributed vastly more to theological enlightenment and the science of religion. Intellectually narrow, theologically bound and seeking to bind, his work was larger than his vision and better than his aim. The value of his thought is inconsiderable; the value of his deed as a providential liberator of thought is beyond computation.

The world has no prevision of its heroes. Nature gives no warning when a great man is born. Had any soothsayer undertaken to point out, among the children cast upon the world in electoral Saxony on the 10th of November, 1483, the one who would shake Christendom to its centre, this peasant babe, just arrived in the cottage of Hans Luther at Eisleben, might have been the last on whom his prophecy would have fallen. The great man is unpredictable; but reflection finds in the birth of Luther a peculiar fitness of place and time. Fitness of place, inasmuch as Frederick the Wise, Elector of Saxony, his native prince and patron, was probably the only one among the potentates of that day who, from sympathy and force of character, possessed the will and the ability to shield the reformer from prelatical wiles and the wrath of Rome. Fitness of time — a generation had scarcely gone by since the newly invented printing-press had issued its first Bible; and during the very year of this nativity, in 1483, Christopher Columbus was making his first appeals for royal aid in realizing his dream of a western hemisphere hidden from European ken behind the waves of the Atlantic, where the Protestant principle, born of Luther, was destined to find its most congenial soil and to yield its consummate fruit.

More important than fitness of time and place is the adaptation of the man to his appointed work. There is an easy, levelling theory, held by some, that men are the product of their time, great actors the necessary product of extraordinary circumstances; that Cæsar and Mohammed and Napoleon, had they not lived precisely when they did, would have plodded through life and slipped into their graves without a record; and that, on the other hand, quite ordinary men, if thrown upon the times in which those heroes lived, would have done as they did and accomplished the same results,— would have overthrown the Roman aristocracy, abolished idolatry, and brought order out of chaotic revolution.

But man and history are not, I think, to be construed so. There is a law which adapts the man to his time. The work to be done is not laid upon a chance individual, the availing of the crisis is not left to one who happens to be on the spot; but from the foundation of the world the man was selected to stand just there, and to do just that. The opportunity does not make the man, but finds him. He is the providential man; all the past is in him, all the future is to flow from him.

What native qualifications did Luther bring to his work? First of all, his sturdy Saxon nature. The Saxons are Germans of the Germans, and Luther was a Saxon of the Saxons, — reverent, patient, laborious, with quite an exceptional power of work and capacity of endurance; simple, humble; no visionary, no dreamer of dreams, but cautious, conservative, incorruptibly honest, true to the heart's core; above all, courageous, firm, easily led when conscience seconded the leading, impossible to drive when conscience opposed, ecstatically devout, tender, loving: a strange compound of feminine softness and adamantine inflexibility. Contemporary observers noticed in the eyes of the man, dark, flashing, an expression which they termed "dæmonic." It is the expression of one susceptible of supernatural impulsion, — of being seized and borne on by a power which exceeds his conscious volition.

In this connection I have to speak of one property in Luther which especially distinguishes spiritual heroes, — the gift of faith. The ages which preceded his coming have been called "the ages of faith." The term is a misnomer if understood in any other sense than that of blind acquiescence in external authority, unquestioning submission to the dictum of the Church. This is not faith, but the want of it, mental inaction, absence of independent vision. Faith is essentially active, a positive, aggressive force; not a granter of current propositions, but a maker of propositions, of dispensations, of new ages.

Faith is not a constitutional endowment; there is no lot or tumulus assigned to it among the hillocks of the brain. It is not a talent connate with him who has it, and growing with his growth, but a gift of the Spirit, communicated to such as are charged with a providential mission to their fellow-men. It is the seal of their indenture, the test of their calling. In other words, faith is inspiration; it is the subjective side of that incalculable force of which inspiration is the objective. So much faith, so much inspiration, so much of Deity.

Inspiration is in no man a constant quantity. In Luther it appears unequal, intermittent; ebb and flood, but always, in the supreme crises of his history, answering to his need; a master force, an ecstasy of vision and of daring; lifting him clean out of himself, or rather eliciting, bringing to the surface, and forcing into action the deeper, latent

self of the man, against all the monitions not only
of prudence, but of conscience as well.   The voice
of worldly prudence is soon silenced by earnest
souls intent on noble enterprises of uncertain issue.
What reformer of traditional wrongs has not been
met by the warning, "That way danger lies"?
But in Luther we have the rarer phenomenon of
conscience itself overcome by faith.   We have the
amazing spectacle of a righteous man defying his
own conscience in obedience to a higher duty than
conscience knew.   For conscience is the pupil of
custom, the slave of tradition, bound by prescrip-
tion; the safeguard of the weak, but, it may be, an
offence to the strong; wanting initiative; unable
of itself to lift itself to new perceptions and new
requirements, whereby "enterprises of great pith
and moment" "their currents turn awry, and lose
the name of action."   Conscience has to be new-
born when a new dispensation is given to the
world.   It was only thus that Christianity through
Paul could disengage itself from Judaism, which
had the old conscience on its side.

In Luther faith was stronger than conscience.
Had it not been so, we should not be called to
celebrate his name.   Of all his trials in those
years of conflict which issued in final separation
from Rome, the struggle with conscience was the
sorest.   However strong his personal conviction

that indulgences bought with money could not save from the penalties of sin, that the sale of them was a grievous wrong; to declare that conviction, to act upon it, was to pit himself against the head of the Church, to whom he owed unconditional allegiance. It was revolt against legitimate authority, a violation of his priestly vows. So conscience pleaded. But Luther's better moments set aside these scruples, regarding them, as he did all that contradicted his strong intent, as suggestions of the devil. "How," whispered Satan, "if your doctrine be erroneous, — if all this confusion has been stirred up without just cause? How dare you preach what no one has ventured for so many centuries?"

Over all these intrusive voices admonishing, "You must not," a voice more imperative called to him, "You must;" and a valor above all martial daring responded, "I will." Here is where a higher power comes in to reinforce the human. When valor in a righteous cause rises to that pitch, it draws Heaven to its side, it engages Omnipotence to back it.

Our knowledge of Luther's history is derived in great part from his own reminiscences and confessions.

His boyhood was deeply shadowed by the sternness of domestic discipline. Severely and even cruelly chastised by conscientious but misjudging parents, more careful to inspire fear than to cherish filial love, he contracted a shyness and timidity which kept back for years the free development of a noble nature. At school it was still worse; the business of education was then conceived as a species of rhabdomancy, — a divining by means of the rod the hidden treasures of the boyish mind. He cannot forget, in after years, that fifteen times in one day the rod in his case was so applied. "The teachers in those days," he says, " were tyrants and executioners; the school, a prison and a hell."

At a more advanced school in Eisenach, where the sons of the poor supported themselves by singing before the doors of wealthy citizens, who responded with the fragments of their abundance, a noble lady, Dame Ursula Cotta, impressed by the fervor and vocal skill of the lad, gave him a daily seat at her table, and with it his first introduction to polite society, — a privilege which went far to compensate the adverse influences of his earlier years.

At the age of eighteen he entered the University of Erfurt, then the foremost seminary in Germany, the resort of students from all parts of the land. The improved finances of his father sufficed to defray the cost of board and books. He elected for himself the department of philosophy, then embracing, together with logic, metaphysic, and rhetoric, the study of the classics, which the recent revival of letters had brought into vogue. The Latin classics became his familiar friends, and are not unfrequently quoted in his writings. He made good use of the golden years, and received in due order, with high distinction, the degrees of bachelor and of master of arts.

With all this rich culture and the new ideas with which it flooded his mind, it does not appear that any doubt had been awakened in him of the truth of the old religion. He was still a devout Catholic; he still prayed to the saints as the proper helpers in time of need. When accidentally wounded by the sword which, according to student fashion, he wore at his side, lying, as he thought, at the point of death, he invoked, not God, but the Virgin, for aid. "Mary, help!" was his cry.

He was destined by his father for the legal profession. It was the readiest road to wealth and power. Accordingly, he applied himself with all diligence to the study of law, and had fitted himself for the exercise of that calling; when suddenly, in a company of friends assembled for social entertainment, he announced his intention to quit the world and embrace the monastic life. They expressed their astonishment at this decision, and endeavored to dissuade him from such a course. In vain they urged him to reconsider his purpose. "Farewell!" he said; "we part to meet no more."

What was it that caused this change in Luther's plan of life? To account for a turn apparently so abrupt, it must be remembered that his religion hitherto, the fruit of his early training, had been a religion of fear. He had been taught to believe in an angry God, and the innate, deep corruption of human nature. He was conscious of no crime; no youthful indiscretions, even, could he charge himself with: but morbid self-scrutiny presented him utterly sinful and corrupt. Only a life of good works could atone for that corruption. Such a life the monastic, with its renunciations, its prayers and fastings and self-torture, was then believed to be, — a life well-pleasing in the sight of God, the surest way of escape from final perdition. Exceptional virtue tended in that direction. To be a monk was to flee from wrath and attain to holiness and heaven.

All this had lain dimly, half-consciously, in Luther's mind, not ripened into purpose. The purpose was precipitated by a searching experience. Walking one day in the neighborhood of Erfurt, he was overtaken by a terrific thunder-storm. The lightning struck the ground at his feet. Falling on his knees, he invoked, in his terror, the intercession of Saint Anna, and vowed, if life were spared, to become a monk. Restored to his senses, he regretted the rash vow. His riper reason in after years convinced him that a vow ejaculated in a moment of terror imposed no moral obligation; but his uninstructed conscience could not then but regard it as binding. In spite of the just and angry remonstrances of his father, who saw with dismay his cherished plan defeated, the hard-earned money spent on his boy's education expended in vain, he sought and gained admission to the brotherhood and cloisters of St. Augustine at Erfurt.

His novitiate was burdened with cruel trials. The hardest and most repulsive offices were laid upon the new-comer, whose superiors delighted to mortify the master of arts with disgusting tasks. To the stern routine of cloister discipline he added self-imposed severities, more frequent fastings and watchings, undermining his health, endangering life. Harder to bear than all these were his inward conflicts, — fears and fightings, agonizing self-accusations, doubts of salvation, apprehensions of irrevocable doom. He sought to conquer heaven by mortification of the flesh, and despaired of the result. Finally, encouraged by Staupitz, the vicar-general of the Order, and guided by his own study of the new-found Scriptures, he came to perceive that heaven is not to be won in that way. Following the lead of Saint Paul and Augustine, he reached the conclusion which formed thenceforth the staple of his theology and the point of departure in his controversy with Rome, — the sufficiency of divine grace, and justification by faith.

In the second year of his monastic life he was ordained priest, and in the year following promoted to the chair of theology in the new University of Wittenberg, where he soon became famous as a preacher.

In 1511 he was sent on a mission to Rome, in company with a brother monk. When he came within sight of the city he fell upon his knees and saluted it: " Hail, holy Rome, thrice consecrated by the blood of the martyrs ! " Arrived within the walls, the honest German was inexpressibly shocked by what he found in the capital of Christendom, — open infidelity, audacious falsehood, mockery of sacred things, rampant licentiousness, abominations incredible. The Rome of Julius II. was the *Roma rediviva* of Caligula and Nero, — pagan in spirit, pagan in morals, a sink of iniquity. It was well that Luther had personal experience of all this ; the remembrance of it served to lighten the struggle with conscience when called to contend against papal authority. But then such contest never entered his mind ; he was still a loyal son of the Church. He might mourn her corruption, but would not question her infallibility. Like other pilgrims zealous of good works, he climbed on his knees the twenty-eight steps of the Santa Scala. While engaged in that penance there flashed on his mind, like a revelation from Heaven, declaring the futility of such observances, the saying of the prophet, " The just shall live by his faith."

Returned to Wittenberg, he was urged by Staupitz to study for the last and highest academic honor, that of doctor of philosophy. The already over-tasked preacher shrank from this new labor. " Herr Staupitz," he said, " it will be the death of me." " All right," answered Staupitz. " Our Lord carries on extensive operations ; he has need of clever men above. If you die you will be one of his councillors in heaven."

I now come to the turning-point in Luther's life, — the controversy with Rome on the subject of in-dulgences, which ended in the schism known as the Protestant Reformation.

Leo X., in the year 1516, ostensibly in the in-terest of a new church of St. Peter in Rome, sent forth a Bull according absolution from the penalties of sin to all who should purchase the indulgences offered for sale by his commissioners. Indulgence, according to the theory of the Church, was dispensation from the penance otherwise re-quired for priestly absolution. It was not pretended that priestly absolution secured divine forgiveness and eternal salvation. It was absolution from temporal penalties due to the Church; but popular superstition identified the one with the other. Moreover, it was held that the supererogatory merits of Christ and the saints were available for the use of sinners. They constituted a treasury confided to the Church, whose saving virtue the head of the Church could dispense at discretion. In this case the application of that fund was measured by pecuniary equivalents. Christ had said, " How hardly shall they that have riches enter the kingdom of heaven." Leo said in effect, " How easily may they that have riches enter the kingdom of heaven," since they have the *quid pro quo.* For the poor it was not so easy; and this was one aspect of the case which stimulated the opposition of Luther. Penitence was nominally required of the sinner; but proofs of penitence were not exacted. Practically, the indulgence meant impunity for sin. A more complete travesty of the Gospel — laughable, if not so impious — could hardly be conceived. The faithful themselves were shocked by the shameless realism which characterized the proclamations of the German commissioner, Tetzel.

Luther wrote a respectful letter to the Archbishop of Mainz, praying him to put a stop to the scandal, — little dreaming that the prelate had a pecuniary interest in the business, having bargained for half the profits of the sale as the price of his sanction of the same. Other dignitaries to whom he appealed refused to interfere. As a last resource, by way of appeal to the Christian conscience, on the 31st of October, 1517, he nailed his famous ninety-five theses to the door of the church of All Saints. These were not dogmatic assertions, but propositions to be debated by any so inclined. Nevertheless, the practical interpretation put upon them was the author's repudiation of indulgences, and, by implication, his arraignment of the source from which they emanated.

It is doubtful if Luther apprehended the full significance of the step he had taken. He did not then dream of secession from the Church. He was more astonished than gratified when he learned that his theses and other utterances of like import had, within the space of fourteen days, pervaded Germany, and that he had become the eye-mark of Christendom. More than once before the final irrevocable act he seems to have regretted his initiative; and though he would not retract, he would fain have sunk out of sight.

But fortunately for the cause, Tetzel, baffled in his designs on Luther's congregation, attacked him with such abusive virulence and extravagant assertions of papal authority that Luther was provoked to rejoin with more decisive declarations. The controversy reached the ear of the Pope, who inclined at first to regard it as a local quarrel which would soon subside, but was finally persuaded to despatch a summons requiring Luther to appear in Rome within sixty days to be tried for heresy. Rome might summon, but Luther knew too well the probable result of such a trial to think of obeying the summons. The spiritual power might issue its mandates, but the temporal power was needed to execute its behests. Would the temporal, in this case, co-operate with the spiritual? There had been a time when no German potentate would have hesitated to surrender a heretic. But Germany was getting tired of Roman dictation and ultramontane insolence. The German princes were getting impatient of the constant drain on their exchequer by a foreign power. Irrespective of the right or wrong of his position theologically considered, the question of Luther's extradition was one of submission to authority long felt to be oppressive. Only personal enemies, like Eck and Emser and Tetzel, would have him sent to Rome. Miltitz, who had been deputed to deal with him, confessed that an army of twenty-five thousand men would not be sufficient to take him across the Alps, so widespread and so powerfully embodied was the feeling in his favor. The Ritter class, comprising men like Franz von Sickingen and Ulrich von Hutten, were on his side; so were the Humanists,—apostles of the new culture, which opposed itself to the old mediæval Scholasticism. The Emperor Maximilian would have the case tried on German soil. Conspicuous above all, his chief defender, was Luther's own sovereign, the Elector of Saxony, Frederick the Wise. Humanly speaking, but for him the Reformation would have been crushed at the start, and its author with it. Frederick was not at this time a convert to Luther's doctrine, but insisted that his subject should not be condemned until tried by competent judges and refuted on scriptural grounds. He occupied the foremost place among the princes of Germany. On the death of Maximilian, 1519, he was regent of the Empire, and had the chief voice in the election of the new Emperor. Without his consent and co-operation it was impossible for Luther's enemies to get possession of his person. For this purpose Leo X., then Pope, wrote a flattering letter, accompanied by the coveted gift of the " golden rose," — supreme token of pontifical good-will. " This rose," wrote Leo, " steeped in a holy chrism, sprinkled with sweet-smelling musk, consecrated by apostolic blessing, symbol of a sublime mystery,— may its heavenly odor penetrate the heart of our beloved son and dispose him to comply with our request."

The request was not complied with, but by way of alternative it was proposed that Luther should be tried by a papal commissioner in Germany. So Leo despatched for that purpose the Cardinal de Vio, of Gaeta, his plenipotentiary, commonly known as Cajetan. A conference was held at Augsburg, which, owing to the legate's passionate insistence on unconditional retractation, served but to widen the breach. The efforts of Miltitz, another appointed mediator, met with no better success.

Meanwhile Luther had advanced with rapid and enormous strides in the line of divergence from the Catholic Church. The study of the Scriptures had convinced him that the primacy of the Roman bishop had no legitimate foundation. The work of Laurentius Valla, exposing the fiction of Constantine's pretended donation of temporal sovereignty in Rome, had opened his eyes to other falsehoods. He proclaimed his conclusions, writing and publishing, in Latin and German, with incredible diligence. His " Address to the Christian Nobility of the German Nation concerning the Melioration of the Christian State," the most important of his publications, anticipates nearly all the points of the Protestant reform, and many which were not accomplished in Luther's day. The writing spread and sped through every province of Germany, as if borne on the wings of the wind. An edition of four thousand copies was exhausted in a few days. It was the Magna Charta of a new ecclesiastical State.

But now the thunderbolt was launched which, his adversaries trusted, should smite the heretic to death and scatter all his following. On the 16th of June, 1520, Leo issued a Bull condemning Luther's writings, commanding that they be publicly burned wherever found, and that their author, unless within the space of sixty days he recanted his errors, allowing sixty more for the tidings of his recantation to reach Rome, should be seized and delivered up for the punishment due to a refractory heretic. All magistrates and all citizens were required, on pain of ecclesiastical penalty, to aid in arresting him and his followers and sending them to Rome. The papal legates, Aleander and Caraccioli, were appointed bearers of a missive from the Pope to Duke Frederick, commanding him to have the writings of Luther burned, and either to execute judgment on the heretic himself, or else to deliver him up to the papal tribunal. The Elector replied that he had no part in Luther's movement, but that his writings must be refuted before he would order their burning; that their author had been condemned unheard; that his case must be tried by impartial judges in some place where it should be safe for him to appear in person.

Miltitz persuaded Luther, as a last resource, to write to the Pope a conciliatory letter, disavowing all personal hostility and expressing due reverence for his Holiness. He did write. But such a letter! An audacious satire, which, under cover of personal respect and good-will, compassionates the Pope as "a sheep among wolves," and characterizes the papal court as "viler than Sodom or Gomorrah."

When the Bull reached Wittenberg it was treated by Luther and his friends with all the respect which it seemed to them to deserve. On the 10th of December, 1520, a large concourse of students and citizens assembled in the open space before the Elster gate; a pile was erected and fired by a resident graduate of the university; and on it Luther, with his own hands, solemnly burned the Bull and the papal decretals, amid applause which, like the "embattled farmers'" shot at Concord in 1775, was "heard round the world."

So the last tie was severed which bound Luther to Rome. After that contumacious act there was no retreat or possibility of pacification.

But though Luther had done with Rome, Rome had not yet done with him. When Leo found that he could not wrest the heretic from the guardianship of Frederick, he had recourse to imperial aid. The newly elected Emperor, Charles V., a youth of twenty-one, in whose blood were blended three royal lines of devoted friends of the Church, might be expected to render prompt obedience to its head. But Charles was unwilling to break with Frederick, to whom he was chiefly indebted for his election. He would not, if he could, compel him to send Luther a prisoner to Rome. He chose to have him tried in his own court, and only when proved by such trial an irreclaimable heretic to surrender him as such.

An imperial Diet was about to be held at the city of Worms. Thither Charles desired the Elector to bring the refractory monk. Frederick declined the office; but Luther declared that if the Emperor summoned him he would obey the summons as the call of God. To his friend Spalatin, who advised his refusal, he wrote that he would go to Worms if there were as many devils opposed to him as there were tiles on the roofs of the houses.

The summons came, accompanied by an imperial safe-conduct covering the journey to and from the place of trial. Luther complied; he had no fear that Charles would repeat the treachery of Sigismund, which had blasted that name with eternal infamy and incarnadined Bohemia with atoning blood. The journey was one triumphal progress; in every city ovations, not unmingled with cautions and regrets. He arrived in the morning of the 16th of April, 1521. The warder on the tower announced with the blast of a trumpet his approach. The citizens left their breakfasts to witness the entry. Preceded by the imperial herald and followed by a long cavalcade, the stranger was escorted to the quarters assigned him. Alighting from his carriage, he looked round upon the multitude and said, "God will be with me." It was then that Aleander, the papal legate, remarked the dæmonic glance of his eye. People of all classes visited him in his lodgings.

On the following day he was called to the episcopal palace, and made his first appearance before the Diet. A pile of books was placed before him. "Are these your writings?" The titles were called for, and Luther acknowledged them to be his. Would he retract the opinions expressed in them, or did he still maintain them? He begged time for consideration; it was a question of faith, of the welfare of souls, of the word of God. A day for deliberation was allowed him, and he was remanded to his lodgings. On the way the people shouted applause, and a voice exclaimed, "Blessed is the womb that bare thee!" But the impression made on the court was not favorable. He had not shown the front that was expected of him. He had seemed timid, irresolute. The Emperor remarked, "That man would never make a heretic of me."

His self-communings in the interim, and his

prayer, which has come down to us, show how deeply he felt the import of the crisis; how "the fire burned," as he mused of its probable issue, knowing that the time was at hand when he might be called to seal his testimony with his blood.

"Ah, God, thou my God! stand by me against the reason and the wisdom of all the world! Thou must do it; it is not my cause, but thine. For my own person I have nothing to do with these great lords of the earth. Gladly would I have quiet days and be unperplexed. But thine is the cause; it is just and eternal. Stand by me, thou eternal God! I confide in no man. Hast thou not chosen me for this purpose, I ask thee? But I know of a surety that thou hast chosen me."

On the 18th he was summoned for the second time, and the question of the previous day was renewed. He explained at length, first in Latin, then in German, that his writings were of various import: those which treated of moral topics the papists themselves would not condemn; those which disputed papal authority, and those addressed to private individuals, although the language might be more violent than was seemly, he could not in conscience revoke. Unless he were refuted from the Scriptures, he must abide by his opinions. He was told that the court was not there to discuss his opinions; they had been already condemned by the

Council of Constance. Finally, the question narrowed itself to this: Did he believe that Councils could err? More specifically, Did he believe the Council of Constance had erred? Luther appreciated the import of the question. He knew that his answer would alienate some who had thus far befriended him; for however they might doubt the infallibility of the Pope, they all believed Councils to be infallible. But he did not hesitate. "I do so believe." The fatal word was spoken. The Emperor said: "It is enough; the hearing is concluded."

The shades of evening had gathered over the assembly. To the friends of Luther they might seem to forebode the impending close of his earthly day. Then suddenly he uttered with a loud voice, in his native idiom, those words which Germany will remember while the city of Worms has one stone left upon another, or the river that laves her shall find its way to the German Ocean: "Hier steh' ich, ich kann nicht anders; Gott hilf mir! Amen!"

By the light of blazing torches the culprit was conducted from the council-chamber, the Spanish courtiers hissing as he went, while among the Germans many a heart no doubt beat high in response to that brave ultimatum of their fellow-countryman.

With the consent of the Emperor, further negotiations were attempted in private, and Luther found it far more difficult to resist the kindly solicitations of friends and peacemakers than to brave the threats of his enemies. But he did resist; the trial was ended. The great ones of the earth had assailed a poor monk, now with menace, now with entreaty, and found him inflexible.

> " The tide of pomp
> That beats upon the high shore of this world "

had broken powerless against the stern resolve of a single breast.

The curtain falls; when next it rises we are in the Wartburg, the ancestral castle of the counts of Thüringen, where Saint Elizabeth, the fairest figure in the Roman calendar, dispensed the benefactions and bore the heavy burden of her tragic life. The Emperor, true to his promise, had arranged for the safe return of Luther to Wittenberg; declaring, however, that, once returned, he should deal with him as a heretic. At the instigation, perhaps, of Frederick, the protecting escort was assailed on the way, and put to flight by an armed troop. Luther was taken captive and borne in secret to the Wartburg, where, disguised as a knight, he might elude the pursuit of his enemies. While there he occupied himself with writing, and among other labors prepared his best and priceless gift to his country,

— his translation of the New Testament, afterward supplemented by his version of the Old.

A word here respecting the merits of Luther as a writer. His compatriots have claimed for him the inestimable service of founder of the German language. He gave by his writings to the New High German, then competing with other dialects, a currency which has made it ever since, with slight changes, the language of German literature, —the language in which Kant reasoned and Goethe sang. His style is not elegant, but charged with a rugged force, a robust simplicity, which makes for itself a straight path to the soul of the reader. His words were said to be "half battles;" call them rather whole victories, for they conquered Germany. The first condition of national unity is unity of speech. In this sense Luther did more for the unification of Germany than any of her sons, from Henry the Fowler to Bismarck. "We conceded," says Gervinus, "to no metropolis, to no learned society, the honor of fixing our language, but to the man who better than any other could hit the hearty, healthy tone of the people. No dictionary of an academy was to be the canon of our tongue, but that book by which modern humanity is schooled and formed, and which in Germany, through Luther, has become, as nowhere else, a people's book."

Returning to Wittenberg when change of circumstance permitted him to do so with safety, he applied himself with boundless energy to the work of constructing a new, reformed church to replace the old; preaching daily in one or another city, writing and publishing incessantly, instituting public schools, arranging a new service in German as substitute for the Latin Mass, compiling a catechism (a model in its kind), a hymnal, and other appurtenances of worship. And, like the Israelites on their return from Babylon, while building the new temple with one hand, he fought with the other, contending against Münzer, Carlstadt, the Mystics, the Iconoclasts, the Anabaptists; often, it must be confessed, with unreasonable, intolerant wrath, spurning all that would not square with his theology, — as when he rejected the fellowship of the Swiss, who denied the Real Presence in the Eucharist. When the fury of the Peasants' War was desolating Germany, he wielded a martial pen against both parties, — arraigning the nobles for their cruel oppressions, reproving the peasants for attempting to overcome evil with greater evil.

His reform embraced, along with other departures from the old *régime,* the abolition of enforced celibacy of the priesthood. He believed the family life to be the true life for cleric as well as lay. He advised the reformed clergy to take to themselves wives, and in 1525, in the forty-third year of his age, he encouraged the practice by his example. He married Catherine von Bora, an escaped nun, for whom he had previously endeavored to find another husband. She was one of the many who had been placed in convents against their will, and forced to take the veil. It was no romantic attachment which induced Luther to take this step, but partly the feeling that the preacher's practice should square with his teaching, and partly an earnest desire to gratify his father, whose will he had so cruelly traversed in becoming a monk. To marry was to violate his monastic vow; but he had long since convinced himself that a vow made in ignorance, under extreme pressure, was not morally binding.

Pleasing pictures of Luther's domestic life are given us by contemporary witnesses and the reports of his table-talk. In the bosom of his family he found an asylum from the wearing labors and never-ending conflicts of his riper years. There he shows himself the tender father, the trusting and devoted husband, the open-handed, gay, and entertaining host. His Kätchen proved in every respect an all-sufficient helpmeet. And it needed her skilful economy and creative thrift to counterbalance his inconsiderate and boundless generosity. For never was one more indifferent to the things of this world, more sublimely careless of the morrow.

The remaining years of Luther's life were deeply involved in the fortunes of the Reformation, its struggles and its triumphs, its still advancing steps, in spite of opposition from without and dissensions within. They developed no new features, while they added intensity to some of the old, notably to his old impatience of falsehood and contradiction. They exhibit him still toiling and teeming, praying, agonizing, stimulating, instructing, encouraging; often prostrate with bodily disease and intense suffering; and still, amid all disappointments, tribulations, and tortures, breasting and buffeting with high-hearted valor the adverse tide which often threatened to overwhelm him.

Thus laboring, loving, suffering, exulting, he reached his sixty-fourth year, and died on the 18th of February, 1546. The last words he uttered expressed unshaken confidence in his doctrine, triumphant faith in his cause.

By a fit coincidence death overtook him in Eisleben, the place of his birth, where he had been tarrying on a journey connected with affairs of the Church.

The Count Mansfeld, who with his noble wife had ministered to Luther in his last illness, desired that his mortal remains should be interred in his domain; but the Elector, now John Frederick, claimed them for the city of Wittenberg, and sent a deputation to take them in charge. In Halle, on the way, memorial services were held, in which the university and the magnates of the city took part. In all the towns through which the procession passed, the bells were rung, and the inhabitants thronged to pay their respects to the great deceased. In Wittenberg a military cortège accompanied the procession to the church of the Electoral palace, where the obsequies were celebrated with imposing demonstrations, and a mourning city sent forth its population to escort the body to the grave.

In the year following, the Emperor Charles, having taken the Elector prisoner, stood as victor beside that grave. The Duke of Alva urged that the bones of the heretic should be exhumed and publicly burned; but Charles refused. "Let him rest; he has found his judge. I war not with the dead."

I have presented our hero in his character of reformer. I could wish, if time permitted, to exhibit him in other aspects of biographical interest. I would like to speak of him as a poet, author of hymns, into which he threw the fervor and swing of his impetuous soul; as a musical composer, rendering in that capacity effective aid to the choral service of his Church. I would like to speak of him as a humorist and satirist, exhibiting the playfulness and pungency of Erasmus without his cynicism; as a lover of nature, anticipating our own age in his admiring sympathy with the beauties of earth and sky; as the first naturalist of his day, a close observer of the habits of vegetable and animal life; as a leader in the way of tenderness for the brute creation. I would like also, in the spirit of impartial justice, to speak of his faults and infirmities, in which Lessing rejoiced, as showing him not too far removed from the level of our common humanity.

But these are points on which I am not permitted to dwell. That phase of his life which gives to the name of Luther its world-historic significance is comprised in the period extending from the year 1517 to the year 1529, — from the posting of the ninety-five theses, to the Diet of Spires, from whose decisions German princes, dissenting, received the name of Protestants, and which, followed by the league of Smalcald, assured the success of his cause.

And now, in brief, what was that cause? The Protestant Reformation, I have said, is not to be regarded as a mere theological or ecclesiastical movement, however Luther may have meant it as such. In a larger view it was secular emancipation, deliverance of the nations that embraced it from an irresponsible theocracy, whose main interest was the consolidation and perpetuation of its own dominion.

A true theocracy must always be the ideal of society; that is, a social order in which God as revealed in the moral law shall be practically recognized, inspiring and shaping the polity of nations. All the Utopias, from Plato down, are schemes for the realization of that ideal. But the attempt to ground theocracy on sacerdotalism has always proved, and must always prove, a failure. The tendency of sacerdotalism is to separate sanctity from righteousness. It invests an order of men with a power irrespective of character, — a power whose strength lies in the ignorance of those on whom it is exercised; a power which may be, and often, no doubt, is, exercised for good, but which, in the nature of man and of things, is liable to such abuses as that against which Luther contended when priestly absolution was affirmed to be indispensable to salvation, and absolution was venal, when impunity for sin was offered for sale, when the alternative of heaven or hell was a question of money.

It is not my purpose to impugn the Church of Rome as at present administered, subject to the checks of modern enlightenment and the criticism of dissenting communions. But I cannot doubt that if Rome could recover the hegemony which Luther overthrew, could once regain the entire control of the nations, the same iniquities, the same abominations, which characterized the ancient rule would reappear. The theory of the Church of Rome is fatally adverse to the best interests of humanity, light, liberty, progress. That theory makes a human individual the rightful lord of the earth, all potentates and powers beside his rightful subjects.

Infallible the latest council has declared him. Infallible! The assertion is an insult to reason. Nay, more, it is blasphemy, when we think of the attribute of Deity vested in a Boniface VIII., an Alexander VI., a John XXIII. Infallible? No! Forever no! Fallible, as human nature must always be.

Honor and everlasting thanks to the man who broke for us the spell of papal autocracy, who rescued a portion, at least, of the Christian world from the paralyzing grasp of a power more to be dreaded than any temporal despotism,—a power which rules by seducing the will, by capturing the conscience of its subjects: the bondage of the soul! Luther alone of all the men whom history names, by faith and courage, by all his endowments,—ay, and by all his limitations,—was fitted to accomplish that saving work, a work whose full import he could not know, whose far-reaching consequences he had not divined. They shape our life. Modern civilization, liberty, science, social

progress, attest the world-wide scope of the Protestant reform, whose principles are independent
thought, freedom from ecclesiastical thrall, defiance
of consecrated wrong. Of him it may be said, in
a truer sense than the poet claims for the architects
of mediæval minsters, " He builded better than he
knew." Our age still obeys the law of that movement whose van he led, and the latest age will
bear its impress. Here, amid the phantasms that
crowd the stage of human history, was a grave
reality, a piece of solid nature, a man whom it is
impossible to imagine not to have been; to strike
whose name and function from the record of his
time would be to despoil the centuries following
of gains that enrich the annals of mankind.

Honor to the man whose timely revolt checked
the progress of triumphant wrong, who wrested the
heritage of God from sacerdotal hands, defying the
traditions of immemorial time! He taught us little in the way of theological lore; what we prize
in him is not the teacher, but the doer, the man.
His theology is outgrown, — a thing of the past;
but the spirit in which he wrought is immortal:
that spirit is evermore the renewer and savior of
the world.

COUNT ZINZENDORF AND THE MORAVIANS.

WHEN the late Dr. Greenwood, the beloved pastor of King's Chapel, Boston, published, in 1830, the collection of " Psalms and Hymns for Christian Worship" still used by that church, he made us acquainted with certain hymns, before unknown to most of us, bearing the title Moravian. Their deep inwardness, their trustful, undogmatic piety, made them at once the favorites of our worshipping assemblies. I need but cite their initial verses : —

> " Thou hidden love of God, whose height,
> Whose depth unfathomed, no man knows."

> " Oh draw me, Father, after Thee !
> So shall I run, and never tire."

> " O Thou to whose all-searching sight
> The darkness shineth as the light."

> " Give to the winds thy fears,
> Hope, and be undismayed."

> " My soul before Thee prostrate lies;
> To Thee, her source, my spirit flies."

. We welcomed these pieces as precious contributions to our stock of devotional poetry. We accepted the title "Moravian" with no adequate understanding, I think, of the import of that term. The geographical appellation taught us nothing as to the tenets, the principles, and discipline of the people so named. Of this sect and their leader, Count Zinzendorf, I now purpose to speak.

The religionists whom we call Moravian are known among themselves as the "United Brethren," *Unitas Fratrum.* Such a fraternity had existed in Bohemia from the days of John Huss, in the early part of the fifteenth century, until 1627, when, amid the desolations of the Thirty Years' War, in common with all non-Catholic churches it was, as an organization, forcibly abolished, though single families here and there still cherished in secret the old tradition.

The Moravian Brotherhood proper had an independent origin in the ministry of Christian David, a zealous evangelist, seceder from the Roman to the Lutheran Church. This man gathered a band of followers in Lusatia, and initiated in 1722 a settlement on one of the estates of Count Zinzendorf, then absent in Dresden, assigned to them by his steward with his written consent. The place was situated at the foot of the Hutberg, and was named Herrnhut, *Lord's-care.* When the existence

of this asylum became known, it attracted not only
Protestant converts from Moravia who were subject to persecution at home, but also the scattered
remnants of the old Bohemian fellowship, and thus
became the historic successor and continuator of
that ancient Brotherhood, witness of a foiled reformation of the Church which antedated that of
Luther by a hundred years.

Herrnhut was planted; but the further developments and triumphs of Moravian Christianity demanded and found a leader who added to the piety
and zeal of Christian David quite other and peculiar
endowments.

Among the heroes of the eighteenth century
there are three who are specially distinguished
as leaders in religion, — Emanuel Swedenborg,
Count Nicolaus Ludwig Zinzendorf, and John
Wesley. Swedenborg, intellectually far superior
to the other two, was not the intentional founder
of a sect. The sect which has based itself on his
doctrine was not of his ordering. He was no
organizer. It was not his design that the New
Church which he proclaimed should pose as a separate body; rather, it was to act as a leavening
and transforming element in existing communions.
The other two possessed in an eminent degree the
gift of practical leadership.

Zinzendorf, our present subject, was born in

Dresden on the 26th of May in the year 1700, — by twelve years the junior of Swedenborg, by three years the senior of Wesley. His father, a nobleman of ancient lineage who held the high position of prime minister at the court of the Elector of Saxony, died six weeks after the birth of his son. The mother, Charlotta Justina, Baroness of Gersdorf, married a second husband; and young Zinzendorf, at the age of four, was committed to the care of his maternal grandmother in Hennersdorf, in Upper Lusatia. This lady, a friend of the famous Pietist, Philip Spener, who had officiated as godfather at Zinzendorf's baptism, made it her chief end to awaken and foster religious sensibility in her charge. In particular she endeavored to impress upon him what to her was the ground truth of Christianity, — that the everlasting God, Author and Ruler of the universe, had suffered and died for our sake, and therefore claimed his uttermost gratitude and devotion. The impression thus stamped upon the soul of the child became the ruling idea of the man, — the master-motive of all his doing and striving. Through life he knew no God but Christ. As a preacher he instructed his hearers that " God, the Father of our Lord Jesus Christ, is not our father proper; to think so is one of the chief errors current in Christendom." " The Father of our Lord is to us what in the world is called a grandfather or father-in-law." "They who preach God the Father are professors of Satan."

At the age of eleven he was put to school at the pædagogium in Halle, of which the pious Francke was then director, and in 1716 was sent to the University of Wittenberg to study law. A proficient in the customary branches of polite learning, especially in the languages, of which he wrote and spoke Latin with great fluency, his chief distinction even then, in those academic years, was that of a religious zealot. He held prayer-meetings in his chambers, organized clubs for mutual edification, strove to convert, and sometimes succeeded in converting, loose associates who would tempt him to vicious indulgence. At the same time his high breeding, his frank, easy manners, and freedom from all that savors of sanctimoniousness precluded the aversion, not to say contempt, which college youth are apt to entertain for fellow-students of the pious type.

After leaving the university, in accordance with the fashion of the young nobility of that day, he spent two years in travel. In the course of his journeying his piety received at Düsseldorf on the Rhine a fresh impulse from the contemplation of Correggio's picture of the Suffering Christ. He read the inscription: "Thus have I suffered for thee: what hast thou done for me?" and then and there renewed his vows of a life devoted to the service of Christ.

In Paris he made the acquaintance of Cardinal Noailles, with whom he afterward corresponded. Evangelical as he was, and unproselytable, he gained the affection of the Romish prelate by virtue of that universalism of the heart which is independent of forms and creeds. His rank procured for him a favorable reception at the court of Philip of Orleans ; but the dissolute manners of the Regency repelled the unspotted youth. He found his best entertainment at the riding-school, where he won admiration by his superior horsemanship.

On attaining his majority, in compliance with the wishes of his uncle and guardian, who had destined him for civil service, he accepted the post of Councillor of Justice in Dresden. But his heart was not in it, and after five years' trial he resigned his office, resolved to devote himself to what he regarded as his true calling, — that of Christian evangelist. He had no desire to separate himself from the Lutheran Church. His purpose was to form within that Church communities of such as desired to lead a more strictly religious life. But finding a community with similar views already established on his own domain, after careful study of their discipline and aims he was finally induced to make Herrnhut the basis of his operations, and in 1727 accepted the office of spiritual superintendent of the colony of which he was already the legal magistrate and liege lord. He had previously taken to wife Countess Erdmuth von Reuss, sister of Count Reuss, his lifelong friend.

Here we have the rare, if not a solitary, example of a youth of noble birth, endowed with wealth and personal graces, high cultured, with all that the world can give at his command, devoting himself in the morning of life, with all his havings and all his being, to the service of Christ, to the building up of the kingdom of Christ on earth. We have precisely the realization of what the young man in the Gospel, whom Jesus loved, failed to realize, turning away sorrowful, "for he had great possessions." The Pietists at Halle, followers of Spener, looked with jealous eye on this great sacrifice, not made distinctively on their basis and in their service. They questioned its value, discredited its influence. "Master, we saw one casting out devils in thy name; and we forbade him because he followed not us." They insisted that the Count had not been converted; he had not passed through the regular stages of penitential struggle and ecstatic new birth; he might be a servant of God, but was not as yet an adopted child of God. Zinzendorf, far from resenting this allegation, took the matter to heart, and made it the occasion of rigorous self-examination. The result of his reflection was that Halle had no right to impose her methods as a universal test and condition of godliness; that one might rightfully attain to be a child of God independently of Halle.

He soon discovered that in order to labor with the best effect in the mission he had chosen, it would be necessary for him to enter the ministry. Accordingly, after some preparatory study he presented himself, under a feigned name, or rather one which really belonged to him, but which he had not been accustomed to use, as a candidate for orders, and obtained the desired license, in virtue of which he preached whenever he deemed it expedient to exercise that function. The step gave great offence to the Saxon nobility, as tending to abolish social distinctions and threatening the stability of their order. A noble in the pulpit was a dangerous innovation, a public scandal. In consequence of which, on some frivolous charge trumped up by his enemies, he was sent into banishment, a royal rescript requiring him to part with his estates and to quit his native Saxony. The sentence was afterward rescinded. Meanwhile the harm resulting from it was less than might have been expected. He made over his estates to his wife, and thanks to her wise administration, suffered no pecuniary

loss. The community at Herrnhut was too well
organized to need his personal supervision, while
the cause of the Moravian Brotherhood could only
gain from the missionary labors he now undertook
on their behalf.

I have said that Zinzendorf did not intend separation from the Lutheran Church. He accepted
without dissent the Augsburg Confession, the creed
of that Church, and only desired a revival of practical religion by means of voluntary associations
within that Confession. Nevertheless it was found
desirable — in view, especially, of Moravian colo-
nies abroad — to have an independent ecclesiastical
organization. For this the old Bohemian episco-
pate, the original constitution of the *Unitas Fratrum*, offered a convenient basis. During a visit
to Berlin the Count was urged by the King of Prussia, Frederic William I., who was strongly attracted
to our hero and interested in his doings, to revive
that Constitution, and obtain for himself episcopal
investiture. Daniel Ernst Jablonsky, the leading
German divine of that day, seconded the royal
counsel, and referred the Count for further advice
to his friend the Archbishop of Canterbury. Zinzendorf went to England and had an interview
with Canterbury, who advised him by all means to
resume and continue the episcopal succession of
the old Bohemian Church. Accordingly, having

previously submitted himself for examination and approval to a committee of the clergy of Berlin, on the 20th of May, 1737, Zinzendorf was ordained by Jablonsky bishop of the Moravian Church. The King immediately addressed a congratulatory letter to the new Bishop, Ludovicus, as follows:

DEARLY BELOVED LORD COUNT, — It was with satisfaction that I learned that, according to your desire, you have been consecrated bishop of the Moravian Brethren. . . . That this transaction may redound to the glory of Almighty God and the salvation of many souls, is my heart's desire. I am always your very affectionate,

FREDERIC WILLIAM.

The Archbishop of Canterbury, in an elegant Latin epistle, cordially extended to him the right hand of fellowship, acknowledging in him a *coepiscopus* and ecclesiastical peer.

Thus royally and prelatically auspicated and authorized, our Count proceeded to labor with added zeal in the service of a Church which, having now disengaged itself from the Lutheran (though still Lutheran in doctrine), and become a distinct and independent communion, might claim, in virtue of its Bohemian antecedents, to be the eldest of the Protestant Churches.

His life thenceforth is a history of administrative work and missionary operations conducted on a large scale in many lands. He visited England,

Holland, Denmark, Sweden, Prussia, Switzerland, the Danish West Indies, and in 1741 came to this country, having previously, in view of so long an absence, at a synod held in London resigned his office of superintendent of the Brotherhood in Germany, causing it to be transferred to an assembly called the General Conference. After landing in New York he proceeded to Pennsylvania, where he spent the better part of two years, residing chiefly in Philadelphia. At a meeting held in the house of the Governor of the province, — where, among others, Benjamin Franklin was present, — he stated that he wished, while travelling in this country, to drop his title, and to be known only as Brother Louis. A large portion of the population of the province were Germans. To those in Philadelphia and in Germantown, Zinzendorf preached in their native language, and was cordially invited to be their pastor. He accepted the office provisionally, until a permanent preacher from Germany could be obtained for their service. He aimed not so much to establish local Moravian churches as to kindle spiritual interest in other communions and to band together such as desired to lead a distinctively religious life. Some, however, he did establish. The Moravian Brotherhood in Bethlehem, Penn., remains to this day a witness of Zinzendorf's American mission.

In 1742 his romantic genius impelled him to undertake, in company with his fellow-laborers Böhler, Conrad, and Anna Nitschmann, who afterward became his second wife, a missionary tour among the Indians, chiefly Iroquois and Delawares. We have entries in his Journal which give us his impressions of savage life. Some of these Indians had been already converted. Concerning these he exclaims: " Oh, how ashamed we feel in the presence of these brethren, who must help themselves in the Saviour's work with a language which is hardly better than the cackling of geese, while we, possessed of a language like that of the gods, can hardly express our hearts' emotions!" Any language which conveys no meaning to the hearer will be apt to have an irrational sound. The Count was not aware that his own godlike German was compared by the Emperor Julian to the cawing of crows. The faces of the Indians, he says, wear a dull, unhappy expression. " They have only one pleasant look, that is when they contemplate the wounds of the Lamb. . . . They are the most determined enemies of labor; they will sooner suffer the most pinching want than engage in any work. If an Indian puts his hand to anything, it is either because he has become a child of God or because from association with the whites he has acquired the spirit of covetousness, which is the root of all evil."

4

He met in this tour a Frenchwoman, Madame de Montoux, widow of an Indian chief who had been killed in battle. "On seeing us she wept bitterly. I spoke of our affairs, and remarked that we had named our town Bethlehem. 'That,' she exclaimed, 'is the name of the town in France where Jesus and the Holy Family lived.' I inferred from this that what is reported of French missionaries is true. They teach that Christ was a Frenchman, and that the English were his crucifiers."

His stay in America was cut short by tidings of what he regarded as a misdirection on the part of the Brethren at home. The authorities intrusted with the management of the churches in Germany had adopted measures which tended to give the Brotherhood a more sectarian and separatistic position than accorded with his views. He was Lutheran before he was Moravian, and more Lutheran than Moravian still. Although for convenience of ecclesiastical functions he had accepted the office of bishop, it was not his design to cut loose from his native communion. In its civil relations the Brotherhood was still to be reckoned a branch of the Lutheran Church. But in his absence the Conference had taken steps which traversed this intent. He had resigned his authority so far as the Church in Germany was concerned, and had no longer any right to act as their bishop; but he now, without consent of any Council, resumed his episcopal function, and with autocratic inhibition reversed so far as possible the action taken in his absence. It is a proof of the astounding overweight of Zinzendorf's personality and of the deep respect with which he was regarded by the Brethren, as well as their humble and peaceable temper, that such dictation was submitted to on their part without remonstrance. With all his piety and genuine devotion to the cause, he could not forget that he was a count, a feudal noble. As such he seems to have expected the same submission in things spiritual which people of his class were accustomed to exact in things temporal. Theoretically meek, as became a disciple of Christ, condescendingly gracious to his inferiors, professing himself their servant for Christ's sake, he nevertheless preferred to serve by ruling. And he ruled in the main, it must be confessed, with consummate ability. The genius of leadership he certainly possessed, — the power to inspire in his followers unlimited confidence in his judgment. There had been in his absence an outburst of fanaticism among the Brethren in Germany, which assumed an antinomian character and threatened to make the name Moravian a synonym for lawless indulgence. This danger he averted by the timely interposition of his authority, exposing the error in which it originated, reminding the Brethren of the high moral standard of former years, and teaching them that the freedom in Christ which they boasted was not to be understood as emancipation from the moral law, but as free obedience.

Zinzendorf did not recross the Atlantic, but while an exile from his paternal estates led an itinerant life, visiting various countries in the service of the cause he had espoused. He spent four years in England for the more convenient supervision of the churches there established, and because England was the natural *entrepôt* between the mother-church in Germany and her missionary stations in heathen lands. Here, in England, a new trial befell the Brotherhood, — a pressing financial embarrassment, due to the want of worldly prudence on the part of the Count himself. He had authorized, through his deacons, liberal expenditures for missionary and congregational purposes, without sufficiently calculating the means at their command. The deacons, unknown to him, had supplemented their means by borrowing. A heavy debt had been incurred. This could not last; credit failed. There came a crisis, hearing of which the Count, though not legally liable, stood in the gap. He assumed the debt, which he pledged himself to liquidate by instalments. The majority of the creditors accepted the terms; but some, who were bitterly anti-Moravian, insisted on* immediate payment, and were minded to send the Count to jail for debt. To prevent this step, which would have been ruin to the Brotherhood in England, the other creditors, friends, and well-wishers of the cause came forward and satisfied the claims of its enemies.

In addition to his other labors, arduous and unceasing, imposed upon him by the daily care of the churches, Zinzendorf was an indefatigable writer. As many as a hundred volumes, still extant in different collections, are ascribed to him. They have never been published in a uniform edition, and — dealing, as they mostly do, with local and ephemeral topics — would have no interest now, except as characteristic of the writer.

He composed, it is said, five hundred or more hymns for the use of the Church. Many of these are still preserved in Moravian collections. Some of them were eliminated on account of the offensive imagery employed in treating the mutual love of Christ and his Church as a sexual relation. Others were rejected as trivial and beneath the dignity of the man and the cause. In the conduct of public worship he sometimes ventured to improvise hymns, which he gave out, verse by verse, to be sung by the congregation after the manner of the so-called deaconing of the hymn in Puritan New England. It sometimes happened that when a verse had been given out and sung, an appropriate rhyming word for the next was not forthcoming. In that case he supplied the defect by a meaningless sound, which met the vocal exigency if it did not satisfy the intellectual requirements of that part of the service. The devout congregation knew that though the Count might not always succeed with his rhymes, he always meant well; and so they obeyed the direction of the Chorus in " Henry V." : —

" Still be kind,
And eke out our performance with your mind! "

His preaching is said to have been marvellously effective, especially in pathetic appeals. From a slight acquaintance, I should say it was often extravagant, and somewhat coarse. Here is an extract from a homily on his favorite topic, the wounds of Christ : —

" There is no more formidable law — the law of Moses and Moses himself was a mere poltroon compared with it — no law more formidable than the thunder-word of the Gospel, the soul-piereing sword of the wounds of Jesus. Well did the women of Jerusalem know it. O word of wounds! thou thunder-word, thou soul-transfixing sword! To think that Jesus was pierced and bored and mangled for all that we behold, for the ground-stuff of time and humanity, for all the horrors that pass before our eyes, and for those that do not pass before our eyes, but within our knowledge, and that fill this earth-ball and desecrate and defile it! And for us, with our wretched hearts, for us who are so vile, whom he has to drag and carry, and must look through an astonishing magnifying-glass in order to see any reality in us! He has to make his own heart, his bridegroom's heart, a microscope, that beneath it our little mite of gratitude, our sun-mote of love, may seem to be all, so that he shall see nothing and care for nothing but that."

The last years of Zinzendorf's life were spent on his own estates and in the neighborhood of Herrn-hut, the edict of banishment having been revoked. There, toiling faithfully to the end in the service of the Brotherhood, he died in May, 1760, in the sixtieth year of his age. His obsequies were cele-brated with the pomp befitting the grandeur and priceless blessing of such a life. A procession of twenty-one hundred mourners, consisting of kin-dred, friends, admirers, the principal dignitaries of the Church from far and near, escorted by a mili-tary company of Imperial grenadiers, and witnessed by two thousand spectators, accompanied his re-mains to their grave in the beautiful cemetery at Herrnhut, where they still repose beneath the marble slab which records his name. It was noted as a happy coincidence that the scriptural watchword for the day was the text: " He shall come with rejoicing, bearing his sheaves with him."

Herder, in the " Adrastæa," says of him, " He left the world as a conqueror, like whom there have been few in the world's history, and none in his own century." A conqueror, indeed, whose conquests, attested by Moravian exploits, have dotted the globe with oases of holiness ; missionary conquests extending in literal verity from " Greenland's icy mountains " to " India's coral strand," from the Cape of Good Hope to the shores of the White Sea, from Tranquebar to Surinam, from St. Thomas to Labrador, and gladdening our own land, in Georgia, North Carolina, and Pennsylvania, with its gardens of peace. Methodism, the strong and many-membered body of the Methodists, may be reckoned one of his conquests. For did not John Wesley kindle his far-flaming torch at the altar of Herrnhut, making the long journey to Lusatia to verify with his own eyes the report which had come to him of the Brotherhood, and writing to them afterward, " We are endeavoring here also, according to the grace that is given us, to be followers of you, as you are of Christ " ?

Zinzendorf was twice married, — first to Countess Erdmuth of Ebersdorf, a lady of his own rank ; and after her death to Anna Nitschmann, who, in her character of deaconess to the Moravian sisterhood, had already proved an efficient helpmate. Three children were born to him from his first wife, — two daughters, and a son of great promise who died in early life.

As to person, the Count's commanding figure drew the admiring gaze of passers-by as he walked the streets of London. His face in picture wears a look of imperturbable calm, with a hint of self-satisfaction in the eyes.

A conqueror, but no seer, no revealer, like Swedenborg, of original truth. Never did a spirit so intense inhabit intellectually so narrow a world. The sinfulness of man, and the wounds of Christ, were the two foci of the little orbit in which his being revolved. All beyond that was barren and void. The majestic volume of the Universe with its sacred scriptures, older than Hebrew or Greek, was unrolled to him in vain. Unknown to him the " sense sublime of something far more deeply inter-fused " than any lore of Palestine. Not through Nature, I think, not consciously through Nature, did God speak to him, but only through Christ. And the Christ whom he worshipped was not the divine teacher, not the high model of a heavenly life, but only the sufferer, the victim,—

> " The Master's marred and wounded mien,
> His hands, his feet, his side. "

And yet, with astonishing self-ignorance, this man could say, "I am not one of those who are satisfied with feeling; I belong to the class of thinkers." He entertained the pleasant conceit of a private correspondence with the Saviour, who brought him temporal aid as well as spiritual blessing. Once at sea, off the Scilly Islands, a violent tempest threatened to drive the vessel on the rocks. Shipwreck seemed imminent. The captain in despair had resigned himself to his fate; but the Count assured him that within two hours the tempest would abate, which it actually did. The vessel was saved. "How could you know," asked the captain, "that the storm would pass so soon?" "The Saviour told me," was the reply.

The Moravians have a custom, much insisted on by Zinzendorf, known as the "watchword." Texts are selected from the Bible and assigned in advance, at a venture, one for each day in the year. Out of three hundred and sixty-five days it would not be strange if occasionally the events of some particular day should fit the text set down for it. Thus, on the day when the Count met his followers in Bethlehem, Penn., to inaugurate the church in that place, the watchword for the day was found to be, "This is the day which the Lord hath made: let us rejoice and be glad therein." Such coincidences were believed to be divinely predetermined.

Another custom is the use of the lot to decide difficult questions,—such as the choice of a chief elder out of two or three esteemed equally competent, the adoption or non-adoption of some doubtful policy or proposed undertaking. I suppose many of us have had recourse to lot in some perplexing alternative. The doing so is a practical confession of the inability of the will to act without a preponderating motive. We refer the matter, as it were, to a foreign agent, which some call " chance," and others accept as the oracle of God. The Moravians, like the first disciples, use it always in the latter sense. But when we consider that the position of the slip on which the choice is inscribed, and the direction of the fingers which select it, if the act is honest, are determined by natural laws and depend on the action of forces, present and past, reaching back through all time, so that the drawing of that slip is a necessary result of the original constitution of things; when we think that the world in all its parts, through all its periods, must have been other than it was and is, had not that slip, but another, been drawn,—when we consider this, the supposition of a special Providence willing that result is a heavy strain on one's faith. But faith is always beautiful, and criticism is cheap.

I have said that the Moravians are the oldest Protestant Church. I will add that, above all others, they most resemble the Church of the first disciples. More than any other, they have reproduced the original unity, the pristine brotherhood, of the followers of Christ. "No brotherhood, no Christianity," was Zinzendorf's motto. He did not care to found a sect; his aim was to gather into one, from all the churches, souls attracted to each other by common faith in the saving efficacy of the blood of Christ, and conscious of salvation through that faith. He regretted the tendency to separatism in the Brotherhood; but separatism was a necessary result of the hostility toward them of other communions.

As a separate fold they still survive and still retain the stamp of Herrnhut in their discipline and way of life. Undogmatic, with no enforced creed, no test of fellowship but their common faith in atonement by the blood of Christ, — secure in that, they cultivate a religion of trust, less passionate than Methodism, less formal than Quakerism, less sulphurous and grim than Calvinism. Heaven, not hell, is the staple of their preaching; love, not fear, the soul of their religion. The rant of the conventicle is not heard in their borders. They rejoice in skilled music and love-feasts; and if, on the one hand, they traverse nature by rigid separation of the sexes, they overcome, on the other hand, the weakness of nature by vanquishing the fear of death, treating it as a joyful return, a *Heimgang*, celebrated with triumphal music from the church tower, and symbolized by the beauty of their burial-places, which they denominate " Courts of Peace."

A religion of peace. Some of the finest spirits of Germany are among its witnesses. Schleier-macher and Novalis were reared in its fold. Goethe, in the " Confessions of a Beautiful Soul," reflects its sweetness. Prince Bismarck, thanks to his Moravian wife, has been touched with its influence.

They survive, but they do not increase. The number of Moravians in Europe and the United States is estimated at twenty thousand souls. But mark, as proof of the expansive force, the spiritual reach, of Moravian Christianity, that this compara-tively small body maintains, scattered among all the remote corners of the earth, eighty-two missionary stations, in which collectively the number of na-tive converts amounts to more than seventy-seven thousand.

Their success with savage nations surpasses all other missionary triumphs. Whom none could in-fluence, they have persuaded; whom none could enlighten, they have made to see. The Hottentot of the Cape, in answer to their patient appeal, cast aside the beast that he was, came forth a man, and entered the kingdom prepared for him too from the foundation of the world. The ice-bound Greenlander opened his tardy bosom to their solicitation as the arctic flora, starting from its long sleep, opens at last to the July sun.

Moravian communities have ceased to multiply. That tidal-wave of spiritual life which swept over Christendom during the first half of the eighteenth century has left its traces in churches that still survive and that mark the height of the swelling flood; but the flood ebbed, and no longer suffices for new creations. Nor is there, perhaps, any need of such. The principle of segregation, of local seclusion, which gave birth to the old Fraternities, as in mediæval time it had given birth to countless monastic institutions, has done its work. It is not needful, it is not well, that the spiritually minded should dwell by themselves in separate folds. Better they should be dispersed, should mix with the world, and act as a leavening principle in secular life. The secular life must absorb the spiritual, must be permeated by it, transformed by it; else would the spiritual have no business in earthly places, and the human world would miss the true purpose of its being, dishonoring Him who willed it to be. The world is not doomed to be a godless world; it is to be the abode of redeemed and perfected man, the realization of all the ideals. Religion is one of those ideals, but not the only one, the chief, but not the only agency in transforming the world. There is a greater word than even religion, a word of farther reach, of more momentous import, including religion with how much else! That word is Humanity.

CHRISTIANITY IN CONFLICT WITH HELLENISM.

[*From the Unitarian Review.*]

THE saddest passage of the world's annals, and also the grandest, according as we fix our regards on its losses and decays, or on the new creations which it witnessed, is the period embraced in the first four centuries of the Christian era. The lover of classic antiquity — Christian though he be in heart and creed — contemplates with a sigh [1] the downfall of ancient temples and the ruin of rites and beliefs involved in the death of Hellenism. On the other hand, the most fervent admirer of those vanished splendors, "the fair humanities of old religion," contrasting, on its social side, what perished with what replaced it in the order of time, must confess that the world was well rid of polytheistic uses, and humanity abundantly compensated for all æsthetic and poetic losses by the spiritual life which streamed from the new dispensation.

[1] The sigh which breathes so pathetically from Schiller's "Gods of Greece."

The histories which treat of this period have been written, for the most part, from an ecclesiastical point of view, and inspired by dogmatic or pragmatical interests. That of Gibbon, written in a spirit of historic indifference, with no apologetic or polemic bias, will always maintain its place, and, so far as it covers the ground, approve itself as a faithful report of the facts of the time. But in Gibbon also I miss the faculty of historic divination, the sense which discerns the deeper meaning of the facts recorded, which interprets historic results in the light of their bearing on the whole of human destiny. We have no history of the origins of the Christian Church from a humanitarian or, if I may use so pedantic a phrase, from an *anthropocosmic* point of view; no history inspired by the questions, What is humanity's debt to the Church; what is Christianity's place in the education of humankind? The time and the man for such a history have not yet arrived. Meanwhile, the histories we have will be found most instructive when studied in that sense.

The Christian Church and the Roman Empire were contemporary, or nearly contemporary, births. The latter came armed from the throes of a naval conflict on the waters of the Ambracian Gulf; the former sprang to life, a babbling babe, in a garret of an inland city shut in by inhospitable hills. What shall be the fortunes respectively of these new-comers on the stage of history? The one is backed and omened by a pedigree of heroes and seven centuries of victory; the other, by the humble if saintly life and tragic death of one who had recently perished as a malefactor. To balance this inequality, the latter is inspired by a faith in its own future, immeasurable, indomitable; the other derives its sole guarantee from favoring circumstance.

Could not the two unite in one dominion? There was a moment when such a coalition seemed possible. The Emperor Tiberius is said to have proposed to the Roman Senate the admission of Christ to a place in the Pantheon, and his consequent solemn recognition as one of the gods of the State. It is a curious question what would have been the effect of such recognition had that proposition been accepted, had Christianity enjoyed at the start the sanction of imperial power. Its spread might have been more rapid, but the strength that was in it, its latent moral force, would never have asserted itself. It needed the hardening by fire to which the wantonness of Imperial cruelty subjected it in its infancy, in order to become the world-subduing power it was destined to be. It could not accept as a gift what it felt itself entitled to by divine right. It

could not "borrow leave to be," but must conquer
for itself — not with sword, like armed Islam in a
later age, but by miracles of patience, by suffering
and dying — an unprecarious throne. Constitutionally exclusive, it must put all things under it. It
must reign supreme, it must reign alone.

Such a consummation seemed, from a worldly
point of view, an impossibility; for though the
dominant religion was inwardly dead, though polytheism as a faith, as personal conviction, had lost
its hold of educated minds, it was still politically
seized of the Roman State, and not to be evicted
but with mortal agony and throes that upheaved
the world. Theodor Keim[1] calls attention to the
fact that the Roman religion, unlike all others,
originated, not with priest or prophet, but with the
secular power. It was therefore from the first
indissolubly linked with the State. Conceive, then,
a government powerful as none ever was before or
since in all the elements of civil strength, and jealous as it was powerful, impatient of opposition,
prompt to crush whatever opposed; a government
whose sleepless vigilance and omnipresent police
not a thing that occurred in any corner of its wide
dominion could escape; a government whose head
was also the head of the national religion, himself
an object of worship, to refuse which worship was

---

[1] In his Rom und Christenthum.

treason to the State, — to such a government comes this vagabond from the East, from a land universally despised, and seeks to establish itself in the capital of the Empire. Ignominiously repulsed, it continues to advance; smitten and cast out, it steadily prevails; and having entered as an outlaw, ends as sovereign of the world. Its triumph is the supreme miracle of history.

The fierce rebuff which Christianity encountered, at the point where it first emerges into secular history, revealed, on the part of the Christians, a power of endurance which should have taught the secular authorities that the "pestilent" novelty was not to be disposed of in that fashion. Meanwhile, by the light of those cruel fires in the gardens of Nero, the "disciples" might see how wide was the chasm which then divided their Church from the State. Three centuries were required to bridge that gulf; and this the Church accomplished by casting into it the children of her bosom, over whose mangled bodies humanity made the dire passage from the old world to the new.

An inscription at the entrance of the Catacombs of St. Sebastian in Rome tells of one hundred and seventy-four thousand martyrs who there repose in peace. It is not necessary to suppose that all these were the immediate victims of civil persecution. But, in any view, this record of a single city suggests an estimate very different from that which Gibbon would have us accept as the number of those who suffered martyrdom throughout the vast extent of the Empire.[2] The precise number does not concern us, nor even the approximate number; enough that torture and death were the frequent penalty of the Christian confession in those centuries, — torture and death the most excruciating that human ingenuity could devise, — and that these were voluntarily incurred and unflinchingly borne by the victims. It was not their belief that the government quarrelled with, it was not their doctrine that was punished, but their insubordination in refusing to sacrifice. In the view of the government the Christians were a political party, insurgents against the State, whose head they refused to honor in the way prescribed. It was not a question of opinion, but one of obedience. Will you or will you not sacrifice to the Emperor? Will you "swear by the genius," that is, acknowledge the divinity, of Cæsar? To the government official it was simply a token of submission to rightful authority; but to the Christian it meant something else, — it meant that Cæsar was before Christ, that Cæsar was God. With that understanding, young and old, delicate women, nursing mothers, suffered their flesh to be

---

[2] " Somewhat less than two thousand persons." See Milman's Gibbon, i. 599.

torn with red-hot pincers, and would not commit
the saving act.

Martyrdom is no proof of the truth of a religion,
that is, of the truth of the opinions held by its
votaries. Quite opposite opinions have had their
martyrs. What it does prove, when it reaches the
scope and strain of the Christian martyrologies, is
— Spirit, — the action of a spirit which transcends
the ordinary limits and capabilities of human nature, takes captive the will, and makes it at once
an invincible bar and an all-conquering force.
The political success of Christianity was the work
of that spirit. The secondary causes by which
Gibbon attempts to explain that success are well
put; but Gibbon does not perceive that those
causes themselves require to be explained. Compact organization. What compacted it? Austere
morals, intolerant zeal, belief in immortality. Yes;
but whence derived, the morals, the zeal, the belief? How came they at that particular crisis to
develop such exceptional potency? They point to
another factor, — inspiration. It is the fashion of
the current philosophy to derive new births from
old antecedents by way of evolution. But there
are births which this philosophy does not explain.
Christianity had no such genesis. It cannot be
said, in any proper sense, to be an evolution of
Judaism, any more than Islam was an evolution of

Christianity. Judaism was its matrix, but not its sire. If in any sense "evolved" from given antecedents, it was as the whirlwind is evolved from atmospheric heat. This great world-force, which came with "a sound as of a rushing, mighty wind" and went cycloning through the lands, was surely no product of Mosaic tradition, but the immediate offspring of a Spirit which conducts the education of the human race and from time to time interpolates the course of events with new motives adjusted to a pre-ordained ascending scale of spiritual life. I say "interpolates," for is not all inspiration interpolation,— a lift that breaks the dead, mechanical sequence of things?

It is not to be supposed that all who joined the Christian confession partook of this spirit. Many were drawn to it by quite earthly motives, — by the hope of a social revolution, the coming of a new kingdom in which, having nothing to lose, they might reasonably hope to gain; by the charm of equality; by the communism which secured them against want, as we learn from Lucian, — an unintentional witness of the charity of the early Church. And there were lapses in times of persecution. The Church could afford them; the Church could afford to take back the lapsed when persecution ceased. It was not the aim of the Spirit to have a faultless Church, a Church com-

posed entirely of the " *Katharoi.*" A mixture of
tares with the wheat was not fatal to the Church,
did not prevent its being a true Church, as Cyprian,
earliest exponent of the Catholic idea, maintained,
in opposition to Novatian purists.

Nor did the Spirit care to have a constituency
of such as are called in worldly phrase " respectable " people. Socially and intellectually they
seem to have been, with few exceptions, a low
class, — " not many wise after the flesh, not many
mighty, not many noble." Paul, the high-hearted
Roman citizen, who bravely cast in his lot with
these people, could see with prophetic vision how
God was going to put to shame the wise and the
strong by means of the weak and foolish and the
low. But how would it strike an outsider ? Is it
surprising that men of culture and good position,
men like Tacitus and Suetonius, should have looked
with contempt on the Christian Church when they
saw what sort of people it drew to its communion,
— restless spirits ; malecontents ; radicals of every
stripe ; occasionally slaves, as we infer from the
allusion to " those of Cæsar's household ; " now and
then an adventurer like Peregrinus Proteus ? Not
the kind of people that a self-respecting citizen
would care to consort with. And I suppose that
few of us, had we lived in those days, and had not
caught, or been caught by, the Spirit, would have

cared to be found in such company. And when I see Christian zealots, proud of their orthodoxy, with conscious holiness looking down upon heretics and flouting new departures in theology, I amuse myself with thinking how heartily, had they been contemporaries of Paul, these respectables would have spurned the writers of the New Testament and all that guild.

In the second century Christianity assumed a new phase. It had developed an intellectual life. It had its men of letters, its learned essayists, its eloquent apologists. It had also developed heresies and schisms. Rival systems had sprung up. Gnosticism asserted its claims, assuming to teach a profounder doctrine than the Gospel. The Church was called to contend with intellectual adversaries as well as civil authority. The latter half of this century witnessed the culmination and incipient decline of the Upper Empire. Marcus Aurelius, standing midway between the first appearance of Christianity and its civil enfranchisement, represents the high-water mark of Roman greatness, as he does the height of Imperial virtue in the annals of mankind. Allen, in his valuable monograph, "The Mind of Paganism," says: "We may have to come down as far as Louis IX. of France to find his parallel." But neither in Saint Louis nor in English Alfred, to whom Merivale compares him, do I find the serene piety, the moral sublimity, which I admire in the Roman sovereign. The piety of Louis was reinforced by the stimulus of Christian memories, of a Christian ideal, in an age of unquestioning faith. Marcus had no such support. He dwelt amid decaying altars ; he flourished in a dying world. I contrast in the two the lunar virtue with the solar. He is accused of weakness in his lenient treatment of Faustina. The justice of the charge depends on the truth of the alleged infidelity of Faustina, which is somewhat doubtful. He is blamed for bequeathing the Empire to Commodus ; but the choice of the natural heir, who might outgrow his youthful follies, seemed less dangerous than the inevitable conflict between rival claimants of the throne.

The character of the man is revealed in his self-communings, which have come down to us, an imperishable volume, the so-called " Meditations of the Emperor Antoninus." Better preaching I have not found, nor thoughts more edifying, in any Christian writer of that time. A sombre spirit, but how sweet, how grand ! No soul was ever more impressed with the vanity of earthly things. As from under the shadow of impending doom, he urges upon himself the pursuit of the one thing needful. " What is immortal fame ? Vanity and an empty sound. What is there, then, to which we may reasonably apply ourselves ? This one thing alone, — that our thoughts and intentions be just, our actions directed to the public good, our words inspired by truth, our whole disposition acquiescence in whatsoever may happen, as flowing from such a Fountain, the original of all things."

That Marcus authorized the persecution of the Christians, is justly reckoned, from the Christian point of view, a blot on his fame. One could wish, indeed, that he had understood Christianity, that he had been in a position to judge it fairly. All he knew of it was that the Christians, in the Roman sense, were atheists, — they neglected sacrifice, they denied the gods. His father, Antoninus Pius, had checked the persecution in Asia, had even written to the authorities at Ephesus to punish the informers, and to let the accused, though Christians, go free. But the son had fallen on other times. A season of national prosperity, unbroken since the reign of Nerva, had come to a close. There was trouble on the German frontiers; the legions had been routed on the Danube, the Marcomanni were pouring down from the Carpathians. Worst of all, at home a raging pestilence, imported from the East, was decimating the people. An inundation which destroyed the public granaries had brought famine and desolation on the land. The horizon was dark all round; the public mind

was agitated with strange fears. In this agony
the religious sentiment, long dormant, was suddenly aroused. It was no longer social antipathy,
but returning piety, that demanded the extermi-
nation of the Christians. For were not they the
true cause of all this misery? They are atheists,
they have denied the gods; and the gods in their
wrath have sent these woes. The only way to
appease the gods and bring back the averted eye
of their blessing, is utterly to destroy the Christians. How far the Emperor shared these views,
it is impossible to say; enough he yielded to the
popular cry: persecution was renewed, and the
Church grew strong and stronger thereby.

In the third century the elemental forces are the
same, but their relative position and prospects have
changed.   The new religion has gained immensely
in extent and repute.   It no longer hides itself in
the bowels of the earth, but moves freely in the
face of day.   It had grown to be a recognized and
powerful member, or rather rival, of the State; no
longer a doubtful adventure, but an accomplished
fact.   In every province, in every city of note,
churches were established,—compact bodies bound
together by laws of their own and a common aim.
They constituted a state by themselves, an *impe-
rium in imperio*, a vast confederation extending
from the Pyrenees to the Caucasus.   Men of all

conditions had embraced the confession. There were Christians in the army, in the senate, and around the throne. Their doctrine could no longer be ignored; it challenged the attention of Gentile scholars, and could match an Arrian and a Celsus with a Clement, a Tertullian, and an Origen.

But Hellenism also presented a new front. It had grown devout; it had "got religion." The religious enthusiasm of the Christians had exerted an influence beyond their ranks. The public mind had sobered as the State declined. A moribund world in its sick dotage craved supports which custom could not furnish, satisfactions which sense could not supply. Sated with the gorgeous spectacles of the circus, on which the treasures of an empire had been lavished, and the world ransacked to furnish some new prodigy, surfeited with earthly splendor, the heart sickened with intolerable weariness of life. From this disease there were only two ways of escape. With the more refined, the selfish and despairing, suicide became the fashion and passion of the time; parties of pleasure were formed to witness, perhaps to unite in, voluntary death. On the other hand, those who still clung to life and hope sought in religion a refuge from the loathing and disgust of their lot. The religion which thus competed with the Christian was not a revival of the old cult; it was not the religion which instituted the Salian priesthood and the rites of Mars Gradivus. That was outgrown and irrecoverable. Mithraism, with its fascinations, its mysteries, and its horrors, had succeeded to the vacant place. This and Neo-Platonic mysticism might soothe the spiritual hunger they could not satisfy. They might resist the attraction of the Gospel, they might even infect the strain of Christian doctrine; but they possessed no binding force, they were powerless against the organic solidarity of the Church.

With the advent of another century the strength of that organism was to be arrayed in a final conflict with the State. In the winter of 303, in the imperial palace of Nicomedia, the question was debated between the Emperor Diocletian and his associate Cæsar, What shall be done with Christianity? The vacillating policy of former years, now rigorous, now lax, was no longer practicable. It must be settled once for all which is the stronger, Rome, or Christianity. And so the bolt was launched. The anniversary of the god Terminus was to be the beginning of the end to the Christians, — demolition of the Christian churches, ejection of Christians from civil and military office, suppression on pain of death of Christian worship, ending with authority of the local magistrates to ferret out, to torture, and put to death refractory believers.

We have no means of knowing how extensively and how exactly in all parts of the Empire during the eight years of ·its operation this edict was obeyed. Its execution must have depended somewhat on the local authorities, whose sympathy would sometimes be with the Christians. Meanwhile Diocletian had set the first example on record of an Emperor voluntarily divesting himself of the purple, — an example followed a thousand years later by his Western successor of the allied houses of Hapsburg and Castile, on occasion of another great revolution in religion. In distant Dalmatia, in that famed palace which covered ten acres with its courts and its peristyles, as tidings reached him of the troubled East and Christianity still unsubdued, he had leisure to reflect on the impotence of Imperial edicts to quench the light of the world.

Galerius, now sole in command, urged on the war, resolved to prosecute it to the bitter end. The end came soon to the baffled sovereign writhing in the agonies of a loathsome and incurable disease, — confession of defeat, acknowledged impotence, revocation of the hostile edict, and a piteous cry for aid from the Christian God, since other gods had proved powerless and other aid unavailing.

The contest is ended; Christianity has passed

the supreme test. A new principle of social life is thenceforth and forever established in the world. To the Church a new era has come. The heroic age, the martyr age, has passed; an age of dogmatism, of definitions, of hair-splitting controversies, under secular rule, succeeds. The Church has now won Cæsar to her cause, and rejoices in imperial patronage. But what she gains by court favor, in the way of temporal prosperity, she loses in spiritual freedom. Her princely benefactor proves unwittingly her worst enemy. This from a moral point of view. But the moral view does not always coincide with the providential order. It was necessary in the counsels of the Spirit that Christendom should have possession of the throne, and the Spirit can bear with temporary evil, and profit by it in the compassing of its ends.

What shall we say of Constantine, the first of the so-called Christian Emperors? As a man of action, in war and peace, he emphatically merits the epithet Great which attaches to his name. Superbly endowed in body and mind, able alike as captain and as statesman, fitted by nature to be a ruler of men, successful in conflict with potent rivals, concentrating and consolidating under one head the vast extent of the Roman Empire, founder of a city which for four centuries was the capital of Christendom, and has been for four centuries

the capital of Islam, — he must be accounted one
of the few great sovereigns on the roll of history.
But in what sense can we speak of him as a Christian? Morally lawless, shrinking from no crime,
guilty of the worst, how could the Church receive
him as such? Toward the close of his life he
received Christian baptism. We may hope that
something of conviction accompanied the rite; as
much, perhaps, as was possible to a nature like his.
But previous to that, on the simple ground of his
patronage, how could Christians consent to submit
to the arbitration of the homicide, the filicide, the
conjugicide, questions of Christian doctrine and
discipline? Their doing so is proof of spiritual
degeneracy consequent on temporal success. Constantine had the sagacity to see the necessity of
conciliating the Christian interest, destined to be
the most influential element in his dominion.
Whatever may be the truth concerning the alleged vision of the cross, there can be no doubt
of his hearty belief in the τούτῳ νίκα.

Before grappling with Maxentius he had his
battle-flag stamped with the monogram of Christ.
After the victory of the Milvian Bridge he issued,
in conjunction with Licinius, an edict which not
only permitted the Christians to rebuild their
churches, but restored to them the property in
houses and lands which under Diocletian had been

confiscated for the use of the State. He ordained a tax on land for the support of Christian worship, he exempted the Christian *clerus* from military service, and forbade labor, excepting agricultural, on Sundays. And when Licinius, abandoning his former position and ranging himself frankly on the side of the old religion, had been overcome and slain in battle, Constantine, then sole Emperor, formally espoused the Christian cause and diverted the funds of some of the Gentile temples to the use of the Christian. But that these demonstrations were acts of State policy, and not of religious conviction, must have been sufficiently evident to all his subjects. His aim was to equalize and, if possible, to harmonize the different confessions. He had no intention, at first, of breaking with polytheism. He still retained the title of pontifex maximus. In the New Rome which he founded on the Bosphorus, moved thereto by Sibylline and other prophecies (that of the "Apocalypse" among the rest), which predicted the fall of Rome on the Tiber, he caused to be erected, along with several Christian churches, a temple to Castor and Pollux, one to Rhea, the mother of the gods, and one to the Tyche, the Fortune of the city. An image of this Tyche occupied the centre of the cross upheld by the united hands of the colossal statues of the Emperor and his mother, Helena.

So far from renouncing the honor of the apotheosis bestowed on his predecessors, he made special provision for it by ordaining that annually, in all coming time, a golden statue of himself should be borne in procession through the city, and that the Emperor for the time being should prostrate himself before it. On the top of a monolith of porphyry he had placed a statue of Apollo, re-dedicated to himself, with a halo of rays formed, it was said, of nails taken from the cross which Helena had brought from Jerusalem. Between the nails the inscription: " To Constantine shining like the sun, presiding over his city, an image of the new-risen Sun of Righteousness." This column, we are told, was long an object of formal worship to the Christians of Constantinople.

All this was polytheism over again. And these measures, conceived in the spirit of the old religion, were subsequent to the Council of Nicæa, at which the Emperor had presided with hands yet red from the recent murder of Crispus.

Constantine was no worse than many a Christian ruler of later time. Our resentment against him is not on account of his crimes as such, but as viewed in the light of the praises bestowed upon him by Christian ecclesiastical historians. Eusebius, the cringing courtier, characterizes him as one "adorned with every virtue of religion." Ecclesiastical policy

forbade the censure of his crimes. The credit of
the Church was more to the historian than the
cause of truth. There is not a more hateful creature in human guise than your typical ecclesiastic.
" Will ye speak wickedly for God ? will ye talk deceitfully for him ?" Job asks of his friends. Talking deceitfully for God, and, where the temper of
the time permitted, killing and laying waste for
God, has been the practice of ecclesiastical policy
in every age. The Christian ecclesiastics of the
new-born Church are no exception. " Lying," says
Maurice, in his Lectures on Church History, " is the
first crime we hear of after the descent of the Holy
Spirit. It is of this that we shall have to hear at
every step as we proceed in the history. . . . I shall
have to tell you of lies uttered by bad men and
by good men. . . . The Church testifies of God as
much through its falsehoods and its sins as through
its truth and its virtues."

The Church of the fourth century could boast
a few choice spirits, — a Gregory Nazianzen, an
Athanasius, a Basil, a Theodore of Mopsuestia ;
but take them in the mass, as they figure in history, the ecclesiastics of that day were a disrep-
utable lot, — conspicuous among them a brutal
George of Cappadocia and a Lucifer of Cagliari.
In the fifth century we have a murderous Cyril, a
Dioscurus, and the incredible atrocities of the two

successive Councils of Ephesus. How they wrangled! Scarce escaped persecution themselves, how they persecuted one another, staking the integrity of the Church on a vocable, an iota, contemptuously indifferent to questions of morality, demanding only correctness of doctrine! A bishop is charged with unchastity. "What do we care about his chastity? Is he orthodox? That is the question." "Worse than a Sodomite is he who will not call Mary the Mother of God! May fire from heaven consume him! May the earth open and swallow him!"

If Christianity were simply Christ-likeness, a life conformed to the precepts of the Gospel, it had well-nigh died out with the triumph of the Church over civil despotism. If the only fruits of the Spirit were those which Paul emphasizes, — love, joy, peace, long-suffering, kindness, goodness, meekness, — then the Spirit might seem, in those years, to have fled up to heaven, like the starry goddess of the Golden Age, and left the Church to her own devices. But the Spirit had not departed; the Spirit has other business besides the cultivation of these moral graces so commended by the Apostle. Through all the turmoil of those angry years, through all the clamor of clashing tongues and crazy Councils, through all the wrangling, the wrath, and the wrong, the Spirit was at work developing in Christian consciousness and assisting to formulate a new conception of Godhead, — of Godhead in its human relations. This conception, partly by instinctive perception and partly by providential conjunction, got itself formulated in the doctrine of the Trinity as enunciated in the Creeds of Nicæa and Constantinople and supplemented by that of Chalcedon, — a doctrine of immense significance, combining what is true in Judaism with what is true in Hellenism, and if not a complete statement of Deity (inasmuch as it leaves material Nature out of view), if not a finality, yet a great advance on former conceptions, connecting, as it does, the human, through identity of spirit, with the divine.[1]

For thirty years the Church had enjoyed the advantage, such as it was, of Imperial patronage. A generation had passed since Christianity had flourished as the Court religion. But now an un-looked-for reverse. The Throne repudiates Christianity and bestows its patronage on polytheism. Christian historians have treated this reaction as something monstrous, and the term "Apostate,"

---

[1] It may seem incongruous, in a "Unitarian Review," to speak favorably of the doctrine of the Trinity ; but the true meaning of the Nicæan-Constantinopolitan creed is something very different from the Trinitarianism justly repudiated by the Unitarian protest.

coupled with the name of Julian, conveys a sentence of reprobation to this day. But the backward step, although politically and philosophically a great mistake, was very natural, and, on the whole, creditable. Consider the circumstances. Deprived in infancy of a mother who might have won him to the Christian cause and given a Christian direction to his life; losing at the age of sixteen his father and all his near kindred, with the exception of his half-brother, by an insurrection of the Imperial troops; placed in confinement and subjected to compulsory Christian instruction, — he learned in early life to judge of Christianity by what he saw of it, which was contemptible, and by what he experienced of it, which was galling; and, on the other hand, to judge of polytheism by what he gathered from the best literature of the ages in which it flourished. His imagination was impressed by the grand traditions of olden time; his intellect was fed and fired by the poets and philosophers of Greece. What had the Church to set off against these for a youth whose heart had never been reached by the Gospel, for whom it was a question between the religion of the Court and that of probably the larger portion of the Empire? All that he knew of the Court religion was petty intrigue and disgraceful broils, quarrels about *homoöusion* and *homoiousion*. Add to this that the chivalrous spirit of the youth was roused in favor of the oppressed by the persecutions with which Constantius harassed the adherents of the old religion.

When, therefore, in 361, the army which he commanded in Gaul, impressed by his military genius and his eminent virtues, proclaimed him Emperor, and when the death of Constantius left him free to follow the promptings of his spirit, he openly espoused the cause of Hellenism, and in all sincerity and with all the zeal of a new convert applied himself to the restoration of the ancient cult. It is curious to consider that precisely the two noblest, the two most religious, in the long line of the Augusti should have been zealous opponents of the Christian cause. Julian ranks next to Aurelius in purity of life and earnestness of soul. His contemporary and fellow-soldier, Ammianus Marcellinus, the sagacious Latin historian of the fourth century, declares that there was in him the material of a hero of the old Greek type; that in other times he might have been an Achilles or an Alexander, but that the age and circumstances in which he lived made him a Sophist. His native ambition degenerated into vanity and love of popularity: " vulgi plausibus laetus, laudum, etiam in minimis rebus, intemperans adpetitor." Gregory Nazianzen ascribed to him the bearing of a madman. Voltaire, in his epigrammatic fashion, characterizes him as "faithless to the faith and faithful to reason, the scandal of the Church and the model of kings." His writings which have come down to us, composed amid the distractions of public life, exhibit a sprightly intellect, more witty than profound. The two satires, "The Cæsars" and the "Misopogon," are the most characteristic; they bear comparison with the writings of Lucian, the wittiest of the ancients. The most important of his productions for the modern Christian reader is the so-called "Defence of Paganism," which in fact is only a criticism of Christianity. The criticism is poor from our point of view, but curious as illustrating the aspect which dogmatic Christianity presented to an outsider of that day. It is noticeable that the author uniformly addresses the Christians as Galileans, and indeed commanded that they should bear that name.

It is not for a moment to be supposed that Julian expected, by his example and Imperial authority, to roll back the tide of opinion and uproot the plant of three hundred years' growth which overshadowed his realm. The uttermost he hoped to accomplish was to infuse new life into Hellenism, to restore to it somewhat of its ancient splendor, to make it an attractive rival of the Christian Church; but even this proved to be beyond his power. The thing was too decrepit to be galvanized into any respectable show of life. It is pitiful to read of his disappointments in this endeavor. He attempted to rebuild the temple of Jerusalem and to consecrate it to Gentile worship. Immense sums were devoted to the enterprise; but the workmen were repelled, as Ammianus relates, by bursting fires, and forced to desist from their labors. He undertook to restore the oracle at Delphos, which had long ceased to give answers. "Tell the sovereign," was the report made to the commissioner, "that the wondrous structure has sunk into dust. Apollo has not so much as a hut left, no prophetic laurel; the speaking fountain has gone silent." He went about to celebrate, after long intermission, the annual festival of Apollo in the grove of Daphne, near Antioch. He repaired to the spot in person, in his character of pontifex maximus, expecting to witness the ancient pomp of sacrifice. " But when I arrived," he says, in the " Misopogon," " I found neither incense nor wafers nor victim. An old priest had brought the god a goose, but the rich city nothing, neither oil for the lamps nor wine for a drink-offering. . . . And yet [addressing the citizens of Antioch] you allow your wives to give everything your house affords to the Galileans, to feed their poor."

All this while the Christians never doubted the result. "'T is a cloud," said brave Athanasius, " which will soon blow over." When the prospect looked most encouraging to the Gentiles, Libanius the philosopher is said to have taunted a Christian acquaintance with the question, "How now about your carpenter's son?" The answer was: "The carpenter's son is making a coffin for him in whom you have placed your hope."

Julian was too wise, perhaps too merciful, to adopt the severe measures of former Emperors against the Christians. He knew too well what kind of harvest springs from the blood of martyrs. But in a mild way he allowed himself to persecute by invidious discriminations in favor of polytheism, and by exclusion of Christians from many of their former privileges. Ammianus himself, though siding with the Emperor in the main, condemns the edict by which Christian scholars were forbidden to teach the classics, and Christian children to receive instruction in Greek lore, on the ground that they could not do justice to writers whose religion they contemned. The prohibition was keenly felt by the Christians, and, to supply the loss of classic literature, Apollinarius wrote a heroic poem on the fortunes of the Hebrew people from the creation of the world to the time of Saul, in which, as honest Sozomen assures us, he far surpassed Homer. He also wrote comedies after the manner of Menander, tragedies in imitation of Euripides, odes on the model of Pindar. "I doubt not," says Sozomen, with exquisite simplicity, "that if it were not for the prejudice in favor of the old authors, the writings of Apollinarius would be held in as high estimation as those of the ancients."

Julian was not so bigoted as not to appreciate the immense superiority of the Christian Church over polytheism as a practical social religion. He saw very clearly where lay the strength of the Gospel, and exhorted his priesthood to imitate the philanthropy of the Galileans by establishing institutions like theirs for the entertainment of strangers, for the care of the poor and the sick, for instruction in the truths of religion; to introduce preaching in their temples, and, generally, to copy Christian manners. It seems never to have occurred to him that the ordering of these things was a virtual acknowledgment of the claims of Christianity. "It is a shame to us," he writes, "that those impious Galileans not only provide for their own poor, but also for ours, whom we neglect." He failed to perceive that only a good tree can bring forth good fruit.

Julian died at the age of thirty-one in an expedition against the Persians from which the warnings of his friends and even his own forebodings could not deter him. He was killed, it is said, by the treacherous spear of a soldier of his own army. The high-hearted, impetuous youth, "the roman-

ticist on the throne of the Cæsars," had lived in
vain for the cause he had espoused, but not in vain
for that which he opposed; for though his apostasy
had occasioned some defections from the Church,
some ignominious backslidings, and many bloody
conflicts between the polytheists who counted on
his patronage and the Christians whom he failed
to protect, it served to reveal the weakness and
decadence — the utter, hopeless decadence — of the
Gentile faith. The experiment in which a Julian
had failed would not be tried again. The old religion was irrevocably doomed; had it only been
allowed to die in peace a natural death; but Christian zeal would not permit.

The time had come when the Christians were in
a position to wreak their vengeance on the Gentiles;
and with the opportunity came the will. They hastened to persecute the children of those who had
persecuted their fathers. In vain the Scriptures
read in their churches — the law of their religion —
commanded: "Avenge not yourselves, but give
place unto wrath;" "Recompense to no man evil
for evil." They perceived another law in their
members. Constantine, as we have seen, while
siding with the Christians, spared the adherents
of the elder faith. It was reserved for a Spaniard,
a native of that land which in after years produced
a Torquemada and blushed with the fires of the

Inquisition, to institute the first *autos-da-fé* for the suppression of Paganism. We pass by an interval of twenty years, from the death of Julian to the reign of Theodosius. The Council of Constantinople had just completed the doctrine of the Trinity, when the new Emperor, baptized into that faith, and, in the language of Gibbon, " still glowing with the warm feelings of regeneration," issued an edict which prescribed the religion of his subjects. "It is our pleasure that all the nations which are governed by our clemency and moderation shall steadfastly adhere to the religion which was taught by Saint Peter to the Romans." " Let us believe in the sole deity of the Father, the Son, and the Holy Spirit, under an equal majesty and a pious trinity." Having thus dictated to his subjects, a large, if not the larger, portion of whom still worshipped as polytheists after the manner of their fathers, he proceeded, by successive edicts, to hunt out and to stamp out every vestige of the faith which for so many centuries had intempled and inspired the two great nations which have scored the boldest characters on the scroll of pre-Christian history, and yielded — the one by its letters and arts, the other by its jurisprudence — such important contributions to the civilization of mankind.

There were still, we are told, in the city of Rome three hundred temples in which sacrifice was

offered.[1] These were now to be suppressed. In the
year 385 an edict of the government ordained that
sacrifices should cease, and forbade on pain of torture and death the function of the haruspex. Then
began a systematic crusade, in which the Emperor
conspired with the local bishops and monks to put
an end to Gentile worship. An Imperial officer
was despatched with full powers to close the temples in the capital cities of the East. But the closing of the temples did not satisfy the blind fury of
Christian zealots. They must not only be closed,
but destroyed. The most magnificent structures
ever dedicated to the service of religion, the costly
marvels of architectural art, — among them the
famed Serapeum at Alexandria, — were ruthlessly
given to the flames or levelled with the ground,
and where resistance was made by the votaries,
the carnage of previous centuries was renewed.
The new religion availed no more than the old
to tame the tiger that has its lair in the human
breast.

The persecutions suffered by Christians under
Roman Emperors of the second and third centuries
are well known. Writers of Church history have
seen to it that they should not pass into oblivion.
Not so well known are the persecutions inflicted by
Christians in power on their Gentile subjects and

[1] Lasaulx, Der Untergang des Hellenismus.

fellow-citizens.   Lasaulx, in a monograph devoted
to the subject,[1] has presented them in one view in
the order of their succession, — a long story, and
profoundly tragic!   If the slaughter was less, the
atrocity was greater, as perpetrated by disciples of
a religion whose plainest precepts were violated by
it.   The Christian conscience of the time appears
to have been less shocked by these enormities than
by the treatment of the orthodox under Arian rule,
although Socrates does admit that the murder of
Hypatia, the beautiful and learned lecturer of Alexandria, whose body was stripped and mangled with
oyster-shells by Christian fanatics, was discreditable
to Cyril and the Alexandrian Church.

It had taken three centuries to place Christianity
on the throne ; two more were required to complete
the extinction by fire and sword of the vanquished
faith.   The final act of the long tragedy was the
closing of the schools of Athens by the Emperor
Justinian.   Already in the same year, 529, the
founder of the Benedictine Order at Monte Casino
had destroyed the last temple of Apollo and the
adjacent grove, in which the pagans still sacrificed
to their tutelar god.

The end had come, the work was accomplished.
The old heaven and the old earth had passed away.
The Spirit had created " a new heaven and a new

[1] Der Untergang des Hellenismus.

earth." Can we add—could Christian consciousness, at that high solstice of the world's history,
add—" wherein dwelleth righteousness"? Alas,
no! The looked-for righteousness was yet in abeyance, far remote in the depths of time. It is still
remote; although nearer, let us trust, than in those
early years of grace.

What, then, was the aim of the Spirit in the
founding of the Christian Church,—a work accomplished at such fearful cost? Not *primarily* good
behavior. Had this been the end, there would
have been a rapid and marked improvement in
the morals of society. But no such improvement
appears. Salvian, a Christian presbyter of Arles,
writing about the middle of the fifth century, complains that " the Church of God itself, which should
be pleasing in the sight of God, is but the provoker
of God's wrath." " With the exception of the very
few who shun evil (*praeter paucissimos quosdam
qui mala fugiunt*), what is the whole body of
Christians but a sink of vices?"

A new world the Spirit had builded; but much
of the old material went into the building. Morality was not its primary aim. That will come
in due season, when the work is complete. The
moral law, by the " Power that makes for righteousness," will finally vindicate itself. The aim of the
Spirit in the founding of the Christian Church I

7

suppose to have been this: to provide a matrix and nursery for certain ideas, notably for these three, — the idea of a divine humanity embodied in the doctrine of the Trinity; the idea of the solidarity of the human race; the idea of a heavenly kingdom in this earthly world. When these ideas have taken full possession of the mind and heart of humanity and have actualized themselves in human life, then Christianity will have fulfilled its mission; then the Spirit will cast aside the sheltering hull of ecclesiasticism; the Church, no longer a separate organism, will be merged in society; the secular and the spiritual, principially and practically one, will realize at last in their full consummation the " new heaven and new earth wherein dwelleth righteousness."

FEUDAL SOCIETY.

IN history there is properly no beginning, no record of a time when civil society was absolutely and altogether new. Society, like the individual, has no knowledge of its own birth. The earliest which history can trace and ascertain is not the earliest that has been, but refers us to something still more remote, unchronicled, inscrutable. Every nation that now exists was the offspring of another. Every nation known to history was the offspring of another; and the eldest are lost in prehistoric night. Every civil and social institution has elements derived from an unexplored and dateless time. Nations, institutions, and events are the varying phases of a stream whose source is unknown, and equally unknown its issues. History reports what appears, and leaves to antiquarian surmise at one end, and to philosophic speculation at the other, the conjectural beginnings and endings.

And as there is no beginning, so in history there is no retrocession or decline. The thousand years which intervened between the fall of the

Western Empire in the fifth century and that of the Eastern in the fifteenth are commonly regarded as a period of arrested development, a halt in the march of humanity, or even a retreat. The arrest we may grant, but only in the sense in which the winter that arrests the vegetation of one season guards the germs of the next. The Græco-Roman civilization was defunct; but a new civilization was steadily forming beneath the frosts of mediæval years. History is never retrograde. Nations may degenerate, arts may perish; but humanity never halts. There is always progress somewhere, in some things. The same nature which produced the Greek and Roman civilities was just as vigorous and just as productive in the age of Hildebrand as in that of Pericles or that of Augustus. If it did not produce the same things, it produced others which were quite as needful. The philosophic historian sees nothing retrograde in all those centuries, but unbroken progress, the steady germination of seed that was sown while Rome was still in the zenith of her power. He sees no perishing world, but a world in genesis, — an immense future struggling into birth. In every falling leaf of the Græco-Roman civilization he sees the forward shoot of the Christian, which pushed it from its stem.

The distinguishing feature of mediæval life is

Feudalism. To understand feudalism, we must study its origin in the semi-barbarous society of the German tribes antecedent to the Christian era. The ancient Germans, as Tacitus describes them, differed from the Romans, the Greeks, and the Oriental nations in not inhabiting cities, but thinly settled rural districts governed by chiefs, who in turn were subject to the king of the nation or tribe. This circumstance gave to the mediæval politics their distinguishing character as compared with the ancient States. The basis of the ancient State was the civic corporation; that of the mediæval was landed possession, the possessor being bound by feudal tenure to the Crown. The king was elective, but chosen from certain noble families, not from the people at large. The leaders under him were selected for their warlike qualities. *Reges ex nobilitate, duces ex virtute sumunt,* says Tacitus. Each king had a hundred followers or associates chosen from among the people, called in Latin *comites (centeni singulis ex plebe comites),* from which our English count, county, country.

In German, the *comites* were called *Gesellen* (companions), from which, it is supposed, our English word *vassal* is derived. Vassal and count are identical terms. Vassalage, etymologically speaking, is not bondage, but fellowship, peerage. The Germans had slaves; but these were captives of war, or such as had lost their freedom in games of chance.

Another peculiarity of the German tribes was their respect for women, to whom they accorded a much higher rank than was ever assigned to them by Greece or Rome. They were the counsellors of the nation, diligently consulted in all matters of public moment. They followed their husbands and brothers to the wars, stimulated them with their cries, and sometimes decided the battle by their interposition. In accordance with this reverence for the " ever womanly," the German, with its cognates, is the only European language in which to this day the sun is feminine and the moon masculine. Guizot makes light of this trait of the German forest, or of Tacitus's testimony regarding it. But I think we have here the prototype of a very marked feature of mediæval civilization, — the loyalty to woman, exhibited practically in the courtesies of chivalry, and poetically in the lays of the Minnesingers.

Once more. The German aborigines were preeminently a nation of warriors. All barbarous nations are given to fighting ; but the Germans seem more than any other to have exemplified the doctrine of Hobbes, that war is man's natural state. *Nihil nisi armati agunt.* They carried war into everything. It was their business, their pastime, their politics, their religion. When there was no foreign enemy to encounter, they made war upon each other; they invaded neighboring territories, and sought in every possible way to keep themselves in training for the great work of life. In these military expeditions the king was attended by his *comites*, or counts, between whom and himself there subsisted an intimate and indissoluble bond. They bound themselves to accompany him through life, and to accompany him in death. He bound himself to stand by them in all straits, to find them food and equipment in return for their services, and to give them their share of the plunder.

We have here the rudiments of the feudal system, — a system in which independence and loyalty were singularly blended, "the system," says Heeren, "of people who had a good deal of fighting to do, and very little money." Suppose, now, a clan or tribe of these warriors at the end of one of their predatory excursions to settle in some province of the Roman Empire. Let that tribe be the Franks, with Clovis at their head. Let that province be the western part of Gaul, which took from them the name of France. There it was that the feudal system was soonest developed and most clearly defined. Clovis is a German prince, attended by his *duces*, or dukes, the leaders next in command, by his and their *comites*, or counts, and other warriors of inferior note. They settle in Gaul. Clovis becomes king of France. The ancient inhabitants are dispossessed. Some of them become serfs or slaves. Others, and especially the clergy, by means of superior ability attain to posts of honor around the Throne. Some of them in process of time become vassals of the Crown.

The land is divided into districts, and over each district is placed one of the counts as magistrate and collector of revenues. Hence the term *compté*, "county." A *dux*, or duke, had charge of several counties. These offices, held originally during the pleasure of the king, were afterward hereditary, and laid the foundation of that power by which the nobles in time became rivals of the Throne. The rest of the warriors received by allotment or obtained by pillage portions of land, which they held in their own right, with power of devise, and subject to no condition but the general burden of public defence. These estates were called *allodial*,—a word denoting absolute property, in distinction from feudal. The feudal estates were benefices or grants made by the king to his favorites (*Gasindi, Antrustions, Leudes*) out of the reserved fiscal or Crown lands, not as absolute property, but as a temporary loan, to be returned on the death or forfeiture of the occupant, who during possession was bound to render fealty and military service, when required, to the grantor. We see here repeated the same principle which connected the *rex*, or the *dux*, in the forests of Germany with his *comites*, or vassals. The holder of such a benefice was the vassal of the Crown.

The benefices in time became hereditary; and then commenced another stage in the feudal process, — *subinfeudation.* The holders of grants from the Crown made new grants of portions of their estates to new beneficiaries, who received them on similar terms, and sustained the same relation to the new grantor which he did to the Crown. They were his vassals; he was their *suzerain*, or *mesne lord*. An estate so held was a *feodum*, or feud. The holder of a feud was bound to follow his lord to battle, albeit against his own kindred, when required, and against his sovereign. He was bound to ride by his side in the field, to lend him his horse when dismounted, and to go into captivity as a hostage for him when taken prisoner. He was liable to certain pecuniary taxes, called "Reliefs and Aids," on taking possession of an hereditary fief, or when his lord made a pilgrimage to Jerusalem or gave his sister or eldest son in marriage, or took a new investiture of his own fief. On the other hand, the suzerain, or feudal lord, was under obligations equally binding to his vassal. He was his vassal's sworn protector, ally, and friend, the helper of his necessity, the avenger of his wrongs. He was required to make indemnification if the tenant was evicted of his land. In Normandy and in England he was his tenant's guardian during minority. In this capacity he was authorized to provide his female wards with husbands; and they, on their part, were bound to accept the husbands, or to pay as much in the way of mulct as the suitor was willing to give for his wife. In the Latin kingdom of Jerusalem, where the feudal system developed some peculiarities, — the result of insulation, — a singular custom prevailed. The lord could compel a female tenant to marry one of three suitors whom he might present to her choice. The candidates must be of equal rank with herself, but one of them she was bound to accept. No avowed disinclination to wedlock in general, no repugnance to the given candidates in particular, could exempt her from this necessity. To females advanced in life, one alternative remained. If the lady would declare herself to be sixty years of age, the right to single-blessedness was not denied her. Of this dilemma it does not appear which horn was preferred in any recorded case.

The feudal system, once established, pervaded the whole structure of society. It embraced the clergy as well as the laity. The dignitaries of the Church and the abbots of monasteries were the vassals of the sovereign or prince, of whom their lands were held in fief. They had their own vassals, who held of them. They were bound, in return for their possessions, to swear fealty and to render military service, if not by taking arms, by sending their vassals into the field.

There was one species of feudal tenure which appears in strange contrast with modern ideas of dignity and rank; that is, the tenure of menial office. Nobles did not disdain to hold such offices about the person or the household of a king or superior, such as cup-bearer, farrier (*maréohal*), stabler (*constable*), bearer of dishes (*seneschal*). Here, again, a marked trait of the old German life. The German loved independence, it was the breath of his nostrils. But with this love of independence he combined a sentiment which might seem at first incompatible with it, — the sentiment of loyalty, enthusiastic devotion to the person of his chief; a devotion which to his mind invested even menial offices, rendered to that chief, with glory. In after times the title remained, while the original function was forgotten. France has still her marshal, although that functionary has no longer the care of stable or stud. His predecessor in the Merovingian era did not disdain that function; he owed to it his title and his estates. The Elector of Saxony was formerly marshal of the German Empire. A symbol of his function long survived in the vessel of oats which the Elector, in person or by deputy, presented to the Emperor at his coronation, as described by Goethe, who witnessed when a boy the coronation of Joseph II. The ascendency of the ecclesiastical power in the twelfth century is illustrated by the fact that the Emperor Frederic Barbarossa held as a fief from the Bishop of Bamberg the office of seneschal, or bearer of dishes.

The basis of feudal polity, as I have said, — that by which it is especially distinguished from ancient civilization, — was landed possession. The ancient civilization was municipal. The Greeks and Romans lived in cities and compact settlements. The Germans, as we learn from Tacitus, lived scattered over large districts, each freeman lord of his own territory, — a custom strictly maintained by their posterity in mediæval Europe, and one which has exercised an immense influence on modern European civilization. The ancient noble, however extensive his landed possessions, was still a citizen, the member of a compact civic body. His property bound him more closely to the State, and the State to him. The property of a mediæval nobleman, on the contrary, tended to seclude him from the rest of the world. The essence of feudalism is insulation. The proprietor, instead of connecting himself with civic organizations, planted himself on his territory, solitary, remote, and became the head and nucleus of a little community of his own which gathered around the feudal castle and subsisted by him and for him. These communities were practically sovereign and independent States. The feudal lord possessed the rights and exercised the three most important functions of a monarch, — the right to make war, the right to coin money, and the right of supreme judicature (*la haute justice*); that is, the right to inflict capital punishment within his domain. In the exercise of this last-named function antiquarians notice a ludicrous distinction between different orders of nobility. Every man who was entitled to a fortified castle might exercise *haute justice*, he might hang offenders within his domain. But the rank of the lord was indicated by the number of posts in his gallows. A baron could hang his subjects on a gallows with four posts. A *châtelain*, or possessor of a castle who was not a vassal of the Crown, was restricted to three posts. A lord inferior to the *châtelain*, the lowest in the scale of nobility, must serve the cause of justice as well as he could with a two-posted gibbet.

Such independence was of course entirely incompatible with the existence of a central and controlling power in the Crown. We read of a king of France, of England, of Germany; but this title previous to the fourteenth century was little more than nominal. The king was merely one noble among many, with perhaps more numerous vassals and a court, but with no more actual power than many of the barons of his realm. The problem of mediæval history was to counteract and overcome this separatism, to develop the nation against the nobles, and to establish the central power of the Crown over feudal independence. This end was soonest and most completely accomplished in that country where feudalism found its earliest and fullest development, — in France, which differed from Germany in having an hereditary instead of an elective monarchy, and from England in the earlier resumption of fiefs by the Crown at the expiration of the feudal tenure. The French sovereign at the close of the thirteenth century had achieved an ascendency which the English did not attain until after the Wars of the Roses.

To this separative tendency of feudalism we owe one of the principal characteristics of modern civilization as contrasted with that of the ancients; namely, the preponderance of the *country* in national polity. The ancient nations were mostly dependencies of capital cities, and are called by the names of their capitals, — as Athens, Rome, Sparta,

Carthage. The destruction of the capital involved that of the nation. Modern nations, on the contrary, are named after their respective races, — France, England, Germany; and notwithstanding the disproportionate influence of the capital in some cases, as of Paris in France, they have an existence independent of the capital, and would continue to exist if the capital were destroyed.

Of later origin than feudalism, but not less widely diffused, was the institution of chivalry, — another marked trait of the Middle Age. It affected profoundly the character and tone of mediæval society, but rather in the way of moral influence than by any organic action on the time. It created no new political Order, but grafted on the class of nobles and freemen an additional social distinction for all who embraced it, as most of the nobles, for lack of other occupation, were fain to do. The title of a knight, or knight-banneret, so long as it represented the reward of valor alone, was the highest distinction known to that period. Kings were proud to add the prefix of Sir to the royal title. It conferred important privileges, among which in some countries was exemption from taxes. But it was not hereditary. It founded no lineage: it expired with the individual on whom it was conferred. It did not modify the organic structure of society. It was bloom and polish, not substance nor form.

Chivalry was eminently a Christian institution. It was the application of Christianity to the business of arms. It was the use of arms for the redemption of society. With it was associated also the old German reverence for women. It gave lustre and sweetness to an age which else had been one of unmitigated barbarism. Morally it is very significant, as illustrating the remedial power of human nature, — that power by which, when evils become intolerable, society reacts on its own excesses and rights its own wrongs.

In our own country, in the new communities of the West, when the law is feeble and the constituted tribunals deficient in authority, the savage but needful Lynch law or vigilance committee supplies the defect. Chivalry was a modification of the same principle more worthily embodied, and authorized with religious sanctions. The knights were self-constituted judges and avengers of social wrong. The knight-errant was a missionary, a military evangelist, operating with spear and sword instead of the word. He was consecrated to his work with solemn and religious ceremonies, and had something of the priestly character. His moral code was not very extensive. It contained but four articles; but these were rigorously enforced. It enjoined truth, hearing Mass, fasting on Friday, and the succoring of dames.

" And thus the fourfold discipline was told.
  Still to the truth direct thy strong desire,
  And flee the very air where dwells a liar.
  Fail not the Mass ; there still with reverent feet
  Each morn be found, nor scant thine offering meet.
  Each week's sixth day with fast subdue thy mind,
  For 't was the day of passion for mankind :
  Else let some pious work, some deed of grace,
  With substituted worth fulfil the place.
  Haste thee, in fine, when dames complain of wrong,
  Maintain their right, and in their cause be strong ;
  For not a wight there lives, if right I deem,
  Who holds fair hope of well-deserved esteem,
  But to the dames by strong devotion bound,
  Their cause sustains, nor faints for toil or wound."[1]

The necessity of such an institution is explained
by the lawless character of the times, by the social
anarchy and predatory violence of a barbarous age.
Europe was everywhere infested with robbers, who
ravaged the country, made travelling unsafe, and
agitated society with perpetual alarms. Peaceably
disposed persons were subject to violence whenever they ventured abroad, and were not always
safe in their own homes. The boldness and nu-
merical strength of these robber bands may be
inferred from the fact that the highest dignitaries
in Church and State, and even royal personages
travelling with large escorts of armed followers,
were attacked by them on the highway, plundered,
and sometimes held prisoners until redeemed by a

[1] The Order of Knighthood, — Way's Fabliaux.

ransom.　In 1285 the town of Boston in England was assailed and pillaged by a party of these marauders.

In splendor and pomp, the customs of chivalry far exceed all that modern life can exhibit in the way of spectacle and festive show.　If mediæval Europe was poor in productive industry, she was rich in knightly splendor and festivity.　When we call up before us the idea of those ages, we have a picture of nodding plumes, resplendent shields, and gay devices, a lavish display of gold and silver in knightly appointments.　We see the compact body of cavaliers drawn up before the baronial castle or pilgriming toward the Holy Land.　We see the gallant tournament with its rich caparisons and pennoned lances, —

> "Where throngs of knights and barons bold
> In weeds of peace high triumphs hold,
> With store of ladies, whose bright eyes
> Rain influence and judge the prize," —

a spectacle which in gorgeous appearance and stirring effect has probably never been surpassed.

On the whole, the institution of chivalry was a wise and beneficent force, opposed to anarchy and violence, — a splendid vindication of human nature against barbarism and social wrong.

Its effect on literature is seen in the metrical productions of the twelfth, thirteenth, and fourteenth centuries. The adventures and the manners of chivalry supplied authors of these productions, the Troubadours, Trouveurs, and Makers, with their materials and topics. And so completely was the mind of the time preoccupied with chivalric ideas that all topics were treated in the same fashion. The worthies of ancient history, the heroes of Plutarch and Homer, were metamorphosed into Christian knights. Even Biblical characters underwent the same transformation. Adam Davie, a poet of the fourteenth century, represents Pilate as challenging our Lord to single combat. In " Piers Ploughman's Vision" the soldier who pierced the Saviour's side is spoken of as a knight who came forth with his spear and jousted with Jesus.

Intimately associated with the institution of chivalry, and characteristic of the time, was the grave importance attached by the higher orders of society to the sentiment of love. Knighthood, from the first, distinguished itself by devotion to woman,— a trait derived from the ancient Germans. Every knight had his lady-love, of whom he professed himself the devoted slave, and whose superiority to every other lady in creation he conceived it his duty to assert, if necessary, with spear and sword. According to the received comparison, a knight without a lady was like a sky without a sun. In this there was often more of affectation than of true sentiment. The pretended passion was not of that practical character which looks to matrimony as its proper consummation, but an aristocratic fancy, perhaps an assumed one, cherished for its own sake,—an idea which served to stimulate valor, and beguiled the tediousness of unoccupied hours; a thing to dream of and to break a lance for, but not to be realized in the way of a domestic establishment.

The most remarkable part of this lady-worship was the mystic importance, the metaphysical subtilties, and minute casuistry which the spirit of the time connected with the subject.

Courts were established for the purpose of adjusting all questions that might arise between lovers or concerning them. Whether they really loved, what were the proofs of affection, what their mutual obligations,—all this was determined by a regular code of love, compiled with great care, and considered as binding as the canons of the Church. All differences between lovers and all questions of gallantry were referred to these courts for adjudication. They were presided over by kings, emperors, and even popes. They had all the usual officers, counsellors, auditors, masters of request. Their decrees were duly reported, and illustrated by commentaries pointing out their conformity to the principles of the Roman Law and the Fathers of the Church.

It may be doubted if the private, domestic life of women in these ages corresponded with this public devotion. Indeed, the whole system of chivalry owes much of its attraction to the medium of tradition and romance through which we view it, and loses its brilliancy on closer inspection, as theatrical illusions are dispelled by a peep behind the scenes. If we could transport ourselves into those centuries, compare their fashions with ours, observe their daily life, and bring it to the test of modern refinement, we should see that the romance of chivalry is partly the effect of distance, which works enchantment in time as well as in space.

If we could witness the scenes which were then exhibited in the way of theatrical entertainment; if we could listen to the lays of the minstrels, or even, it is probable, to the language of the hall and bower; if we could follow lady and knight in all the details of their daily life, and notice every point in the manners of the times, — we should find that the age which, as mirrored in novel and song, shows so courteous and fine, was in fact extremely coarse, indecent, and disgusting. The knight whose costly armor shone so gayly in the lists would not, when stripped of his outer case, have seemed to modern refinement a very fascinating object. He often sacrificed to the splendor of helmet and hauberk what might have been more profitably spent on a comfortable wardrobe, and was richer in iron than in linen. Civet or other coarse perfume was needed to disguise the effects of hard exercise in woollen garments under iron armor. But mediæval taste was not curious in such matters. When the knight arrived at a castle where he was to lodge as guest, the ladies of the house came to meet him in the court-yard, divested him of his armor, and clothed him in the loose upper robe which was worn within doors, and of which every family kept a supply for visitors.

The lady whom the knight elected as the mistress of his heart and life, and for whose charms he was ready to defy the world to mortal combat, could neither read nor write. She possessed none of the accomplishments or resources of a modern lady. Not that the want of intellectual culture was the lot of all the women of that age. Where it did exist, in convents and in some of the cities, it was carried to a greater extent than with us, as we see in the case of Héloïse. But these were exceptions. Inability to read and write was the usual condition of the high-born as well as of the lowly.

It is fearful to think what ennui those high-born dames must have suffered when left to their own devices in the absence of their knights and of out-door diversions. They lived in rooms which were bare not only of paint and paper, but also of plaster or other internal architectural finish. The hall, and perhaps the ladies' bower, were hung with tapestry; that is, with pieces of figured canvas suspended upon hooks extending along the sides of the apartment, at a distance of about two feet from the wall. When the family removed, these were taken down and left only the bare stone walls. The floor was usually covered with straw or with rushes, not too often renewed, and harboring fragments of food and all manner of impurities. Our fine lady's wardrobe and household appointments, though not wanting in jewels and other splendors for festive seasons, were lamentably deficient in what are now regarded as the necessaries of life. She had no stockings to her feet, most likely no cloths to her table, possibly no sheets to her bed. If she had handkerchiefs, the supply was exceedingly limited, consisting of one or two for state occasions, and none for common use. She had no accommodations for sitting in her bower, except, perhaps, a stone seat in the embrasure of the window, and her bed. Chairs were unknown. At meals, the company sat on rude wooden benches around coarse wooden tables. Waiters were abundant, but the table furniture was scanty and vile to a degree very shocking to modern sensibility. A few pieces of plate, hereditary or plundered, graced the tables of the wealthy; but the dishes were mostly wooden trays, and the plates or trenchers were of the same material. The custom of a plate to each person was a luxury undreamed of. One plate for two was the utmost allowance; and at festive entertainments the gallantry of the age contrived to couple the sexes, so that each gentleman should share his plate with a lady. In the novel of "Launcelot du Lac," a lady whom her jealous husband had compelled to dine in the kitchen complains that it is a very long time since any knight has eaten off the same plate with her. Gentleman and lady have a plate between them, but no fork. The fork is altogether a modern invention. Knightly and fair fingers came into primary relations with boiled and roast, — a fashion more primitive than nice, especially when we add the absence of napkins.

On the whole, mediæval life appears more attractive in the field than it does within doors; it shows better at a distance than it does on close inspection; and loses much of the bloom of its romance when we bring it fairly before us in its practical details.

And yet we see only its best features as it passes before us in the current history of the time. We see knights, nobles, and priests, — that class which in every age is most independent of circumstances, most able to help itself. We see little or nothing of the weaker classes, which form in every age so large a constituent of society. In mediæval as in Greek and Roman civilization, the laboring classes, distinctively so called, were mostly slaves.

The origin of slavery in the Middle Age was various. We find it existing among the German aborigines before their migration. Their slaves were either prisoners of war or criminals, or such as had staked their liberty at the gaming-table, and who probably lost nothing by exchanging bondage to a passion for bondage to an individual. The German tribes, when they migrated, took their slaves with them. They found slavery existing in the territories which they conquered. The Franks found *servi* and *coloni* in Roman Gaul, and the Normans found *thralls* and *ceorls* in Saxon England. Thus mediæval bondage was in part the continuation of a previous institution. Another source of bondage, which seems strange to us, was self-sale. In that terrible period of anarchy, violence, and famine which preceded the age of Hildebrand, many a poor freeman was induced to sell his liberty for a maintenance, his person for bread. It was a choice of evils, in which, provided the master were humane, the servile alternative to a hungry and peaceably disposed man was the more tolerable. A North American savage would have chosen differently.

Another cause of self-sale, and another source of bondage still more abhorrent to modern ideas, was the piety which induced some to sell themselves to monasteries and religious establishments for the benefit of their prayers. In this case we know not which more to admire, — the price of intercession, or the faith in intercession which was willing to pay that price.

The condition of the Jews in the Middle Age was a kind of bondage peculiar to that period. The Christian world conceived itself charged with the duty of avenging on this wretched people the sins of their fathers. General massacres, sanctioned or connived at by government, from time to time gave vent to this retributory spite. In the absence of these, all kinds of exactions and oppressions distinguished the hated race. In the city of Toulouse it was customary for a priest at the Easter festival publicly to smite a Jew on the cheek at the gate of the principal church. Sismondi relates that on one occasion a powerful ecclesiastic felled to the earth and killed his victim with this paschal blow. The Jews in each city had a separate quarter assigned to them for their residence, where they were locked up at nightfall. They were forced to wear a yellow patch or horned hat, or other distinguishing badge, which indicated at the first sight the abhorred people. Two remarkable facts illustrate the indomitable vigor and vitality of this wondrous race. One is that, with such inducements to abandon the religion of their fathers, they seldom embraced the Christian faith. The other is that, with all these oppressions and obstructions, they still throve, they grew rich. The commerce of the time was chiefly in their hands. They supplied the exchequer of kings and nobles, and are said in the time of Philip Augustus to have possessed one half of the city of Paris.

Such was the state of society in Europe between the ninth and fourteenth centuries. Its distinguishing feature, as compared with modern life, is rigid separation, seclusion, no central power, no free communication, no social flow, no point of union but the Church. The few cities were sharply defined against the surrounding country by protecting walls. Within those walls the various classes and vocations were jealously screened and confined by traditionary guilds and corporations. In the country, instead of the open villages, hamlets, and farms of modern civilization, the traveller found here and there the secluded monastery, with its offices and patches of cultivation, or the feudal castle perched on the brow of a hill, with its clustering huts nestling in anxious dependence around its base, the communicating drawbridge ever up, the warder on the tower forever on the watch to detect the distant enemy. The City, the Monastery, the Castle,—these were the three enclosures which contained the three forms of mediæval life. All around and between a blank wilderness; and each of these settlements, the civic, the ecclesiastic, and the feudal, self-contained, self-complete, and as separate from the rest of the world as if divided by intervening seas,—no openness, no expansion, no public, no society but the pent-up life contained within the precincts of each particular fold. Feudalism developed individuality, it made marked and strong men; but all its conditions were adverse to civil order.

There is nothing so difficult in history as to form a correct idea of the private life of past ages. Public life records itself in public monuments and written chronicles. But that which we most desire to know is precisely that which history does not reveal. What humanity most desires to know of the past is man,—humanity in its common domestic aspects and functions, the daily ordinary life of ordinary men. Not how monarchs ruled and warriors fought and nobles feasted, but how John and Thomas sped and fared in their daily tasks and fortunes; what was their programme for the day and for the year; how they amused themselves in the intervals of labor; what clothes they wore, and what was the cost of them, and what they had for breakfast, dinner, and supper. Of battles fought by nations and tribes on public fields the old chronicles have given us abundant details. We accept these with all gratitude; but we would also know of the daily battle of life, with what conditions and with what success it was fought on the common level by common men. Of this no record has survived; but we are safe in assuming that the net result and absolute gain in this warfare was the same to mediæval man that it is to modern, — that, with all their defects of means and accommodations, they extracted as much of the pure juice of life from their hard condition as we do from ours.

With all the progress humanity has made in other arts and kinds, there has been no progress in the art of life, if the art of life is to fill the twenty-four hours with the greatest number of pleasing sensations or the greatest amount of profitable experience or profitable action. Every facility and every accommodation — mechanical, economical, literary — which advancing civilization brings with it, is compensated by corresponding requisitions; and the labor of life for the individual is nowise superseded by it. The conditions may change, but the problem of life is ever the same. In every age the problem for the individual is how to make the most of a day, — to fill up the given mould of existence with an adequate flow of conscious life. The mould is the same in the nineteenth century that it was in the ninth; and the filling up is no easier now than it was then, and no more likely to be satisfactory.

The question which humanity asks of an age is not how fast it travels, nor with what despatch it gets tidings from abroad, nor how many printed sheets or yards of cloth it can turn out in a given time by steam-press and power-loom; but what has it added to the sum of human ideas and human well-being, what spiritual growths have been perfected by it. Tried by this test, it is doubtful if steam, gas, and electro-magnetism have done more for man than feudalism and chivalry. They have multiplied the facilities of life without changing in the least its essential quality. They have shortened the distance from point to point in space, but there is no railroad to happiness. No art has yet been discovered to shorten the distance between the ideal and the real, between desire and satisfaction, between here and there.

Historic progress is not of men, but of man. Individuals are relatively no wiser and no better from age to age; but humanity advances all the while with sure and steady pace, receiving contributions from each successive period, and gaining something with every century which it adds to its dateless life. The ages we have been considering have contributed their full share to this millennial growth; and, dark as they seem compared with our own, they record themselves as real and substantial additions to humanity's increase. The final result of all these contributions — the great human product, the consummate fruit of history — may require for its full maturation and perfection as many ages, perhaps, as were needed to prepare the earth for the first of human kind. Geology traces the steps of that process through all its periods and formations, and shows how each successive revolution contributed its part, how each age deposited its layer and arranged the materials and adjusted the mixture, until the mountains were brought forth, the valleys scooped, the minerals baked, the loam matured, and the finished planet, with all its earths, ores, granite, slate, coal, iron, gold, was compounded and compacted, clothed with vegetation, and delivered up to its human occupant to subdue, replenish, and enjoy. So period-wise and complex, as witnessed by history, will be the composition and growth of historic man. Stratum upon stratum of knowledges and ideas the centuries will deposit in him. Revolution upon revolution will compact his culture. One civilization after another will be absorbed in his blood. Indian and Egyptian myths, Hebrew faiths, Greek and

Italian art and song, feudalism, chivalry, mediæval sanctities, will melt into the heart of him. Whatever of promise and of blessing the travails of humanity have brought forth, whatever of enduring worth the accumulated labors of all generations have compiled, whatever the tempest and the calm of time have proved and perfected, will make up the funded wealth of his complex nature. And, so replenished and matured, he will come in his kingdom, a universal Man, with the wisdom of all time for his intelligence, with the art of all time for his faculty, and the riches of all time for his estate.

CONSERVATISM AND REFORM.

AN ORATION DELIVERED BEFORE THE Φ. B. K. SOCIETY OF HARVARD COLLEGE AT THEIR FIRST MEETING AFTER THE CHANGE IN THEIR CONSTITUTION ENLARGING THE TERMS OF MEMBERSHIP.

GENTLEMEN OF THE Φ. B. K. SOCIETY, —

WE are met for the first time under the new and more liberal aspect which this association now wears. I congratulate you on the change in our Constitution and on the unanimity with which it has been adopted. If in yielding up something of that exclusiveness which heretofore characterized us we have seemed to compromise our ground-idea, the original import of this institution, that compromise is not a forced capitulation to popular prejudice, but a free surrender to the genius of the age, before whose progress old limitations are fast disappearing, as the charmed circle which bounds our dreams dissolves with the morning sun.

A good spirit prompts these concessions, which forestall by a wise policy the revolutions of time. It is well to greet the sun at his coming, to court the blessing of the morning with early vows.

There comes a time when the Past must give
account of itself to the Present, when existing customs and institutions must judge themselves or be
judged. Whatsoever lacks vitality enough to ac-
commodate itself to the new ideas that rule the
time is judged by those ideas and thrust aside, as
the new foliage judges and extrudes the last year's
growth.

Progress is the characteristic of modern Christian civilization, which herein, as Guizot and others
have shown us, is chiefly distinguished from the
fixed ideas of the Asian mind. Our culture is Oriental in its origin; but who distinguishes the features of the parent in the fortunes of the child?
We gaze upon the river as it hastens to the sea,
city-skirted, traffic-swarming; but who remembers
the "mountains old" in whose silent bosom that
river had its rise?

Eternal movement is the characteristic and destiny of the modern mind. Or shall we rather say,
the movement is old like the earth's movement in
space, and only the discovery of it new? The
earth's movement in space, it is now believed, is
not merely the ever-repeated cycle which constitutes the solar year, but a portion of some vaster
orbit which is carrying us toward unknown firma-
ments. Let us believe also that history is not
merely periodical, but progressive. But the prog-

ress of society is never wholly a unanimous movement; its judgment is never a unanimous verdict.
Our motion in time, like motion in space, is subject to a contrary power. All civilization is a conflict of opposite forces. While Faith instinctively
gravitates to the new, Fear, with eyes behind, as
instinctively clings to the old. According as one
or the other of these elements predominates, the
mind is drawn into one or the other of two opposite directions, — Conservatism, Reform. These
two tendencies at present divide the world, — Conservatism and Reform; the old and the new. All
forces, opinions, men, and things are enlisted in
this conflict, arrange themselves around one or
the other of these opposite poles. A word as to
the scholar's place and function in this warfare
has seemed to me the topic most apposite to the
present occasion.

In Germany and France, where letters constitute the first interest in the State next to the
State itself, the learned are easily drawn to new
views, and are usually reformers in their respective spheres. In England, on the contrary, and
in this country, where letters are subordinate to
business and to property, the conservative influence predominates, and the scholar is seldom quite
abreast with his time. The superior ability dis-
played in the Tory journals of Great Britain, com-

pared with those of the Liberal party, shows clearly
to which side, in politics, at least, the literary talent of that nation inclines.   The same illustration
may not hold with us, yet is our own literature
too deeply imbued with English influence not to
exhibit essentially the same trait.   Strong attachment to existing forms, and a consequent distrust
of all that wants the authority of age and numbers,
must be regarded as the characteristic tendency
of the educated classes in either country.   It is
impossible to say how much of this tendency, in
our own case, may be owing to near contact with
an unlettered democracy which acts repulsively on
the scholar, or how much, in either case, may be
the natural growth of the English mind, — a form
of intellect, in all periods, more conversant with
facts than with ideas.

However this may be, let us honor whatever is
praiseworthy in Conservatism, — its deference to
authority, and its veneration for the *Past.*   Let us
honor authority.   Not that which another imposes,
but that which ourselves create.   We must not
look upon authority as something incompatible
with the rights and freedom of the individual
mind, compelling assent to forms of belief which
the mind, if left to itself, would never adopt.   This
view of the subject confounds the effect with the
cause.   It is not authority that usurps, but the

sluggish, slavish mind that concedes such power.
It is not the idol that makes the idolater, but the
reverse. The power of authority is purely subjective. Its character is our own. On ourselves it
depends whether it shall be to us a law of liberty
or a law of restraint; a goad or a guide. With
well-regulated minds it is the natural expression
of a noble sentiment, the testimony of a reverent
and grateful spirit to intellectual or moral power;
the confidence we feel in an individual or a system, founded on personal experience of their wisdom and worth, — a conviction that what has
approved itself in one particular is trustworthy
in all, as the stamp of a well-known manufacturer
guarantees the article so marked.

No doubt this faith may sometimes mislead.
We may carry our confidence too far. We may
exaggerate the worth of a name, and do injustice
to ourselves in our implicit reliance on another's
thought. Still, the principle is one on which the
majority of mankind have always acted, and will
always act. The first glance at society shows us
how little men are disposed to rely on themselves,
and how, with the greater portion, authority seems
to be a necessity of their nature. The common
mind instinctively flies to some accredited source
in quest of the light which it does not find in
itself. The existence of oracles, Christian and

pagan, from ancient Dodona to modern Rome,
attests this fact. Those oracles have ceased or
are ceasing; but the faith in oracles is no whit
abated. There is no difference here between Radical and Conservative. However they may differ
in the authorities to which they appeal, however the one may build on an ancient church and
the other on a modern heresy, the need of authority is felt equally by both. Whether this ought
so to be, we have not now to decide. Such is the
fact; all our civilization is built upon it. All
civilization consists in a series of provisions to
meet this want. The merit of Conservatism is
that it recognizes this want, and gives it its place
among the facts of the soul.

There is another view of this subject. Authority
is not only a guide to the blind, but a law to the
seeing. It is not only a safe-conduct to those (and
they constitute the larger portion of mankind)
whose dormant sense has no intuitions of its own,
but we have also to consider it as affording the
awakened but inconstant mind a security against
itself, a centre of reference in the multitude of its
own visions, in the conflict of its own volitions a
centre of rest. Unbounded license is equally an
evil and equally incompatible with true liberty,
in thought as in action. In the one as in the other,
liberty must bound and bind itself for its own pres-

ervation and best effect; it must *legalize* and determine itself by self-imposed laws. Law and liberty are not adverse, but different sides of one fact. The deeper the law, the greater the liberty; as organic life is at once more determinate and more free than unorganized matter, a plant than a stone, a bird than a plant. The intellectual life, like the physical, must bind itself in order that it may become effective and free. It must organize itself by means of fixed principles which shall protect it equally against encroachment without and anarchy within. It is in vain that I have been emancipated from foreign oppression, while I am still the slave of my own wayward moods. We want not only liberty, but *direction;* not movement only, but method. Our speculations have no absolute ground or evidence in themselves, but vary with the moods they reflect. To-day I am occupied with one set of opinions, to-morrow with another. Now my faith is equal to the most attenuated mysticism; anon first axioms will seem doubtful. Every thought justifies itself to the state which produced it; but there is none which answers to all states. Who will insure me that the clearest convictions of to-day shall abide the criticism of to-morrow? Or where, in this heaving and shoreless chaos, shall I find the system and repose which my spirit craves? It is precisely here that authority

comes in, not as a hostile, but a voluntary power,—
a fiat of the will like that which projected a universe in space, an original determination in the
mind itself, a constructive principle around which
speculation may gather and grow to an articulate
faith, and the blind chaos become an intelligible
world.

Such is the value of authority to the *individual*
in forming his *individual* faith. But we are to
consider, farther,— what should never be forgotten
in these inquiries,— that man is not an individual
merely. He is not complete in himself; like a
single organ, an eye, a leaf, he is perfect only in
connection with the system to which he belongs.
It was written of old, "It is not good for man to be
alone;" and therefore he was made many, and appears, in the ancient *mythus*, to have first become
conscious of his own nature when he saw himself
reflected in a kindred form. Man is still many,
and not one. He is not complete in himself, he is
not intelligible in himself alone. Whether we consider him as animal or as spirit, society is the complement and solution of his individual nature. His
relation to society is twofold. On the side of his
earthly nature he belongs to the State; on the side
of his intellectual he belongs to the Church. By
Church is not meant the particular communions
which are usually designated by that name, but the

whole circle of ideas and influences within which
the spiritual culture of an age or people is comprised, as Islamism, Mosaism, Christianity. And
when I say that man belongs to the Church, I do
not mean that the individual may not in some cases
feel himself more at home without it; as in some
cases he may please himself by withdrawing from
the State and shutting himself out from all communion with his kind. But such cases are exceptions. The rule is that the individual finds in
Church, as in State, his most congenial sphere.
Within this sphere, in the Church as in the State,
authority is the regulative and even constitutive
principle, without which no society could exist.
But here, too, authority is not to be conceived as a
hostile, compulsory force, but as a necessary reference in the uncertainty of clashing views and
minds, as an appeal of the Spirit from itself to
itself, from its lower instances to its higher, from
its morbid states and wild wanderings, its incon-
sistencies, doubts, and errors, to the standing monuments of its own inspiration, — old Tradition,
and the written Word of those prophetic souls
whom the Church reveres as "foremost of her true
servants,"

"Among the enthroned Gods on sainted seats."

This I take to have been the idea intended in the
Catholic Church when that Church asserted its own

infallibility. It could not have meant to assert absolutely and unconditionally what the very fact of
its deliberative councils disproved. The infallibility assumed was only a more emphatic announce-
ment of that authority by which every society
provides for the final arbitrament of litigated questions in its own sphere, and which the Catholic
Church could claim, with peculiar propriety, on the
allowed supposition of a Divine Spirit copresent to
every period and phase of its development. The
design was not to subject the mind, but to build it
up; not to enforce a particular scheme of faith, but
to offer guidance and repose to darkling and weary
souls. The Protestant eye detects the danger to
individual liberty which lurks in this pretension,
but not its deeper reason in the nature of a Church,
nor its justification in the fact that every Protestant Church has, in substance, repeated the claim,
with no greater modification than the temper of
the times required.

There is another element in Conservatism, intimately associated with its deference to authority,
and equally entitled to respect. I mean its veneration for the Past. Veneration for the Past
must not be confounded with that slavish attachment to ancient uses, into which, it must be
confessed, the conservative spirit too easily degenerates. Here, as elsewhere, a good principle is dis-

honored by excess, and here, as elsewhere, it is
common to visit the excess on the principle itself.
The true veneration for the Past consists in a vivid
sense of what we owe to the Past, — a devout
acknowledgment of the good amassed by the ages
which preceded us, and the influence which they
have on our own well being and doing. This acknowledgment is particularly incumbent on the
scholar, for he, above all men, is most indebted to
the Past. Him all the ages have conspired to
mould and to train. His education comprises the
flower of all time. How many minds have gone to
educate that one! What wealth of genius and of
toil has been spent in rearing the harvest which he
reaps! The legacies of nations compose his library. The whole of civilization is condensed in
his text-books. For him Athenian art and Roman
virtue. For him the victors at Corinth and Olym-
pia won their crowns. For him ancient Tragedy
composed her fables. For him Herodotus observed,
and Plato mused, and Cæsar commented, and Cicero
plead. His culture, — which who of us does not
feel to be our better part, the life of our life,
the whole astounding difference between the ripe
scholar and the naked savage? — what is it but the
concentration in one individual of unnumbered
minds?

And not the scholar only, but the individual in

every walk of life, is the product of all that has transpired before his day. His ancestry comprise the whole family of man. All ages and men unite in every influence which goes to form his character and to shape his destiny. He is born into certain relations, traditions, opinions, institutions, all of which, if we trace their growth through all preceding generations, will be found to involve the larger portion of the world's history in their formation and descent. To select one instance out of this complex mass, let us look at language, which affects so powerfully the character and life of civilized man. The individual is born to the use of a certain language, we will say the English. That language is compounded of how many races and climes! It comes to us through how many channels of Roman, Saxon, Norman history! All the nations whose dialects have emptied into this vocabulary have imparted to it some peculiar trait. Had there never been a Hengist or a Cæsar, there never could have been an English tongue. We cannot open our mouths without commemorating, in the very sounds we utter, events and names of distant renown. The household words which first strike our ear are echoes of another age and a pagan world.

But this is not all. What more particularly concerns us in this connection is the fact that language is thought, fixed and crystallized in signs and sounds, conditioned by all the peculiarities, historical and organic, of the nation which uses it. The mind of a people imprints itself in its speech, as the light in a picture of Daguerre. The English language is the English mind. We who use the language partake of this mind. Our individual genius, be it never so individual, is informed by it, and can never wholly divest itself of its influence. It may be doubted if the most abstract and original thinker, in his attempts to construct an absolute system of philosophy, can so abstract himself in his speculations, can reason so absolutely, but that the *genius* of his *language* shall appear as a constituent element in his system. For the words he employs are not algebraic signs which every new speculator may employ at pleasure to express ever new relations. They are constant quantities; they have a fixed value imparted to them by other minds, which he who employs them must accept, and which will go far to modify the results of his speculations. Hence the difficulty of expressing the poetry or the metaphysics of one nation in the language of another. The most successful efforts in this kind are but a compromise between the native and the foreign mind.

Again, the individual is born into some particular church or form of faith, which, whether he

accepts it or not in after life, must needs exert a
very important influence in the formation of his
mind. He is born, for example, into Christianity,
— into a Protestant Christian Church. Here, too,
we notice the same confluence of relations extending through all regions and times. Besides the
doctrine and the life of Jesus, how many systems
and traditions, creeds and facts, have gone to make
or modify that Church! Jewish theology, pagan
philosophy, Romish councils, Ghibbelline factions,
and Protestant reforms, — these influences again
are connected with others, and still others, and so
on through a boundless complexity of cause and
effect, reaching back to the Flood.

Such is the individual; so compounded and conditioned, he comes into life. He is the product of
all the Past. However he may renounce the connection, he is always the child of his time. He
can never entirely shake off that relation. All
the efforts made to outstrip time, to anticipate the
natural growth of man by a violent disruption of
old ties and a total separation from the Past, have
hitherto proved useless, or useful, if at all, in the
way of caution rather than of fruit. The experiment has often been tried. Men of ardent temper
and lively imagination, impatient of existing evils,
— from which no period is exempt, — have re-
nounced society, broken loose from all their moor-

ings in the actual, and sought in the boundless sea
of *Dissent* the promised land of Reform. They
found what they carried, they carried what they
were, they were what we all are, — the offspring of
their time.

The aëronaut who spurns the earth in his puffed
balloon is still indebted to it for his impetus and
his wings; and still with his utmost efforts he
cannot escape the sure attraction of the parent
sphere. His floating island is a part of her main.
He revolves with her orbit, he is sped by her
winds. We who stand below and watch his motions know that he is one of us. He may dally
with the clouds awhile, but his home is not there.
Earth he is, and to earth he must return.

The most air-blown reformer cannot overcome
the moral gravitation which connects him with his
time. He owes to existing institutions the whole
philosophy of his dissent, and draws from Church
and State the very ideas by which he would fight
against them or rise above them. The individual
may withdraw from society, he may spurn at all
the uses of civilized life, dash the golden cup of
tradition from his lips, and flee to the wilderness
" where the wild asses quench their thirst." He
may find others who will accompany him in his
flight; but let him not fancy that the course of
reform will follow him there, that any permanent

organization can be based on dissent, that society will relinquish the hard conquests of so many years, and return again to original nature, wipe out the old civilization, and with *rasa tabula* begin the world anew.

Man's progress is a natural, not a voluntary growth. A divine education is evolving in eternal procession the divine soul. The pupil of the ages, he proceeds in the fore-written order of events to recover his faded image and his lost estate. The true reformers are they who accept this divine order and humbly co-operate with it, instead of seeking to originate one of their own; who sow, like Jesus, the kingdom of God in the midst of the kingdoms of the world, and trust to

> " Blossoming time,
> Which from seedness the bare fallow brings
> To teeming foison."

There is no stand-point out of society from which society can be reformed. " Give me where to stand," was the ancient postulate. " Find where to stand," says modern Dissent. " Stand where you are," said Goethe, " and move the world."

In this defence of Conservatism it has been my aim to discriminate, in the general confusion of false and true which accompanies that tendency, the two principles on which it may fairly ground a claim to the sympathy and support of educated men. I have endeavored to do full justice to a cause, whose real significance, there is reason to fear, is as little appreciated by the mass of those who espouse it as by those who oppose. But let Conservatism, on the other hand, do justice to Reform.

In approaching this part of my subject I feel bound to confess that the actual Conservatism of the present day is in the great majority of cases based on no such ground as that which I have indicated. It is with most men a mere prejudice, which does not care to justify itself in its own eyes. Its advocates, so far from recognizing the ideas expressed in the various reformatory movements which are going on around them, will not even recognize those on which their own cause depends. Ideas of all kinds are distasteful to them. Their ritual palate abhors these Gentile meats. They relish no arguments but appeals to custom and to fear. Approach them with philosophical explanations of their own views, and their sour looks confess how much they loathe the bitter drug : *et ora tristia tentantium sensu torquebit amaror ;* all philosophy is to them *suspect*, and has a guilty, revolutionary look. They see a traitor beneath the stole. You are not for a moment to admit that their cause can require such support, as if tradition were not sufficient for itself. You are expected to assume the whole burden of the Past on the simple credit of the Past. Take no counsel of modern discoveries. Once admit an argument based on the soul, and you betray the cause. It is only substituting a ruse for an onset, sap for storm. All such weapons are forged by the adversary. "We are not ignorant of his devices." The only safety is in planting yourself immovably on the letter, and availing yourself of such protection as property and numbers, popular prejudice and the fear of change, the anathemas of the Church and the terrors of the law, have thrown around you. But beware how you parley with Reason. You must not tamper with ideas. To speculate is to surrender, to reason is to capitulate, to examine is to yield.

However practicable this method of maintaining orthodoxy may once have been, it is not practicable now. The age of menace and high-toned defiance in matters of faith has set, never to rise again on this quarter of the globe. The order of the old world is reversed. Inquisition has gone over to the side of Freedom. Reason is the grand inquisitor in these latter days. Her high court of last appeal is holding a long assize on all human things. Every opinion must come to that bar. The only policy for an enlightened Conservatism, in this day

of judgment, is to confront Reason with Reason,—
to show the philosopher that his philosophy is com-
prehended and seen through by a philosophy older
than his, and that beneath those inquiries which
he deems so profound, deeper than Schelling
sounded or Hegel drew, below the storm and the
strife of the schools, there lies a region of perpetual calm, where rest the rock-foundations of Church
and State, and where gushes in secret the everlasting fountain which he who drinketh shall thirst
no more.

Let the conservative do justice to Reform, and
while he guards with priestly care the ancient
sanctities of heart and life, let him cheerfully concede whatever of falsehood and corruption and
obsolete value has gathered around them, whereby Truth, in the language of Lord Bolingbroke, is
made to resemble " those artificial beauties who
hide their defects under dress and paint." *Pars
minima est ipsa puella sui.* To deny the existence
of errors and the need of reform in Government
and Religion, is only to repeat the folly and renew
the evils of past centuries; it is only to provoke
a violent disruption where timely concessions might
heal the breach. Consider, too, what manner of
men they are who engage in the work of Reform.
Some of them, doubtless, men of depraved ambition, whose only aim is to ride into power on the

top of some excitement into which they have lashed
the public mind.   But there are others of a different spirit,—men of rare virtue and austere lives,

> " Who by due steps aspire
>   To lay their just hands on the golden key
>   That opes the palace of eternity; "

men who resist not evil, but encounter force with
meekness, and oppose the breastplate of an indomitable patience to gibes and sneers ; men who have
learned to subdue and deny themselves, simple
livers, who know neither flesh nor wine, and taste
" no pleasant bread," but nourish their great souls
with earnest faith and living hope.

Think how vain, in dealing with such, are menace and persecution and all power but truth.   Men
who can live on roots and ideas are not easily
daunted or overcome.   They may be counted upon
as sure to effect something, provided they keep
themselves sane.   It is related of Benjamin Franklin that when opposed in some literary enterprise,
he invited his opponents to supper, and setting
before them his usual coarse fare, bade them take
notice that the man who could subsist on such diet
was not to be put down.   Such are the resources
and qualifications which these reformers bring to
their task.   Grounded in principles and armed with
ideas, by ideas and principles only can they be

overcome. Concede to them what is just, that you may the better resist their unjust demands, and imitate the conservative policy of physical science by guiding the heaven-born fire which you cannot quench. The wild forces of Nature yield only to Nature's laws.

Avoiding particular applications of this policy to the controverted questions of the day, let me speak of it generally, as it relates to men and to ideas.

First, as it relates to *men.* There is no one point in which the moral difference between the Past and the Present is so conspicuous as it is in the growing respect for Humanity now manifest wherever the spirit of modern civilization is distinctly heard. Every authentic movement of that spirit asserts, in ever more emphatic terms, the divine idea of human brotherhood, the worth of the individual, the identity of our common nature in all its guises, and the fundamental equality which exists under all the adventitious distinctions of social life. It is chiefly as the largest and most adequate expression yet given to these ideas that the form of government under which we live is entitled to our regard. It is as the champion of these ideas that the democratic element has acquired such prominence among us, and is even made attractive to some whose early associations point in a different direction.

Seldom does it happen, however, that this attraction is felt to any considerable extent by the scholar, or that the ideas in question obtain, with the educated men of our country, that practical acknowledgment which they deserve. The scholar is apt to stand aloof from the people, as if, in cultivating the " humanities," he had laid his own humanity aside ; not considering that the popular interest is made his peculiar trust by those very advantages on which his exclusiveness is based.

It is not necessary, nor is it desirable, that the scholar should become a demagogue, that he should "give up to party what was meant for mankind," that he should " so completely vanquish all the mean superstitions of the heart" as to sully himself with the vile details of electioneering campaigns ; least of all that they who have been called to be " fishers of men," in the high, apostolic sense of that calling, should quit their proper sphere to cast secular nets in the muddy waters of political intrigue. Vain were our colleges if such the destination of those whom they train. It needs no learned institutions to institute men in arts like these, where the graduate of the bar-room shall render ridiculous the diplomas of Harvard or Yale.

But it *is* necessary to his own growth and influence that the scholar should honor Humanity, and greet it frankly in whatsoever guise ; that he should respect his own likeness in the common mind, and in every debasement of conventional life meet his brother man without reserve, in the name of that common image and the sympathy of that one blood which binds and equals all. It is desirable that the American scholar should practically acknowledge those ideas and institutions whose contemporary and subject it is his privilege to be; that he should not falsify his nativity by affecting to despise the peculiar blessings it confers. He must not coquet, in imagination, with the dowered and titled institutions of the Old World, and feel it a mischance which has matched him with a portionless Republic. Let him rather esteem it a privilege to be so connected, and glory in the popular character of his own Government as a genuine fruit of human progress, and the nearest approximation yet made to that divine right which all Governments claim. Let him not think it shame to be with and of the people in every genuine impulse of the popular mind, not suffering the scholar to extinguish the citizen, but remembering that the citizen is before the scholar, the elder and higher category of the two. He shall find himself to have gained intellectually, as well as socially, by free and frequent intercourse with the people, whose instincts, in many things, anticipate his reflective wisdom, and

in whose unconscious movements a fact is often
forefelt before it is seen by reason; as the physical changes of our globe are felt by the lower
animals before they appear to man. Let the
scholar of every profession think that he does
injustice to that profession, and still greater injustice to his own manhood, whenever he cherishes
any habit of thought or feeling which tends to
seclude him from the people, when he relucts to
mingle with them on equal terms as man with
man, or when, in any division between the moneyed
and the popular interest, he attaches himself ex-
clusively to the former. However he may avoid
them, they will not avoid him. He may shun their
fellowship, but he cannot escape their control.
As a citizen he is their equal, as a functionary
he is their servant. On all sides he is amenable
to their judgment. On all sides they exercise a
jurisdiction over him which it is vain to resist and
impossible to escape. The only way to secure a
favorable verdict is to form one of the council.
It is the worst of all policies to cherish exclusive
feelings where it is impossible to lead an exclusive
life. The *odi profanum vulgus*, always an un-
worthy sentiment, becomes ridiculous where the
arceo is impracticable.

The same liberality which an enlightened policy
demands of the scholar in relation to men, let him

exhibit also in relation to ideas and the progress of inquiry on all topics connected with the spiritual nature and destination of man. A certain reserve in relation to new views may be justly expected of him in proportion as his own views are based on personal investigation. The pains bestowed on his inquiries have made him tenacious of their results, as men love money the more, the greater the labor expended in its acquisition. It is only when this reserve degenerates into peevish intolerance or fierce denunciation, when it assumes to decide questions of a purely speculative character on practical grounds, that it ceases to be philosophical or pardonable or safe. Nothing is more natural than that men who have contributed something in their day to illustrate or extend the path of discovery in any direction should cling with avidity to those conclusions which they have established for themselves, and which represent the natural boundaries of their own mind, — " the butt and sea-mark of its utmost sail ; " nothing more natural than that they, for their part, should feel a disinclination to farther inquiry. But it ill becomes them to deny the possibility of farther discovery, to maintain that they have found the bottom of the well where Truth lies hid because they have reached the limits of their own specific gravity. One sees at once that in some branches of inquiry this position is not only untenable, but the very enunciation of it absurd. It would require something more than the authority of Herschel to make us believe that creation stops with the limits of his forty-feet reflector. Nor would the assertion of Sir Humphry Davy be sufficient to convince us that all the properties of matter have been catalogued in his report. By what statute of limitations are we forbidden to indulge the same hope of indefinite progress in every other direction, which remains to us in these?

Besides, our opposition to new views must not overlook that the course of human thought, on the controverted subjects of philosophy and religion, is not a voluntary movement. The prevalence of certain views at certain periods does not depend on the caprice of those who adopt them. Ideas are not maggots of the brain generated at pleasure, nor must we suppose that a system of philosophy gains currency in the world because certain individuals who *choose* to think thus, have *set* it in motion. These things are ordered by a higher Power. Ideas do not spring from the ground. They are not manufactured, but given. Man is not their author, but their organ. No one who traces with philosophic eye the progress of opinions through successive ages can fail to perceive a causal relation between each epoch and the opinions it represents. He will see the presence of law in the intellectual creation as in the material. The history of the human mind, like all the processes of planetary life, has its appointed method, and is from beginning to end a series of evolutions, in which every phase is connected by necessary sequence with every other phase, and the first movement contains the last.

" Omnia certo tramite vadunt
    Primusque dies dedit extremum."

It does not follow, however, that because certain opinions characterize certain epochs, the individual has no choice of opinions, but must necessarily accept those which belong to his time. The general movement does not *preclude* individual liberty, but *includes* it, as all the motions on the earth's surface are included in the earth's orbit. Nor are we justified in supposing that a system of philosophy is necessarily true because a divine order in human affairs has connected the ideas embodied in it with the period in which they appear. The inference is rather that no philosophy is absolutely true, and none entirely false. They are all but so many factors in that process by which truth is continually approximated, and never reached. They alternate one with another, now the sensual, and now the spiritual, as one or the other element in our complex nature requires.

For the intellectual man, like the physical, can advance only by putting one foot before the other.

It is from this point of view that we are to judge of the *transcendental philosophy* (so called), on which the mind of this century divides, and which, though very different views are included in that name, may in some sort be regarded as one system. Regarding it in this light, we shall find it to be neither so glorious nor so vile an apparition as one side and the other would make it. It is not the " pure spirit of health " which its advocates suppose, nor yet the " goblin damned " with the dread of which its adversaries have so needlessly afflicted their souls. It is not destined to supersede other systems, but it is destined to take an equal rank by their side. Setting aside its method and its critique, which constitute its real merit, it has produced nothing as yet which after ages can quote as discovery; but these may be regarded as an actual advance on ages past. As a science of the *Absolute* it has failed to redeem its high promise, and to place itself on a footing of equality, in point of demonstration, with the exact sciences. In the enunciation of its doctrines, its disciples are liable to the charge of not having sufficiently regarded the wholesome precept of the ancient rhetorician, *tanquam scopulum vites insolens verbum.* But with all its faults it will be found, in the final judgment, to have answered, in its degree, the true purpose of metaphysical inquiry, in furnishing a new impulse to thought, and enlarging, somewhat, the horizon of life. If Utility object that its sphere lies too remote from earth, let Utility consider it as an observation of the heavens by which the wanderer here below is enabled to shape more correctly his terrestrial course.

The real or supposed hostility between the prominent conceptions of this philosophy and the Christian religion has given it an interest in the minds of some which its own merits would not have procured for it. It is on this ground that war is waged against new views by conservative minds. Were it possible, in the nature of man, that religion could ever cease from the earth, or that any particular form of it could cease, so long as it satisfies a real want of the soul, then the posture of philosophy at this time, as in all time, and not more than in all time, might seem to justify the apprehensions it has caused. We may derive great encouragement, however, from the fact that these fears and fightings are not new. All philosophies have encountered the same. When Mr. Locke published his "Essay on the Human Understanding," which the more cautious among us are now disposed to regard as the only safe philosophy, it was impugned, on precisely the same ground, by the wise and pious men of that day; and we are told that the Heads of the several Houses in the University of Oxford, at a special meeting called for that purpose, resolved, if possible, to prevent its being read in their respective colleges. All philosophy which does not assume revelation for its basis will be deemed hostile to revelation by some. Meanwhile Religion and Philosophy have each their separate path, and the gradual progress of human culture can alone mediate between the two. May we not suppose a threefold development of religion, corresponding with three successive stages of the individual mind, — sense, sentiment, and reason? A religion addressed to sense we have in the forms and ceremonies of the Catholic Church. A religion addressed to sentiment we have in the vehement emotions of the Protestant sects. May we not expect, as the complement of these two, a third epoch, — a religion addressed to Reason, a religion of ideas? Assuredly Christianity contains within itself the elements of such a church.

On the whole, we may leave these sacred concerns where they have been left by their Guardian and ours. We may trust to Heaven to protect its own, without laying our rash hands upon the ark.

Nor need the educated dread, on account of others, a tendency which they feel to be innoxious as it respects themselves. There is too much of this groundless apprehension, this superfluous and officious concern in behalf of the popular faith, and too little confidence in the native instincts and clear judgment of the common mind. There is a class of men among us who seem to possess an organic alacrity in scenting out what is noxious in the opinions of their neighbors, and in raising the alarm whenever anything is uttered that does not square with the old standards, — as if, in emulation of those conservative birds in Roman history which once saved the Capitol, they supposed the welfare of the Church to depend on their timely cackling. Neither the views in question nor the apprehensions respecting them, neither the heresy on the one side nor the consternation on the other, are shared to any considerable extent by the people at large, who for the most part are too much occupied with their own practical concerns to trouble themselves with either. "Because half a dozen grasshoppers under a fern," said Burke in relation to certain contemporary speculations, "because half a dozen grasshoppers under a fern make the field ring with their importunate chink, while thousands of great cattle, reposed beneath the shade, chew the cud and are silent, do not imagine that those who make the noise are the only inhabitants of the field, that they are of course many in number, or that after all they are other than the little, shrivelled, meagre, hopping, though loud and troublesome, insects of the hour."

Let this too have its weight, that no system or tendency or speculation is rightly discerned or fairly judged when seen in conflict with opposite views. Every philosophy which springs up in an earnest soul, which is born of faith and uttered in love, will be found instructive to those who view it in its own light, and innoxious when received in its own spirit. But when, urged with harsh contradiction, it is thrown into a hostile attitude and becomes polemic, its whole character is changed. Every good trait is suppressed, every doubtful trait is more pronounced. What was radical, becomes blasphemous; what was mystical, absurd. Every man's word should be stated without reference to opposite views, and heard without contradiction, in order to produce its full effect.

> " The current that with gentle murmur glides,
>   . . . being stopped, impatiently doth rage ;
>   But when his fair course is not hindered,
>   He makes sweet music with the enamel'd stones,
>   Giving a gentle kiss to every sedge
>   He overtaketh in his pilgrimage.
>   And so by many winding nooks he strays
>   With willing sport to the wild ocean."

Whatever conclusions speculative philosophy, in the ebb and flow of its own unstable element, may advance or overthrow, on the *terra firma* of practical wisdom there is *one* conclusion which will always stand fast, one fact which all reason and all experience conspire to enforce; that is, the inexpediency of opposing the tendency of thought, in an individual or a nation, with visible antagonism and direct contradiction. As far as the individual is concerned, such opposition is as unreasonable in point of justice as it is inexpedient in point of policy. If a man is earnest in his thinking, if he is serious in his convictions, his thoughts — aye, and the expression of them — are as much a part of him as the form or features of his physical man. You might as well quarrel with your neighbor's nose and expect him to suppress it for your sake, as expect him to change or disguise his opinions because they are an offence in your eyes.

But is there then no appeal from noxious sentiments? Is there no remedy against dangerous heresies? The remedy and the appeal lie in stating your own convictions, with all the ability you can command, whenever and wherever you can find voice and ear. But state them without reference to others. Publish your opinions, but not your dissent; and take no notice of opposite views, but simply and steadily ignore them. Controversy on any subject is seldom productive of much profit; but to controvert abstractions, to oppose speculative philosophy on practical grounds, is to outdo the hero of La Mancha, — it is tilting, not with wind-mills, but with the wind.

It was a principle with Goethe, and one among the many proofs which that great genius gave of his practical wisdom, to avoid contradiction, to deal as little as possible in negations, to state his view as if the opposite had never been stated, to work out his own problems in his own way, and let the world take its course. In the midst of con-flicts, civil and religious, which agitated his time, with the din of battle always in his ear, he main-tained a strict neutrality, and held in silence his steady course, well knowing that these controver-sies would decide themselves, and that for him to take part in the fray was only to postpone their decision. He felt that to produce somewhat of his own was better than to quarrel with the work of others; that to plant for the future was better than to war with the past. So he trode the fierce battle-field of his age with the implements of peace in his hands, and sowed philosophy and art in the upturned sod.

Peace, and not controversy, is the true and genial element of the scholar's life. The Goddess of Wisdom was sometimes represented with the ægis and the lance; but the olive was the emblem assigned her by her favored votaries in later times.

In the conflict between the old and the new which is raging around him, let the scholar attach himself wherever instinct may draw or conscience drive, happy if he can find a point of reconciliation common to both, and minister as mediator between the two. Having found his own position, let him gladly concede to others the like freedom, and rejoice that there is wisdom enough on both sides to do justice to both. However the controverted question may divide itself to the intellect, let no division be recognized by the heart. Let no technicalities stand between us and our brother's soul. Let no mean prejudice, no paltry apprehension baffle our serene intuition or mar the full and free enjoyment of whatever is quickening in our brother's word. Wherever in the many-mansioned house of philosophy or religion the understanding may lodge, let the affections be everywhere at home. The understanding is essentially protestant, — always defining, dividing, exclusive; but Love should be catholic as Nature and Life.

REV. WILLIAM E. CHANNING, D.D.,

ON OCCASION OF THE CELEBRATION OF THE TWENTY-FIFTH ANNI-
VERSARY OF HIS DEATH.

WE are following the usage of the ancients in
commemorating the anniversary of our prophet's death.   The modern custom has been to celebrate the birthdays of distinguished men, but the
ancients celebrated their death; and what is remarkable, considering the imperfect views of a future existence which we ascribe to them, they called
the death-day the birth-day,—*dies natalis;* for they
held that it was the birth of the soul into nobler
fellowships and a freer life.   And certainly, if to
any who have passed away within our remembrance
decease from this earthly world has been a heavenly
birth, in commemorating the death of Channing we
are celebrating a great nativity.   Who in our remembrance needed less of transformation in order
to translation?   He had as little to put off, in putting on immortality, as any of the old pillar-saints
or mediæval devotees who tried to wean themselves
into glory by refusing the breast of Mother Earth,
—the homely nurse, who, as Wordsworth says,
does all she can—

" To make her foster-child, her inmate man,
   Forget the glories he hath known,
  And that imperial palace whence he came."

Not that there was in him anything of the ascetic, anything of that morbid spirit which looks upon the body as a house of penance, and embraces, in one trinity of damnation, "the world, the flesh, and the devil." His view of life was healthy, genial; his habit cheerful, joyous even, so far as physical debility permitted joyousness. He differed from the rest of us not so much in severity of practice as in spirituality of mind. In that, he had no equal among all the men whom I have known. And that I conceive to be the characteristic thing in Channing, — spirituality; living in the contemplation and pursuit of the highest; the habit of viewing all things in reference to the supreme good. All questions, movements, institutions, enterprises, all discoveries and inventions, he judged by this standard. Their spiritual bearing was the measure of the interest he felt in them. Even matters of science — and he loved to read and hear of science — interested him only as they served to illustrate the goodness of God, or as he saw in them an opening into a better life for man. His intellectual orbit had two foci, around which it forever revolved, — the goodness of God, and the dignity of man. How to make the true nature of God believed against the distortions of a false theology ; how make men conscious of their divine image and calling, and anxious to realize it, — this was the one perpetual quest of that steady-burning, never-flaring, always-flaming, adoring spirit. In this spirituality lay the secret of his strength, and especially of that overwhelming personality which pervades all his speech, so that you can nowhere separate between the word and the man. By virtue of this he spoke to us, and we listened to him as one having authority. And curious it was How this man — without learning, without research, not a scholar, not a critic, without imagination or fancy, not a poet, not a word-painter, without humor or wit, without profundity of thought, without grace of elocution — could, from the spiritual height on which he stood, by mere dint of gravity (coming from such an elevation), send his word into the soul with more searching force than all the orators of his time. I said, "by mere dint of gravity;" but his speech had another quality which made it effective. That was a singular perspicuity, the result of a rare combination of calm and intense. Nothing is so eloquent, addressed to the intellect, as luminous statement ; nothing addressed to the sentiments so eloquent as intense conviction. Channing had both, by reason of that singleness of mind which begets both. When the thought, which is the eye, is single, the whole speech, which is the body, is full of light. In conversing with the writings of Channing, we move in a world of exceeding day. There are no dark corners in his thought, no cloud-shadows on his discourse, no *chiaroscuro*, no twilight mysteries; it is all clear sky, and broad, effulgent noon, — owing in part, it must be confessed, to the singular want, in so distinguished an intellect, of all speculative proclivity, and consequently of all metaphysical scruples. He saw no difficulties, or none of the deeper difficulties, which perplex metaphysical minds. The imaginary objections which he considers, the imaginary opponents against whom he argues in his essays, are all of the most superficial kind. His lofty Theism, which lies at the basis of all his teaching, was assumed apparently without question. His Christology, his doctrine of Christ, so edifying on the moral side, is loose on the critical. A scientific theologian he certainly was not, not a profound thinker; but, what is vastly more important, a very clear thinker and a wonderfully luminous writer. The critic and metaphysician may be disappointed in his writings, but they find an unfailing response and abundant justification in the common-sense of mankind.

Side by side with the spirituality so characteristic of Channing I place his scarcely less characteristic honesty. The action of this quality in private made conversation with him, to a young man especially, somewhat embarrassing. You missed those smooth insincerities which hide or soften milder disagreements and facilitate colloquial intercourse. You made your statement : if he accepted it, it was well ; he was sure to furnish, from the riches of his mental experience, some apt comment, illustration, or application. If he rejected it, it was equally well ; there was then opportunity and scope for friendly debate. But the chances were that he would neither accept nor reject, but receive it with dumb gravity, turning upon you that calm, clear eye, and annoying you with an awkward sense of frustration, — as when one offers to shake hands, and no hand is given him in return. But, as speaker and writer, this honesty established for Channing a peculiar claim, through the confidence it inspired, that the unadulterated sense of the man was in his speech. He might not see very far in some directions; but he saw with unclouded eye, and reported only what he saw. His judgment took no bribes. That is what can be said of very few of the writers or speakers of our time, I fear, or of any time. In theology, at least, I know very few whose judgment does not seem to be vitiated, corrupted, by one or another influence, from within or from without, by position or passion. Some are warped by sectarian

bias, some by worldly interest, some by fear of
public opinion or of loosing the bands of authority;
and a great many more by lust of distinction, by
jealousy of ecclesiastical domination, by impatience
of traditional beliefs which they want the power to
comprehend. Conservatives are bribed by the love
of stability; radicals are bribed by the lure of
novelty and the charm of defiance. Channing was
unbribable. He had no interest to serve, aside of
the truth; no crotchet of the brain to pamper or
defend. He was neither conservative nor radical,
but a simple child of the light, bringing to the truth
no prism, but a mirror, and giving back, without
color or shade, the illumination he received. This
honesty declares itself in his style. What a remarkable style it was! No purer English has
been written in our day. So colorless, and yet so
impressive, so natural, yet so exact. He never
courted attention by the turn of a sentence or trick
of words; he used no flavors; he practised no distortions to make truisms pass for more than they
were worth. If his thought was commonplace, he
said it in a commonplace way. He never tried to
disguise it by a pert and perky way of putting
it, by smart phraseology or inverted syntax; if his
thought was weighty, its simple weight sufficed,
and a perfectly colorless style sufficed for its presentation. He never aims to be smart, he never

aims to be quaint, but just walks through his pages with a sober, steady, dignified gait, and never capers and never struts.

His faith in humanity was another characteristic trait. He cherished an immense hope for the race. He believed in liberty; he glowed for it; if need were, I think he would have died for it. A characteristic anecdote was told of him, that in the year 1830, when the tidings came of the revolution in Paris which dethroned Charles the Tenth, he hurried from Newport to Boston to exchange congratulations with his friends on the subject, but found them unexpectedly cold and unsympathizing. He could not understand it. Meeting one of them, he said, "Are you, too, so old and so wise as to feel no enthusiasm for the heroes of the Polytechnic School?" "Ah!" replied his friend, "you are the youngest man I have met with." "Yes," said Channing, "always young for liberty."

What — now that twenty-five years have rolled over his grave — what is the present and what is to be the final significance of Channing? In the world of letters, in the world of scientific theology, not so great as that of many of his contemporaries; in the world of ideas and ideal characters, a most weighty name and a sempiternal power. Of all the men of modern time, he stands for spiritual freedom. Although not an iconoclast, not a denier, but eminently an affirmative spirit, he represents the emancipation of the mind from all unrighteous thrall. His theology was never popular, and I suppose it never will be. What Renan says of it is probably true : "It demands too great intellectual sacrifices for the critic, and too little for those with whom it is a necessity to believe." But the final judgment of posterity will know how to separate between the creed and the man, as it does in the case of Saint Augustine and of Fénelon. The creed is costume, the spirit is the man. No man by accident wins enduring fame. Circumstances, popular illusion, may confer a transient and local repute ; but the heroes who outlive the applause of their day, the heroes whom posterity accepts, whom the wise of other lands install in their Valhalla, have a right to their pedestals. Hear the judgment of one of the most learned, acute, and Christian scholars of this century concerning Channing, pronounced many years after his· death. The late Baron Bunsen, in a work entitled " God in History," selects from the Protestant Church five worthies who stand pre-eminent, in his judgment, as representatives of the Divine presence in man, — Luther, Calvin, Jacob Böhme, Schleiermacher, Channing. And this is what he says of Channing: "In humanity a Greek, in citizenship a Roman, in Christianity an apostle. . . . If such a man, whose way of life, in the face of his fellow-citizens, corresponded to the Christian earnestness of his words and presents a blameless record, — if such a one is not a Christian apostle of the presence of God in man, I know of none."

SCIENCE AND FAITH.

ADDRESS AT THE CELEBRATION OF THE FIFTIETH ANNIVERSARY
OF THE AMERICAN UNITARIAN ASSOCIATION.

MR. PRESIDENT,—The fiftieth anniversary
of this Association suggests, perforce, a
comparison of the ecclesiastical outlook of to-day
with the aspects and auspices of fifty years ago.
And here the thing which first strikes me is a
change in the topics and points of view which
occupy the leading minds not only of our own
but of other communions. The questions which
interested our fathers in 1825 have lost, in a great
measure, their interest for us. The topics then
debated with so much heart and heat, Triunity
of the Godhead, Vicarious Atonement, Original
Sin, Eternal Damnation, have almost dropped out
of sight. The lines of theological separation between ourselves and other Protestant sects, once
so rigidly maintained, are getting lax, are wavering, fading, vanishing. The Protestant sects
are less concerned to define their position one
toward another than to vindicate their common
Christian heritage against a common enemy. Protestant Christendom itself is assailed, and that on

both sides, behind and before. Protestant Christendom finds itself wedged between two hostile powers, of which our fathers made little account, but which in our day have acquired a portentous significance,—the Church of Rome on the one hand, and scientific scepticism on the other. The most pressing question between us and the Church of Rome is not a theological one, but a question of liberty or bondage, of progress or stagnation, of *intellectual* life or death. The question between us and science is one of religion or no religion; of possible commerce with the unseen, or confinement within the bounds of sensible experience,—*spiritual* life or death. The little I have to say connects itself with the latter question, — the relation between faith and science.

The half century whose expiration we commemorate has been, as you all know, a period of unexampled progress in scientific discoveries and inventions. Four of the most memorable of these are comprised in its limits, — communication by electric telegraph (which my friend who has just taken his seat so eloquently characterized), photography, anæsthetic surgery, and spectral analysis, assuring the physical unity of creation. In consequence partly of these splendid achievements, and partly from other causes, Science in our day has assumed toward Theology a tone of conscious superiority, as if she were the world's leader, the light of life, the mainstay of civilization, and Theology an anachronism, a ghost of other days, at best an off-interest, belonging, as Mr. Tyndall says, to the region of the emotions, outside of the domain of knowledge, and entitled to no voice in the forum of the understanding. Well, it must be conceded that Theology no longer occupies the place she did in ages past, when she gave the law to secular beliefs as well as spiritual. Science has overruled her *dictum* on many questions of space and time. Astronomy has opened a world above, and geology a world below, before whose revelations Biblical statements of cosmogony and chronology have fled like dreams of the night. But the realm of Theology, although restricted by Science in certain directions, is not dissolved. Within her own realm she is still supreme; and when Science invades that realm with her theories, she proves herself as incompetent, as much out of place, as Theology does when she dogmatizes about the order of creation and the genesis of brute and plant.

What, on the whole, are the grounds on which Science vaunts, as against Theology, her superior claims? Mainly, I think, these two, — greater certainty, and greater utility. Will they stand the test of ultimate reason? Science boasts, in com-

parison with Theology, the advantage of greater
certainty, as dealing with realities; while Theology,
in her judgment, gropes in the dark, and is "mov-
ing about in worlds not realized." Now, the truth
of that claim must depend on our definition of
"certainty." Consult your dictionaries, and you
will find that "certainty" means, for one thing,
"freedom from doubt." If we accept that definition, the claim is void; for, not to speak of the uncertainties, the notorious uncertainties, of Science,
the moment she ventures beyond the region of
sight and touch, not to speak of the wavering
views of scientific men on grave questions, such
as the nebular hypothesis, the atomic theory, the
origin of species, — not to speak of these, the
assurance of faith in the religionist is just as
strong as the assurance of demonstration in the
scientist. The devout Roman Catholic whom I
met in Cologne was just as sure that certain
bones preserved in the "Dom" of that city were
the bones of the three wise men of the East, —
Caspar, Melchior, and Balthasar, — as the chemist
is that water is composed of two parts hydrogen
to one part oxygen. My friend the ghost-seer is
just as sure that he has interviewed the shade of
his deceased wife as the mathematician is that a
body acted upon by two forces at right angles
with each other will describe a diagonal between

the two. Now, it avails not to say that in the one case we have facts, established facts, and in the other only beliefs. To the common man, the unlearned, who cannot verify the facts, they are but beliefs after all, received on authority, resting on human testimony; while to the believer, on the other hand, his beliefs are facts. The certainty in either case is the same. I do not say there is no difference in the *kind* of certainty, but I do say there is no difference in the *degree;* and I say, moreover, that the faith of the religionist furnishes as sure a ground to build upon in spiritual things as the knowledge of the scientist does in material things. Science no more than religion can claim to build on reality. For what is reality? Who will define it? Who will prove it? Do not all proofs refer us at last to subjective tests?

Sensible experience is no more a proof of reality than spiritual experience. The scientist builds on sensible experience. He claims for that experience an answering reality; he supposes a world external to himself, corresponding to his sensations. But the existence of such a world is a mere hypothesis. Profoundest thinkers have called it a vulgar prejudice, — a prejudice with which I confess I am somewhat infected. But when we come to demonstration, there is absolutely none. A convenient working theory for scientific and daily use: that is the best we can say of it. The religionist builds on spiritual experience. He claims for that experience an answering reality; he supposes a God external to himself, as well as internal, — an intelligent Will over all, corresponding with the voice in his soul. Such a being is not demonstrable in a scientific sense. There is no mathematical demonstration of it; but surely we can say of it, and the least we can say of it is, that it is a good working theory for spiritual uses, — those uses without which man, with all his endowments, is little better than the brute. The being of God is incapable of demonstration, — but the existence of an external world is equally so. Nay, I think more so; I would sooner undertake to demonstrate the former than the latter. So far from inferring the being of God from an external world, as theologians have attempted to do, I need the belief in a God to assure the existence of things without.

I come now to the second of those grounds on which Science bases her supreme claim, — greater utility, a more needful service. The world is not likely to forget the debt it owes to Science. That is a daily and hourly obligation for most of the comforts and conveniences of life. I have no desire to make light of that debt. But I see that the grandest things the world contains are not the products of Science, but of Faith. Science could have had no beginning had not Religion first lifted man out of the dust and tamed his fierce passions, and given him an interest in life which made it worth his while to study the secrets of Nature, and to learn the reason and constitution of things. And not only so, not only the world's emancipation from brutal ignorance and savage enslavement to animal life, but those material products which are justly esteemed the ornaments of earth; those works of the hand, those wonders of art which draw the curious across the globe, — temples, pyramids, statues, paintings, things which travellers compass sea and land to behold, — are due to the same source; they owe to religion the impulse which gave them birth. Of these the poet could say (what may not be said of the railway or the telegraph) that —

> " Nature gladly gave them place,
> Adopted them into her race,
> And granted them an equal date
> With Andes and with Ararat."

And even those discoveries and inventions of which Science claims the credit could never have been accomplished by Science alone without the aid of Faith; for Science can only see, not do. *She* is the ghost, rather than theology. " Star-eyed Science " has speculation in her eyes, indeed, but no force

in her hand, no blood in her veins. Not one of
those improvements by which man becomes civilized, and more civilized from age to age, could
ever have been achieved without the aid of Faith.
It was Faith that first ventured out of sight of
land in a ship, trusting to a bit of quivering iron
and the stars. It was Faith that first thrust a steel
lancet into the eye to remove a cataract. It was
Faith that first introduced poison into human veins
to forestall a greater evil by a less. Geographers
in the fifteenth century had divined the existence
of another earth beyond the Atlantic waste; but it
needed the faith of Columbus to follow the setting
sun across the deep, and unlock the gates of the
West. The philosophers of the eighteenth century
had conjectured the identity of lightning with what
was then called "the electric fluid," but it needed
the faith of Franklin to send up the kite which
brought confirmation of that conjecture from the
skies. Dr. Jackson, in our own day, had discovered the anæsthetic properties of ether; but it
needed the faith of Morton first to administer the
drug which disarms the surgeon's knife of its
terrors.

Faith and Science, Religion and Science, together
have built up the world in which we live, — this
social, civil, intellectual, ecclesiastical world of
mankind. Both were needed to make the world

what it is, — a fit abode for rational beings. It would be hard to say which in time past has been the more needful, the more indispensable agent of the two. But if it be asked which now of the two could best be spared, it seems to me that the question is not difficult. If now and henceforth the alternative for man were the end and arrest of scientific progress, or the death of Faith, the shutting up of our churches, the choking forever of the voice of prayer, the derubrication of the calendar, the equalization of the week, the utter secularization of life, then I say that the arrest of Science would be the lesser evil of the two. For society can exist without more knowledge; but take away Faith, and you snap the mainspring in the clock-work of life. You take away that without which "star-eyed Science" herself would soon become blind. You spread darkness over all the face of the earth, and make universal shipwreck of man's estate. For this human world, I maintain, with never so much Science at the helm, cannot be sailed by "dead-reckoning" alone. There must be somewhere an observation of the heavens, or the ship which bears us all will founder.

One thing more, and I have done. There has been much talk of a conflict between Religion and Science; a learned *savant* of our own country has written a work on the subject. I take it upon me to say that there never has been, and never can be, any such conflict, any conflict, between Religion and Science. In the loose way of speaking which the use of abstract terms is apt to engender, other conflicts have taken that name. Conflicts there are between the speculations of scientific men and the convictions of religious men. There are conflicts between scientific facts, if you will, and religious prejudices; conflicts between discoveries and traditions; conflicts between certain Biblical statements and the testimony of the rocks: but between Religion proper and Science proper, each on its own legitimate beat, there never has been nor can be any conflict, no more than there can be a conflict between Kepler's Third Law and the first verse of the Fourth Gospel. When, thirty years ago, Leverrier, with his mathematical divining-rod, discovered the latent planet, now a known constituent of our solar system, Religion thanked God who had given such power unto man, and congratulated Science on the triumph of her great detective. When Mr. Tyndall published his exposition of the laws of Light and Heat, the pulpit had no fault to find with his teaching. But when this same Tyndall proposed to test the value of prayer by statistics, then Religion indignantly rebuked the man for meddling with a matter of which, to borrow a comparison from the late

Father Taylor, he knew as little as Balaam's ass did of Hebrew. That was not a conflict of Religion with Science, but a conflict with Nescience.

Let Science pursue the path marked out for her by her own great leaders, — the path, not of vague speculation, but of firm and patient induction, and Religion will rejoice with her in all her discoveries, will thank her, and thank God, for every fact which she adds to the sum of human knowledge ; and when belated theologians bring up their Hebraisms and pit them against her assured conclusions, Religion will join her in every rebuke which shall teach Theology to know her place.

CLASSIC AND ROMANTIC.

[*From the Atlantic Monthly.*]

TOWARD the close of the eighteenth century there appeared in Germany, under the lead of Tieck, Novalis, and the Schlegels, a class of writers and of writings known as the Romantic School.

The appellation gave rise to wide discussion of what precisely is meant by that phrase, and what distinguishes " romantic " from " classic," to which it is opposed. Goethe characterized the difference as equivalent to healthy and morbid. Schiller proposed " naïve and sentimental." The greater part regarded it as identical with the difference between ancient and modern, — which was partly true, but explained nothing. None of the definitions given could be accepted as quite satisfactory.

What do we mean by "romantic"? The word, as we know, is derived from the old Romanic, or Romance, languages, which formed in mediæval times the transition from the Latin to the dialects of modern Southern Europe. The invaders of Italy found a *patois* called *Romana rustica*, thus distinguished from the pure Latin of the cultivated Roman. Romance is a fusion of this *Romana rustica* with the native speech of barbarous tribes. It attained its most perfect development in Southern France in the country of Provence, where it became the *langue d'oc;* that is, the language in which "yes" is *oc* (German *auch*), while in the Romance of Northern France "yes" is *oïl,* in modern French *oui.*

Poems and tales in the Romance language took the name Romàn,—in English, "romance" or "romaunt."

Originally, then, "romantic" meant simply writings in the Romance language, as distinguished from writings in the Latin tongue, the better sort of which were called classic, from *classici;* that is, "first-class."

But the difference was not one of language merely. There was manifest in those Romance compositions—as compared with the classic—a difference of tone, of spirit, and even of subject-matter, which has given to the term "romantic" a far wider significance than that of literary classification. We speak of romantic characters, romantic situations, romantic scenery. What do we mean by this expression? Something very subtle, undefinable, but felt by all. If we analyze the feeling, we shall find, I think, that it has its origin in wonder and mystery. It is the sense of something hidden, of imperfect revelation. The woody dell, the leafy glen, the forest path which leads one knows not whither, are romantic; the public highway is not. Moonlight is romantic as contrasted with daylight. The winding, secret brook, "old as the hills that feed it from afar," is romantic as compared with the broad river rolling through level banks.

The essence of romance is mystery. But now a further question. What caused the Romance writings more than the classic to take on this charm of mystery? Something, perhaps, is due to the influence on the writers of sylvan surroundings, of wild Nature, as contrasted with the civic life which seems to have been the lot of the Latin classic authors. But mainly it was the influence of the Christian religion, which deepened immensely the mystery of life, suggesting something beyond and behind the world of sense.

The word " classic " is more commonly employed in the sense of style. It denotes the manner of treatment, irrespective of the topic. The peculiarity of the classic style is reserve, self-suppression of the writer. The romantic is self-reflecting. In the one the writer stands aloof from his theme, in the other he pervades it. The classic treatment draws attention to the matter in hand, the roman-

tic to the hand in the matter. The classic is passionless presentation, the romantic is impassioned
demonstration. The classic narrator tells his story
without comment; the romantic colors it with his
reflections, and criticises while he narrates.

"Homer," says Landor, "is subject to none of
the passions, but he sends them all forth on
their errands with as much precision as Apollo his
golden arrows. The hostile gods, the very Fates,
must have wept with Priam before the tent of
Achilles; Homer stands unmoved."

Schiller draws a parallel between Homer and
Ariosto in their treatment of the same subject,—
an agreement between two enemies. In the Iliad,
Glaucus and Diomed,— a Trojan and a Greek,—
encountering each other in battle, and discovering
that they are mutually related by the binding law
of hospitality, agree to avoid each other in the
fight, and, in token thereof, exchange with each
other their suits of armor. Glaucus, without hesitation, gives his gold suit, worth a hundred oxen, for
Diomed's steel suit, worth nine. Schiller thinks
that a modern poet would have expatiated on the
moral beauty of such an act; but Homer simply
states it, without note or comment. Ariosto, on the
other hand, having related how two knights who
were rivals,— a Christian and a Saracen,— after
mauling each other in a hand-to-hand combat, make

peace and mount the same steed to pursue the fugitive Angelica, in whom both are interested, breaks forth in admiring praise of the magnanimity of ancient knighthood : —

> " Oh, noble minds by knights of old possessed!
> Two faiths they knew, one love their hearts professed.
> While still their limbs the smarting anguish feel
> Of strokes inflicted by the hostile steel,
> Through winding paths and lonely woods they go,
> Yet no suspicion their brave bosoms know."

There is no better illustration of the reserve, the passionless transparency and *naïveté*, of the classic style of narrative than that which is given us in the Acts of the Apostles, — not the work of a recognized classic author, but beautifully classic in its pure objectivity, its absence of personal coloring. In that wonderful narrative of Paul's shipwreck the narrator closes his account of an anxious night with these words: " Then fearing lest they should have fallen upon rocks, they cast four anchors out of the stern, and wished for the day." Fancy a modern writer dealing with such a theme! How he would enlarge on the racking suspense, the tortures of expectation, endured by the storm-tossed company through the weary hours of a night which threatened instant destruction! How he would dwell on the momentary dread of the shock which should shatter the frail bark and engulf the de-

voted crew, the angry billows hungering for their
prey, eyes strained to catch the first glimmer of re-
turning light, etc.! All which the writer of the
Acts conveys in the single phrase, "And wished
for the day."

Clear, unimpassioned, impartial presentation of
the subject, whether fact or fiction, whether done
in prose or verse, is the prominent feature of the
classic style. The modern writer gives you not so
much the things themselves as his impression of
them. You are compelled to see them through his
eyes; that is, through his feelings and reflections.
The ancients present them in their own light, without coloring. They would seem to have possessed
other powers of seeing than the modern, who, as
Jean Paul says, stands with an intellectual spy-glass
behind his own eyes. Certainly they possessed the
art of so placing their object as not to have their
own shadow fall upon it.

The difference is especially noticeable in poetry,
where each style unfolds itself more fully, and both
are perfected in their several kinds. Ancient poetry is characterized by sharp delineations of individual objects, modern poetry by the color it gives to
things, and the sentiments it associates with them.

The healthy nature of the ancients cared little
for anything beyond the visible world in which
they moved. The finer their organization, the

clearer the impressions which they received from surrounding objects. The modern, estranged from Nature, is thrown back upon himself; the finer his organization, the more feelingly he is affected by his environment. The ancient lived more in phe-/nomena, the modern lives more in thought. Hence, as Schiller says, classic poetry affects us through the medium of facts, romantic through the medium of ideas.

In the thought of the ancients — I speak particularly of the Greeks — soul and body, spiritual and material, were not divided, but blended, fused in one consciousness, one nature, one man. This identity of matter and mind which they realized in their life is expressed in all the creations of Grecian art.

For us moderns this harmony is lost. The beautiful equilibrium of matter and spirit is destroyed. We are divided within ourselves, our nature is rent in twain. We have discovered that we exist. We are become aware of spirit, and, like children of a larger growth, would pick the world to pieces to find where it hides. To the Greeks the world was a fact; to us it is a problem. Where they accepted, we analyze; where they rested, we challenge and dispute; where they lost themselves in contemplation, we seek ourselves in reflection; where they dreamed, we dream that we dream. They enjoyed the ideal in the actual; we seek it apart from the actual, in the vague inane.

It must not, however, be supposed that ancient and classic on one side, and modern and romantic on the other, are inseparably one, so that nothing approaching to romantic shall be found in any Greek or Roman author, nor any classic page in the literature of modern Europe. What has been said is to be understood as indicating only the prevailing characteristics respectively of the earlier and the latter ages.

Moreover, the word "ancient" is not intended to include all writers of Greek and Latin. The literary line of demarcation is not identical with the chronological one which divides the old world from mediæval time. On the contrary, the pagan writers of the post-Augustan age of Latin literature have much in common with the modern. The story of Cupid and Psyche in the "Golden Ass" of Apuleius. is as much a romance as any composition of the seventeenth or eighteenth century. The Letters of the younger Pliny and the "Attic Nights" of Aulus Gellius have very little of the savor of antiquity. The exquisite poem of the last-named writer, which gives the psychology of a kiss, beginning with, —

"Dum semihulco suavio
Meum puellum suavior,"

is intensely modern. Even Tacitus, as a historiographer, is reflective, and so far modern, as compared with Livy. Of Greek writers, also, Lucian and Plutarch, — especially the former, — if classic in style, are modern in spirit.

On the other hand, Dante and Milton are classic in their objective particularity of presentment. Dante in his vision of Malebolge, where public peculators are punished by being plunged in a lake of boiling pitch, gives a Homeric description of the Venetian dock-yard where boiling pitch was used for the repair of vessels.

Milton is not satisfied with comparing a warrior's shield to the full moon, as other poets have done, but, Homer-like, adds : —

> " Whose orb
> Through optic glass the Tuscan artist views
> At evening from the top of Fiesole,
> Or in Valdarno, to descry new lands,
> Rivers, or mountains in her spotty globe."

Ancient and modern are not more sharply contrasted than are Gibbon and Carlyle as historiographers. Mark the calm, impersonal style in which Gibbon recounts the horrible slaughter of the family of the Emperor Maurice by the decree and in the presence of the usurper Phocas: "The ministers of death were despatched to Chalcedon; they dragged the emperor from his sanctuary, and the five sons of Maurice were successively murdered before the eyes of their agonizing parent. At each stroke which he felt in his heart he found strength to rehearse a pious ejaculation. . . . The tragic scene was finally closed by the execution of the emperor himself in the twentieth year of his reign and the sixty-third of his age." Compare this with Carlyle's account of the slaughter of Princess Lamballe: "She too is led to the hell-gate, a manifest Queen's friend. She shivers back at the sight of the bloody sabres, but there is no return. Onwards! That fair hind-head is cleft with the axe, the neck is severed. That fair body is cut in fragments. . . . She was beautiful, she was good; she had known no happiness. Young hearts, generation after generation, will think with themselves: 'O worthy of worship, thou king-descended, God-descended, and poor sister woman! Why was not I there, and some sword Balmung or Thor's hammer in my hand?'"

Modern English poets, from Cowper on, with few exceptions, are strictly romantic, compared with their immediate predecessors. Most romantic of all, Scott in his themes and Byron in his mood.

Among prose-writers romanticism has reached its climax in recent novelists, as shown in their attempted descriptions of scenery, particularly sky

scenery. The elder novelists, from Richardson to
Scott, attempted nothing of the sort. They describe persons and scenes, but not *scenery* in the
commonly received sense of the word. Though
Scott indulges in descriptions of landscapes, he
abstains altogether from sky*scapes*, if I may be
allowed the phrase, — I mean such pictures as Black
undertakes in " The Strange Adventures of a Phae-
ton," and the author of " The Wreck of the ' Gros-
venor,' " in his maritime tales. In one of the most
popular of living novelists I find, among others,
this extravaganza: " In the whole crystalline hollow, gleaming and flowing with delight, yet waiting
for more, the Psyche was the only life-bearing
thing, the one cloudy germ-spot afloat in the bosom
of the great roc-egg of the sea and sky, whose
sheltering nest was the universe with its walls of
flame." What classic writer would have perpetrated this amazing bombast ?

The choicest examples of the classic style in
modern English literature, I should say, are Swift,
Defoe, Goldsmith, and more recently Landor, the
last of the classicists.

If in these comments I have seemed to disparage
the romantic style in comparison with the classic,
I desire to correct that impression. The two are
very different, but neither can be said, in the abstract and on universal grounds, to be better than

the other,—better in and for every province of literature. For history one may prefer the cold reserve and colorless simplicity of the classic style, where the medium is lost in the object, as the light which makes all things visible is itself unseen. In poetry, on the other hand, the inwardness, the sentimental intensity, the subjective coloring, of the romantic style constitute a peculiar charm which is wanting in the classic. This charm in Childe Harold, for example, abundantly compensates the absence of pure objective painting which one might expect in a descriptive poem.

Romantic relates to classic somewhat as music relates to plastic art. How is it that painting and sculpture affect us? They arrest contemplation and occupy the mind with one defined whole. In that contemplation our whole being is for the time bound up. Consciousness excludes all else. Past and future are merged in the *now*, real and ideal are blended in one. Music, on the contrary, not only presents no definite object of contemplation, but just so far as it takes possession of us precludes contemplation; it allows no pause. Instead of arresting attention by something fixed, it carries attention away with it on its own irresistible current. It presents no finished ideal, but suggests ideals beyond the capacity of canvas or stone. Plastic art acts on the intellect, music on the feelings; the one affects us by what it presents, the other by what it suggests.

This, it seems to me, is essentially the difference between classic and romantic poetry. I need but name Homer and Milton as examples of the one, and Scott or Shelley as representative of the other. Instead of occupying the mind with well-defined images, romantic poetry crosses it with "thick-coming" fancies.

Rhyme, a characteristic property of modern poetry, favors this tendency, hindering clearness and fixedness of impression, perpetually breaking the images it presents, as the ripples which chase each other on the surface of a lake, though beautiful in themselves, prevent clear reflections of sky and shore. The classic poet is satisfied if his language exactly covers the idea; the romantic would give his words, in addition to their logical and etymological import, a suggestive interest: they must not only indicate the things intended, but must be the keynotes to certain associations which he himself connects with them. The first couplet of the "Corsair," —

" O'er the glad waters of the dark blue sea,
Our thoughts as boundless, and our souls as free," —

is not so much intended to paint the ocean as to convey the feeling which that element inspired in the poet. Of the same character are those lines in Scott's " Rokeby " : —

> "Far in the chambers of the West
> The gale had sighed itself to rest."

In his " Mazeppa," Byron puts into the hero's mouth the following experience of sunrise : —

> " Some streaks announced the coming sun:
> How slow, alas, he came!
> Methought that mist of dawning gray
> Would never dapple into day.
> How heavily it rolled away
> Before the eastern flame
> Rose crimson and deposed the stars,
> And called the radiance from their cars,
> And filled the earth from his deep throne
> With lonely lustre all his own ! "

We have here no distinct image of sunrise, such as a classic poet would present, but we have, what is better, the sensations with which the phenomenon is watched by the unfortunate victim. It is not the vision, but the heart's response to it, which the lines convey.

The analogy with music is aptly illustrated by the larger function which sound performs in romantic verse. The best passages of Paradise Lost would lose little if rendered in prose; but what would become of Scott, Moore, and Byron if stripped of prosody and rhyme? All poetry by its rhythmical form addresses itself to the ear; but romantic poetry depends so much on the co-operation of that organ — on sound if read aloud, or the representation of sound if read silently — for its true appreciation that a deaf and dumb reader would lose the better part of the enjoyment we derive from such pieces as the " Burial of Sir John Moore " and Campbell's lyrics. To deny that this musical charm of romantic poetry is an excellence, is to contradict the æsthetic consciousness of the greater part of the reading world, and to pass condemnation on some of the most cherished productions of literary art. By how much music is more potent than painting, by so much romantic poetry will exercise an influence surpassing that of the classic on the popular mind.

Goethe in his " Helena " — an episode which constitutes the third act of the Second Part of " Faust " — has attempted a reconciliation of the controversy then raging between the classicists and romanticists as to the comparative merits of either style, by showing that love of the beautiful and interest in life are common to both, and that what distinguishes them is merely formal and accidental. Helena represents classic beauty, Faust modern culture; Lynceus, the ancient pilot of the Argonauts, officiates as mediator between the two. Dialogue and chorus proceed, after classic fashion, in unrhymed

verse until Lynceus appears on the stage. He an-
nounces the advent of the romantic by discoursing
in rhyme. Helena declares herself pleased with
that new style of verse, where sound matches sound,
and the verses " kiss each other." She asks how
she may learn to discourse in such pleasant wise.
Faust answers, it is very easy ; it is the natural
language of the heart. He begins,—

> " And when your breast with longing overflows,
>   You look around and ask,"

(Pause. Helena breaks in)

> " Who shares my throes ? "

So they play crambo until Helena has caught the
trick.

Goethe seems to have meant by this that the
beauty of ancient poetic art, so extolled by the
classicists, can take on a modern form without loss
of what is most essential in it ; and on the other
hand, that the deeper feeling which characterizes
the romantic — the language of the heart — may
ally itself with classic elegance, and add a new
charm to antique beauty.

Much of the symbolism of this strange poem
(for the " Helena " is a poem, complete in itself) is
obscure, and some of it misleading. In strict consistency, Euphorion, the offspring of Helena and
Faust, ought to represent the fusion of the classic

and romantic in one. And such appears to have been Goethe's meaning. But Euphorion confessedly stands for Byron; and Byron is simply and wholly romantic, with no tincture of classicism in his nature or works.

Not Byron, but Goethe himself, above all modern poets, combines the two under one imperial name. What is most characteristic in each kind may be found in unsurpassed perfection in the ample treasury of his works, — nay, in a single work; for is not the First Part of "Faust" the very essence of romance, and is not the larger portion of the Second Part a reproduction of the classic Muse?

The "Iphigenie auf Tauris" was called an echo of Greek song; but a still purer classicism meets us in the Elegies, in the "Pandora," and in the "Alexis and Dora." What a gulf divides these compositions from the "Sorrows of Werther"! There Goethe anticipates by a quarter of a century the rise of the Romantic School in Germany, which was nearly contemporaneous with the same fashion in England: inaugurated in the latter country by Scott, in the former by Novalis and Tieck. The birthyears respectively of these three poets, Scott, Novalis, and Tieck, are 71, 72, 73 of the eighteenth century. The "Sorrows of Werther" first appeared, I think, in 1772.

When I say that Scott inaugurated romanticism

in England, and Novalis and Tieck in Germany, I
do not mean that the new turn which poetry took
in those countries was due to them alone. The
movement had a deeper origin than personal caprice or the efforts of a clique. The revolution in
literature was the outcome of a revolution in the
spirit of the age, of which these writers were the
unconscious exponents. Literature and life are
never far asunder. Every age enacts itself twice, —
first in its acts and events, then in its writings.
The struggles and aspirations which agitated Europe at the close of the eighteenth century elicited
an echo in the breasts of her poets. The French
Revolution, following our own, electrified the nations, causing them to thrill and heave as never
before since the Protestant Reformation. It star-
tled England out of her placid acquiescence in the
pompous pedantry of Johnson and the boasted
supremacy of Addison and Pope. In Germany it
roused a protest against the shallow *Aufklärung*
of the Universal German Library. Its effect in
England was conspicuous in a richer diction, recov-
ering somewhat of the opulence of the Elizabethan
age. In Germany it made itself manifest in a
more believing spirit and a deeper tone of thought.

Other influences conspired to this end. The
publication of the "Reliques of Ancient Poetry," by
Bishop Percy, in 1765, presented, in the strains of

the old romantic time, a refreshing contrast with the polished tameness of contemporary verse. A similar service was rendered in Germany (Lessing having broken the spell of French classicism) by Herder's publication of the " Cid," his " Völkerstimmen," his " Andenken an einige ältere deutsche Dichter;" by Clemens Brentano and Achim von Arnim's publication of " Des Knaben Wunderhorn;" by Wieland's " Oberon;" and by the re-editing of the " Nibelungenlied."

Another power on the side of romanticism, not commonly recognized, was " Ossian." The poems bearing this name were given to the public a short time previous to Percy's " Reliques," in 1763, and made a great sensation, partly on account of their novelty, and partly because of their reputed source. The ardor with which they were welcomed in England was soon damped, it is true, by doubts concerning their authenticity. The English people are constitutionally afraid of being " gulled," and when Samuel Johnson, the literary dictator of the day, pronounced them spurious, they were indignantly cast aside,—as if the authorship, and not the character, of the poetry determined its value! The question of genuineness does not concern us in this connection; all I have to say about it is that if Macpherson wrote " Ossian," he had a good deal more poetic feeling than most of the poets of his time, — certainly a good deal more than Dr. Johnson had. In spite of all objectors, Wordsworth included, who condemns the poems on technical grounds, they have the effect of poetry on most readers. If they do not satisfy the critical sense, they breathe a poetic *aura*, and awaken poetic feeling in the breast. Nothing else can explain the enthusiasm with which at first they were everywhere received. On the Continent especially, where no question of authorship interfered, they charmed unprejudiced minds. But what particularly concerns us here is the romantic tone of these compositions. Whether uttered by an ancient Celtic bard, or composed by a modern antiquary, they were thoroughly romantic, and confirmed the romantic tendency of the time. Napoleon, in whose rocky nature a wild flower of romance had found some cleft to blossom in, carried them with him in his expeditions, as Alexander did their literary antipodes, the Iliad and Odyssey.

A marked feature of modern romanticism is love of the past, — that passionate regret for by-gone fashions which prompts the attempt to patch the new garment of to-day with the old cloth of former wear. The feeling which, early in this century, found inspiration in mediæval lore, and loved to present the old chivalrics in novel and song, is the same which inspires the practical anachronisms of

recent time, which in England seeks to reproduce
the old ecclesiastical sanctities, which astonishes
American cities with a mimicry of Gothic architecture ; the same which forty years ago restored
the long-disused beard, which now ransacks second-
hand furniture-stores and remote farmhouses for
claw-footed tables and brass-handled bureaus, which
drags from the lumber-room the obsolete spinning-
wheel, which rejoices in many-cornered dwelling-
houses with diminutive window-panes, — the more
unshapely the better, because the more picturesque.
A mania innocent enough in these manifestations,
but in its essence identical with that which inspired
the knight of La Mancha, — the typical example for
all generations of romanticism gone wild.

It would be unjust, however, to maintain that
the reaching back after old things is the sum of
romanticism, as if what we so name were mere
conservatism or reactionism. This worship of the
past is only an accidental manifestation of a principle whose most comprehensive term is *aspiration*,
— a noble discontent and disdain of the present,
which in the absence of creative genius, of power
to originate new forms, seeks relief in the past
from the weary commonplace of the day.

The essence of romanticism is aspiration.
'Whether it look backward or forward, there is in
it a spirit of adventure, — as much of it in the

Crusaders who sought a sepulchre in the East, as in the Spanish navigators who sought an Eldorado in the West; as much in the arctic explorers who would force a way through eternal frost, as in the Knights of the Holy Grail; as much in the nineteenth century as in the twelfth, in Garibaldi and Gordon as in Godfrey and Tancred.

The romantic schools of German and English literature were transient phases already outgrown; but the principle of romanticism in literature is immortal, — it is the spirit asserting itself through the form. Classicism gives us perfection of form, romanticism fulness of spirit. Both are essential, seldom found united; but both must combine to constitute a masterpiece of literary art.

THE STEPS OF BEAUTY.

(From the Unitarian Review.)

BEAUTY is that quality in the objects of our contemplation which pleases irrespectively of use or any profit to ourselves resulting therefrom. Æsthetic philosophy does not, as usually received, embrace in its view of the beautiful the satisfactions of the palate; yet, strange to say, it borrows from the palate the name of the faculty which regulates and constitutes æsthetic enjoyment in all its kinds, — the word "taste." Kant ascribes this to the idiosyncrasy and seeming wilfulness of æsthetic judgments, where, as in the matter of food, individual preference plays so important a part. "You cannot," he says, "make me like a dish by reasoning about it and showing why I ought to like it; I judge it with my tongue, and from that judgment there is no appeal. So, in the realm of art, no rules established by critics, and no majority of voices, can force my delight in any object in spite of myself." There is this analogy, but it does not, in my view, satisfactorily explain the use of the word "taste" in its application to beauty. A simpler explanation is that taste, in the physical sense, being the most active and positive of our sensations, by a natural symbolism furnishes a convenient metaphor for those of a more ethereal kind.

For the purpose of this essay I include in the word "beauty" whatever gratifies taste, in the metaphorical sense of the term.

But tastes differ; what one condemns, another approves. Is beauty, then, a merely subjective experience, with no ground or reason in the object? Is one man's taste as good as another's? Is there no absolute beauty? Reason protests against such a conclusion. The alleged divergency of taste is, after all, superficial, very confined in its range, and overbalanced by a general uniformity of taste in things essential. We may differ in our preference of this or that style of architecture or dress; but there are forms which all will agree in pronouncing beautiful, if only comparatively so, and there are monstrosities which all will condemn. No one will say that a satyr is as beautiful as the Belvidere Apollo, or a crab as comely as a gazelle. We speak of deformity: deformity implies a model, it presupposes normal forms of universal acceptance. We say ridiculous: our sense of the ridiculous is proof of a law of beauty or propriety to which all that we term ridiculous is consciously or unconsciously referred. When we pronounce a thing ridiculous, we affirm an ideal, the departure from which makes it ridiculous. And when the aberration from ideal beauty exceeds certain limits, we resent the incongruity as a moral offence; the author is judged to have sinned against a law in *his* mind as well as ours, and passes into like condemnation with the work of his hands.

A noted sinner in this kind was Prince Pallagonia, a Sicilian nobleman of the last century, who made his palace a museum of all sorts of monstrosities, exhausting his ingenuity in ugly inventions, and gaining as much celebrity by his systematic warfare against taste as others have achieved in its service. The lodge, as you entered the grounds, presented four huge giants, with modern gaiters buttoned over the ankle, supporting a cornice on which was depicted the Holy Trinity. The walls leading from the lodge to the castle were disgraced with every imaginable deformity,—beggars, men and women in tattered garments, dwarfs, clowns, gods and goddesses in French costume, mythology caricatured; Punch and Judy cheek by jowl with Achilles and Chiron; horses with human hands, horses' heads on men's shoulders, dragons, serpents, misshapen monkeys, all sorts of paws on all sorts of figures, with duplicates of single members, and heads that did not belong to them. In the court-yard and castle, new enormities, — the walls not straight, but inclining to this side and that side, affronting one's sense of the horizontal and the perpendicular; statues lying on their noses, rooms finished with bits of picture-frames with every variety of pattern. In the chapel, swinging from the ceiling by a chain fastened to a nail in the head, was a kneeling figure in the attitude of prayer.[1]

What shocks us in these enormities is not the strangeness, which would only surprise, but the violation of a standard, an ideal of beauty which we have in our minds, and with which we unconsciously compare them. The more that ideal is developed, the more sensible we are of beauties and defects. Thus, Nature reveals beauties to the painter which are missed by the uninformed eye. And this explains the fact that a painted landscape seems often more beautiful than the original, and promises to one who sees it first more than the original fulfils. In the painting the beauty is disengaged, so to speak, from the substance, and made more apparent. For the beauty resides not in the material objects, the woods and the water, hill and vale, as such, that make the landscape, it is the reflection of something in ourselves, an idea which we bring to its contemplation. The more

---

[1] The description is from Goethe's Italienische Reise.

14

refined that idea, the more beautiful the landscape to our eye. The painter, carrying into Nature his own quick sense, has seized her deeper meaning; he sees the pure form of things abstract from the substance, and gives it on the canvas. He enables us to see the landscape as he sees it, he brings us into communion with his and its idea.

Kant maintains that the Beautiful interests us only in society, that a man left alone on a desert island would neither adorn his hut nor himself.[1] I hold, on the contrary, that the love of beauty belongs to man as man, and in no human being can be utterly wanting or wholly inactive. Let the individual be entirely secluded from his kind; let him dwell in a desert shut out from the world, so that no influence from without shall disturb the pure spontaneity of his action: if you could look in upon him so situated, you would find in his arrangements, I fancy, some slight sacrifice to the eye, some faint regard for order and form. The sense of beauty is wanting in none, but no faculty is less perfect by nature. The germ only is given; the rest is discipline.

We may distinguish five grades or modes of beauty, — color, form, expression, thought, action.

The perception of the beautiful begins with color. The eye rejoices in brilliant hues, — scarlet, purple,

---

[1] Kritik der Urtheilskraft, Analytik d. Erhabenen.

green, and gold. It needs no culture to appreciate these; they are patent to the child and the savage. But when we come to combinations of color, and a right selection in order to the best effect, the child and the savage are at fault. A degree of cultivation is needed to select the purest tints, and so to arrange them as to produce a harmonious whole. A happy choice of colors in the making-up of a costume, in the garniture of a drawing-room, or the composition of a bouquet, betokens always a measure of æsthetic refinement.

To the gratifications of color succeeds the more intellectual enjoyment of form. The pleasure derived from color, at least from single colors, is purely sensuous, passive, the action of refracted light on the nerves through the medium of the eye, the least sensual of the senses. The relish of beautiful forms presupposes something more than sense. Mental co-operation is here required. The mind must construe the form to itself, and reflect upon it so as to seize its idea. It is true we are not conscious of any such process in ordinary cases; but a careful analysis of our impressions of formal beauty as distinct from grandeur — which yields a merely passive delight, the mind contributing only the sentiment of wonder — will show them to be intellectual products.

What constitutes beauty of form? Why are

sphere and oval, and even cube, more satisfactory than shapeless masses; the full moon and the crescent moon more pleasing than the gibbous; a vaulted roof than the flat ceiling of an ordinary dwelling? The answer is given in the word "proportion." Proportion — in compound forms, symmetry — is such a relation of part to part in a given body as shall produce in the beholder the feeling of equipoise. It answers to harmony in music. Schelling calls architecture "a music in space, . . . as it were a frozen music." We might call it an arrested dance. Some feeling of this sort may have given rise to the Greek myth which presents Amphion building the city of Thebes by making the stones dance into place to the sound of his lyre. Sand strown upon a plate may be made to arrange itself in symmetrical figures by means of musical vibrations, — a fact which shows that the relation of form to music, the connection between symmetry and harmony, is not a mere fancy, but is founded in the nature of things.

The beauty of symmetrical forms may be figured as the result of a double movement, the balance of two opposite tendencies, — centrifugal and centripetal, expansion and concentration. First, motion outward in different directions from a common centre. This motion itself we contemplate with pleasure, — the pleasure experienced in beholding a cloud dispart and disperse into delicate lichens and gauze-like films, which grow more and more filmy as we watch them until they vanish in the far blue ; or the similar enjoyment of seeing a volume of smoke on a still, bright day unroll itself with a lazy, cumbrous grace, and stretch contentedly away into invisibility. But this enjoyment is partial, and soon wearies. Motion outward does not long satisfy. The mind is not content to lose itself in endless departure, it tires of evolutions which come to nothing. It is forced back upon itself, it craves a result. This craving is met by a counter-motion from the circumference toward the centre. The first essays of that return movement give us Hogarth's line of beauty, — the wavy motion of a streamer in the wind. Its completion gives us the beautiful form.

We have here the ground-plan of formal beauty as an object of visual and mental contemplation, — radiation in all directions to form an outline, and reference of all points in that outline to a common centre, the mind unconsciously going forth and re-turning to that centre in its contemplation. In the balance of these two tendencies or move-ments consists the feeling of proportion. All forms which yield this mental equipoise we pro-nounce well-proportioned, beautiful. What consti-tutes deformity in any object is the disturbance of this harmonious relation between the perimeter and the centre.[1]

The next grade in the scale of beauty is expression. Here, beauty assumes a decidedly intellectual character. Form pleases by affording the mind an agreeable pause, by throwing us back on ourselves in a state of tranquil contemplation. Expression tempts us forth from ourselves into communion with what we contemplate. Expression constitutes the compound beauty of natural scenery as distinguished from that of single objects. The sky, earth, and water which compose a landscape interest us not as individual phenomena, but by their grouping, their blending together in one expression, one face, — as it were the face of a spirit akin to our own, and answering our gaze with reciprocal greeting. The beauty of expression reaches its acme in the human countenance, which in its perfection is the fairest of material creations, the last link in the chain which connects the visible

---

[1] If beauty of form, as exemplified in symmetrical structure, is rightly termed visible music, then, conversely, music may be said to be audible symmetry. The enjoyment derived from it through the practised ear is resolvable into a fine sense of proportion. Beauty as predicated of music I venture to class under the head of form. It is not the ear in its primary function, but, as De Quincey, following Sir Thomas Browne, remarks, the reaction of the mind on the notices furnished by the ear, that gives the enjoyment of music. But is not the same true of the enjoyment of beauty through the medium of the eye?

with the invisible. Heaven and earth meet in the face of a beautiful woman, where the beauty is of that supreme type which plastic Nature alone cannot fashion, mould she never so cunningly ; where a spiritual grace supervenes, and native intelligence, high culture, sweetness, and moral majesty transfigure fleshly tints and lines.

Feminine beauty, it is true, is not all of this supreme type. There is an animal beauty in which spirit has no part, where physical perfection of tint and feature, grace of form and movement, lack the crowning grace of moral inspiration. And this carnal beauty, it must be confessed, has exercised a more potent sway in human affairs than the spiritual. Such must have been the beauty of Grecian Helen, of Thespian Phryne, of Cleopatra, of Herodias' daughter, of Waldrada, of Rosamond, of Agnes of Meran, of Nell Gwynn, and Pompadour, —

" Quick and skilful to inspire
Sweet, extravagant desire."

What a power it has been in the history of nations, — a spell of fate turning the heads of men or dancing them off their shoulders, enslaving monarchs, impoverishing States ! Yet see on what trifles the mere physical merit of facial beauty depends. How infinitesimally small the difference in lines and angles which divides beauty from ugliness ! Lavater has demonstrated the distance be-

tween the face of a frog and the normal human
countenance by a scale of but twelve types, in which
any member of the series differs by a scarcely perceptible change from that which preceded and that
which follows. If only twelve stages intervene between the frog countenance and the human, judge
how slight must be the measurable difference of
contour between the human ugly and the fair. It
is not the physical conformation of the face, the
curve of the eyebrow, the curl of the lip, the length
of the chin, the angle of the nose, the setting of the
eyes and their color, the moulding of cheek and
forehead; it is not the features in and of themselves, minute varieties of a common pattern, quaint
freaks of the flesh, — it is not these, but something
behind which lights and inspires them, that gives
those exquisite phases of expression which painting
and sculpture reach after, but never quite compass :
the maiden's rapt devotion, the beam of divinity
in the eye of maternal love, the hero's triumph, the
seer's ecstasy.

The fugitive expression of a beautiful soul in a
human countenance transcends the scope of chisel
or brush.

The beauty of expression is the highest beauty
which matter takes on. To rise above this, we
must leave the material and enter the realm of
thought, specifically of literary art.

But literary æsthetic is a special topic, foreign to the plan of this essay. I pass at once to the last and crowning beauty of humanity, — beauty in action.

By beauty in action I mean conformity with the moral ideal, a beauty identical with goodness in the more restricted use of that word. Goodness expresses the relation to the actor, beauty the relation to the mind that contemplates the act. Goodness denotes the substance, beauty the form. It is not, however, to all good actions in the ratio of their goodness that we accord indiscriminately the praise of beauty. We bestow that title more especially on those in which disregard of self and absence of calculation are most conspicuous. Actions prompted by the instinct of natural affection please us more than those in which the affections are sacrificed to duty. When the magistrate in the Eastern tale condemns the guilty father to be scourged in his presence, we are disgusted with the act while commending its justice. But our disgust is turned to admiration when, after the infliction, the son descends from the dignity of his office, lays aside his magisterial robe, dresses his father's wounds with his own hands, and bathes them with his tears. We recognize a fearful beauty in the lofty defiance of wrong with which the Roman father seizes a knife from the shambles and slays his daughter to

save her from outrage worse than death ; we admire
the unflinching justice with which another Roman
condemns to death his guilty sons : but, in either
case, we are shocked by the act. If in these and
similar instances the beautiful and the good appear
to conflict, there are others which combine the two,
and satisfy at once the utmost delicacy of feeling
and the utmost rigor of the law, and which neither
on the side of nature nor on the side of reason leave
anything to wish. When Scipio Africanus dismisses
unharmed

"In his prime youth the fair Iberian maid;"

when Caius Marcius at the gates of Rome yields to
the entreaties of his mother and his wife and the
tears of his fellow-citizens, renounces his vengeance
and spares the city; when Regulus dissuades his
countrymen from accepting the treaty which offered
salvation to himself, but compromised the safety of
the State, and then, true to his plighted faith, re-
turns to Carthage to meet the cruel death which
awaits him there ; when Pompeius refuses to tarry
the storm, and against the advice of his friends, at
the risk of his life, ships for Africa in quest of corn,
saying, " It is not necessary that Pompeius should
live, but it is necessary that Rome, if possible,
should be saved from famine," — we feel, regarding
these acts as phenomena merely, a satisfaction akin
to that which we experience in contemplating a

perfect work of art, where it would be impossible to add anything or to take away anything without impairing their complete beauty. Our better soul sees itself reflected in their perfect fitness. We feel that here is truth drawn from our common nature. This lay in us too, could we but have uttered it. This is what we believe and feel and are.

But while the feeling derived from beauty in action has something in common with the satisfactions of art, it has also something higher and better than art can give. We feel that this beauty is not like the beauty of art, phenomenal merely, but real and essential. It is not a charm residing in the soul of the spectator, but something inherent in the nature of the thing. In art, it is merely the form that pleases ; but here the form and the substance are one. Moral beauty possesses the peculiar attribute of necessity. Through the freedom of the actor we revere the obligation of the law. Our sense of beauty in other things can afford to lie in abeyance and be often disappointed; but the moral sense is imperative, and must not be gainsaid. Truth in art we welcome gladly when it appears ; still, it is but a luxury, a thing that may be or may not be, without affecting materially the issues of life. But truth in action we cannot spare; it is the salt of the world: life would rot without it. Moral beauty can stand by itself; it needs no background, it asks no embellishment from any other source to set it off. When Phocion declines the hundred talents sent him by Alexander, and being urged to name some favor which he would accept as reward for his services, asks that some slaves who were confined iu the citadel of Sardis should be set free, we care not to know what manner of man this was in his outward appearance, whether comely or deformed, whether elegant or rude; we are satisfied with the act. But where, on the other hand, this grace is wanting, or where it is violated and set at naught, all other grace and beauty and splendor vanish like the prismatic colors of the spectrum when a cloud comes over the sun. You visit a fine house, splendidly furnished and appointed, with all kinds of costly embellishment, and, while admiring these things, it is whispered in your ear that the owner has obtained them by unjust means, by peculation or extortion, or that the tradesmen or artisans who supplied them remain unpaid, and that they and their families are pining for want of the necessities of life. Would not these costly ornaments then lose their lustre? Would not your admiration be turned to disgust? Would you not sicken at the splendor which covered such wrong? In human life we cannot separate the phenomenal from the

real, the show from the man. I defined beauty as
that which gives pleasure irrespective of use; but
here, in its highest phase, we see that beauty, as
being identical with good, is one with use.

Beauty is the great mediator between the flesh
and the spirit. Its function is co-ordinate with
that of religion: the office of both is to win mankind to the love of the true and the good. It was
doubtless a feeling of this relation which suggested
the use of the arts in religious worship.

Well may beauty minister in temples made with
hands; for see how constant its ministry in the un-
walled temple of the universe, and how it clothes
creation as a garment! No one can think lightly
of its value in the economy of life who marks the
place it occupies in the economy of Nature. If
utility object to art that it offers but a world of
shows, let utility observe that the universe itself is
a show. All creation addresses itself to the eye. It
is but the smallest part that the other senses can
appropriate of external objects, and that small portion is lessened by exclusion or exhausted by use.
But the eye has the entire universe for its fee-
simple. Sun, moon, and stars, and earth and sea,
are articled in its boundless fief. No use can exhaust its sumless income. To it all things are
tributary. For it the sun paints, the sky curves,
the clouds roll, the landscape glows. Day by day

the morning's crimson process, the evening's funeral pomp, and all the wealth of chaliced flowers and plumed birds and insect dyes, and all that the ocean reveals of its pearly secrets, are tributes to the eye. From the diamond star in the deep above to its diamond image in the deep below, from the rainbow cloud to the rainbow shell, all vision glitters and blooms and waves with thousand-fold unspeakable beauty.

The lesson which Nature teaches, shall it not inspire our philosophy of life? What a world it would be from which that lesson were banished! Imagine a State in which life should exhibit no love of beauty, no æsthetic aspiration. The supposition implies the rudest aspect of savage life. It recalls the forest and the cave, from which men would never have emerged but for the humanizing influence of taste. To that we owe all our civilization. From the savage wigwam to the thronged city, the race has been guided by the hand of beauty. The first thing which the wild man does when he has filled his belly is to paint his skin. The next is to shape his garment; and the earliest office of the garment is not protection, but ornament. And so painting and shaping, he grows in all the dimensions of art to the perfect stature of civilized man. His wigwam becomes architecture; his feathered girdle, elaborate costume; his hollow log, a ship. And what he gains by this process is not so much comfort as decorum. An instinct of our nature demands that we add decency to comfort, and grace to necessity, and fling the drapery of art around the meanest of our enjoyments and the commonest uses of life. Food snatched from the hearth where it is cooked, and devoured without ceremony, would nourish the body as well as when accompanied with those formalities which civilization has appended to the sensual act. But those formalities have converted the animal necessity to a social institution, which entertains the mind while it nourishes the flesh.

Farther still, and upward ever, it is the office of Beauty to lead her votaries. Not only from savage uses to polished civility, from wigwam and kraal to palace and towered city, from the rudest earthly to the most refined, but higher yet, from the earthly to the heavenly. The worship of a beauty above earthly shows is the highest homage of a true religion. It is not the custom of public worship to apply to God the epithet "beautiful." We call him almighty, and magnify his power; but is not beauty as true a manifestation of Deity as power? And is not our sense of beauty as near divine as the wonder and awe which infinite power inspires?

Whatever the nominal object of our worship, there are two things which all men everywhere instinctively adore, — strength and beauty : the former embracing all possible demonstrations of creative and ruling energy ; the other including all the attributes of love and goodness which stamp that energy divine.

The Christian Church has no traditional likeness of Jesus ; but a pious instinct taught the old painters to give him a face of beauty, so close the connection which their art divined between the holy and the fair.

Michel Angelo pronounced beauty to be "the frail and weary weed" which Truth in this world puts on, in pity for human weakness. But can we conceive of any state in the infinite future, of any date in the eternal ages, when Truth will not clothe itself with beauty ? For is not all beauty resolvable into truth ? Aspire how we will, we can never transcend the union of the two. Higher than beauty thought cannot mount.

ETHICAL SYSTEMS.

[*From the North American Review.*]

ETHIC is the science of right behavior, — its ground in human nature, and its application to conduct. The subject presents two topics, — first, the reason of right behavior, or the ground of moral obligation; second, the criterion of right behavior, or rectitude in action.

What do we mean by "moral obligation"? Why ought I to act in a certain way, to do this or that, and not to do otherwise? The answers to this question are mainly three, and characterize three different systems of ethic. We may call them the selfish, the politic, the ideal. The first finds the ground of moral obligation in self-love; the second in social relations; the third, theologically speaking, in the will of God, or, — what is the same thing philosophically expressed, — in the moral nature of man.

The selfish system is essentially that of the Epicurean philosophy, — each one's happiness the supreme good. This principle recurs with different modifications in some later systems, and notably in that of Paley, whose " Moral Philosophy " was once an approved text-book for the use of students. To the question, Why am I bound to act in a certain way?— *e. g.*, to keep my word, — Paley answers, Because if I do, I shall be rewarded for it in another life; if I do not, I shall be punished for it in another life. We distinguish, he says, between an act of prudence and an act of duty. Wherein does the difference consist? " The only difference is this, that in the one case we consider what we shall gain or lose in the present world; in the other case we consider also what we shall gain or lose in the world to come." According to this view there would be no duty; moral obligation would not exist for one who should be so unfortunate as not to believe in a future life. Paley, then, is an epicurean, differing from the sage of Athens only in seeking satisfaction in another world instead of securing it in this.

The system of Hobbes, who preceded Paley by a century or more, partakes partly of the politic and partly of the selfish. It is politic inasmuch as it identifies right with civil authority, and denies any higher law. It is selfish inasmuch as it identifies moral obligation with the good to be gained by obedience to civil rule.

The politic systems, distinctively so called, are those in which the sole ground of moral obligation is the good of society, which measure duty by utility. The best representative of these is Jeremy Bentham, a stalwart intellect, a *Hobbes redivivus;* in my judgment superior, in all that concerns social science, to modern Positivists. Bentham assumes utility to be the fundamental principle of morals. "By the principle of utility is meant," he says, "that principle which approves or disapproves every action whatsoever, according to the tendency which it appears to have to augment or diminish the happiness of the party whose interest is in question."

"If the principle of utility be a right principle to be governed by, and that in all cases, it follows that whatever principle differs from it in any case must be a wrong one. To prove any principle a wrong one, there needs no more than just to show it to be what it is, — a principle of which the dictates are in some point or other different from those of the principle of utility."

"Of such principles there are several; but they all agree in not accepting utility as the ultimate standard of right.

"One man says he has a thing made on purpose to tell him what is right and what is wrong, and that it is called a moral sense. And then he goes to work at his ease and says, Such a thing is right, and such a thing is wrong. Why? Because my moral sense tells me it is. Another man comes and alters the phrase, leaving out moral, and putting in common. He then tells you that his common sense tells him what is right and what is wrong as surely as the other man's moral sense did; meaning by common sense a sense of some kind or other which he says is possessed by all mankind, — the sense of those whose sense is not the same as the author's being struck out of the account as not worth taking. This contrivance does better than the other; for a moral sense being a new thing, a man may feel about him a good while without being able to find it out; but common sense is as old as creation, and there is no man but would be ashamed to be thought not to have as much of it as his neighbors. Another man comes and says that as to a moral sense, indeed, he cannot find that he has any such thing, but he has an understanding, which will do quite as well. This understanding, he says, is the standard of right and wrong; it tells him so and so. All wise and good men understand as he does; if other men's understandings differ in any point from his, so much the worse for them, — it is a sure sign that they are either defective or corrupt. Another says that there is an eternal and immutable rule of right; that the rule of right dictates so and so; and then he begins giving you his sentiments upon anything that comes uppermost, and these sentiments you are to take for granted are so many branches of the eternal rule of right."

These extracts indicate the spirit and intent of the utilitarian system of ethics as represented by Bentham, — a system in which there is no recognition of any other source of moral obligation than the comfort of society, of any other right than that which consists in augmenting the pleasures and diminishing the pains of our fellow-men.

The latest form of utilitarian ethics is the outcome of that system of philosophy known as Positivism. Here, as in Paley and Bentham, there is no recognition of absolute right and an aboriginal sense of right in moral agents. Instead of that, we have a modification of the brain resulting from hereditary experience of utility accompanying certain modes of action.

" Moral institutions," says Herbert Spencer, " are the results of accumulated experiences of utility. Gradually organized and inherited, they have come to be quite independent of conscious experience. Just in the same way that I believe the intuition of space possessed by any living individual to have arisen from organized and consolidated experiences of all antecedent individuals who bequeathed to him their slowly developed nervous organization ; just as I believe that this intuition, requiring only to be made definite and complete by personal experiences, has practically become a form of thought, apparently quite independent of experience, — so do I believe that the experiences of utility, organized and consolidated through all past generations of the human race, have been producing corresponding nervous organizations which, by continued transmission and accumulation, have become in us certain faculties of moral intuition, certain emotions corresponding to right and wrong conduct, which have no apparent basis in individual experiences of utility."

The view presented in this statement I regard as a curious example of the extravagances into which a strong mind may be driven by pursuing to its ultimate one line of thought, by the despotism of a system. The analogue chosen by way of illustration — the hereditary origin of our sense of space — suggests the question how primitive man came by his space-perceptions, which, one would say, must have been rather essential to him in the operations by which he won his subsistence and got himself lived, after a fashion, in those dim years ; and further (since heredity is cumulative), whether your and my sense of space is any more perfect than that of Pythagoras when he discoursed of the ἄπειρον two thousand five hundred years ago. As to the physiology of this hypothesis, it seems to me that if our moral perceptions are nervous modifications derived from inheritance, the sons and grandsons of upright ancestors should be pre-eminently gifted in that kind. But we have proof that the moral sense in such subjects is no finer than in persons of less honorable descent, in spite of the *noblesse oblige* of the French aristocrat. Conduct, I know, may be determined by other influences than that of moral intuition ; but surely it might be expected to bear some appreciable relation to such intuition.

There is, however, a truth, a very important truth, involved in Spencer's theory. That truth is the fact of an accumulation of moral capital in civil society, — a capital handed down from one generation to another, and to which each generation contributes its own experience in works and lives. The growth of this capital is coëval with history; it is vested in historic records, in biography, in literature, in churches and other institutions for the education and edification of human kind, but not, I think, in the intracranial ganglia of the human animal. It acts for the good of society, not as a physically plastic force, but as moral attraction, repulsion, incentive, guidance.

One investment of this capital is custom. Under this head I will name an instance in which social influence acts with almost physical force, and comes near to verifying Spencer's doctrine of nervous modification. It relates to the intercourse of the sexes. In the earliest stage of human society, when polyandry prevailed, brothers of one family did not shun to mix with a sister in wedlock according to such form as was known to that rude time. The custom was found to be attended with evil· consequences; it became obsolete; the moral sense was enlisted against it, and that so effectually that now it is regarded as one of the blackest of crimes, and what may be called an instinctive aversion has made it one of the rarest. Here is a strong case — a solitary one, unless parricide be another — of an hereditary sentiment ripening into a moral conviction, or, if you please, a moral intuition, whether through connate cerebral formation, as Spencer claims, or, as I prefer to believe, through overpowering social influence affecting domestic education.

But Spencer's doctrine teaches that man has originally no moral perceptions, no sense of right, — in effect, no moral nature; not differing in this from the brute. If this be allowed, it follows, I think, that man has no moral nature now. For civilized man differs from primitive man, not in the ground-elements of his constitution, but in training, development, habit. He acquires by heredity the habit of acting, the disposition and impulse to act, in conformity with social well-being. But where does he get the feeling that he ought so to act, that such action is right, that he is bound to it, however adverse to his own inclination, however it may seem to conflict with his own advantage? Whence does he derive the idea of duty? The mere perception that a given line of action is conducive to social well-being will not compel a man so to act if he sees no benefit, but, on the contrary, injury accruing to himself from such action. That perception will never induce him to sacrifice himself for the common good, unless reinforced by a strong sense of moral obligation. What do I

care for the common good ?   My own gain is more
to me than any benefit the public may reap from
my action.   Or suppose I feel some interest in the
common weal, some public sympathy : there is in
that sympathy no force sufficient to counteract my
selfish inclination, no categorical imperative.   But
Duty comes in and says, " You must."   A voice
in my conscience, which I feel to be the voice
of God, commands, and woe to me if I disobey.
Herein precisely consists the difference between
moral and political : the former finds its law within ; the latter, without.

There is a radical distinction which we all feel between " right " and " expedient."   That distinction
the utilitarian ethic overlooks.   The terms " right "
and " wrong " have no true place in that system ; they
are borrowed from a higher plane of human experience, and surreptitiously grafted on the stock of utilitarianism.   Take, for example, the virtue of honesty.
The moral sense enjoins honesty as a form of right
irrespective of use.   According to Mr. Spencer the
duty of honesty results from the experience of
many generations that honesty, as the proverb
goes, is the best policy.   The saying is not true in
the unqualified universality in which the proverb
affirms it.   Cases may be supposed in which, so far
as the temporal prosperity of the individual is concerned, rigid honesty is not the best policy.   But

let that pass; grant the truth of the proverb. How was it first discovered that honesty is the best policy? How came it ever to be tried? The carnal instinct is against it. When in early ages the carnal man saw an advantage to be gained by deception, and that deception not likely to be detected, and thereby to injure him in the end, he would be sure to deceive, unless a principle, other and higher than policy, restrained him. The first man who resisted the strong temptation to deceive was certainly not moved to such resistance by the accumulated experience of ages that honesty is the best policy wrought into his nervous structure, otherwise he would not have been the first honest man. He must have obeyed an imperative voice within, which said to him, " You must not deceive, you must speak and act the truth;" and doubtless he experienced a sharp conflict with himself in obeying that mandate, as the conscientious man does now when honesty and seeming advantage collide. If it were always as distinctly seen, as clearly understood, as firmly believed, that honesty is the best policy, as it is that fire burns and water drowns, honesty would cease to be a virtue, and an honest act could not with any propriety be termed a moral act. In the words of Sir John Lubbock, " It is precisely because honesty is sometimes associated with unhappy consequences that it is regarded as a virtue. If it had always been directly advantageous to all parties, it would have been classed as useful, but not as right."

I think we have abundant evidence of an aboriginal sense of moral obligation, a feeling of the difference between right and wrong, as old as the eldest and rudest form of society, older than the State, as old as the tribe, — very imperfect, indeed, very crude, limited to very few topics, but not wholly dormant, not utterly inactive. There was never, I guess, a state of society so rude in which a man could wrong a friend or betray confidence without suffering remorse for so doing.

I oppose, then, to the utilitarian view of the origin of moral obligation the doctrine of a moral sense proper to man as man, and constituting a part of the original dower of human nature. The feeling of remorse which follows wrong-doing can be accounted for in no other way. An injury done to an individual or society would not awaken that feeling except the moral sense had pronounced such injury a sin against one's self. And, on the utilitarian principle, remorse should never arise where no such injury has been perpetrated. Dr. Darwin, referring to the case of the dog which, while suffering vivisection, licked the hand of the operator, remarks that "the man, unless he had a heart of stone, must have felt remorse to the last day of his life." But why remorse, if the utilitarian doctrine is true? The man was contributing, or intending to contribute, to the uses of science, which are the uses of society. Satisfaction, not remorse, should follow such action.

I shall not undertake to prove to those who deny it the existence of an innate sense of right; but let me recall to the reader's memory a beautiful illustration of it from Grecian history. Themistocles had announced to the people of Athens that he had in his mind a project which, if put in execution, would be of great use to the State, but that the thing was of such a nature that it could not, before the execution, be made public. The assembly deputed Aristides to be the recipient of Themistocles's confidence, and, if he approved, to have it done. The project was to burn the Spartan fleet, then massed at Gythium, and thus to secure to Athens the supremacy on the seas. Aristides reported to the agora that what Themistocles proposed would be eminently useful, but would not be right. Whereupon the Athenians concluded that what was not right was not expedient, and rejected without a hearing the proposal of their greatest general. Says Emerson: "As much justice as we can see and practise is useful to men and imperative, whether we can see it to be useful or not."

Let us pass to the third, the ideal theory of moral obligation. The ideal theory is that which finds the ground of moral obligation in the simple idea of right. Plato, and after him the Stoics, are its chief representatives among the ancients. Plato's philosophic system is based on the assumption of eternal ideas, — ideas which are not perceptions or states of the human mind, but which have an existence entirely independent of the human mind. Of these ideas the first category consists of the Beautiful, the Just, the Good. These are different aspects of one and the same fundamental reality. And man's vocation, according to Plato, is to realize and embody these ideas in his life. This is duty, this is virtue. Hence, so far from basing morals on polity, Plato's system, on the contrary, bases polity on morals.

The philosophy which during the days of its prevalence exercised unquestionably the greatest practical influence on its votaries is that of the Stoics. The atmosphere of that school, after converse with utilitarian and eudæmonistic theories, comes bracing to the soul as a nor'-wester in dog-days braces the nerves. The sublimest ideas have sprung from its theory, the grandest souls have been ripened by its training. We find them at the opposite poles of the social scale. Epictetus the slave, Aurelius the sovereign lord of the world,—milk-brothers, suckled by the same high-hearted nurse who freed her foster-children with a freedom which bondage could not bind, and bound them with bonds from which thrones could not free.

The first principle of the Stoic philosophy was that virtue is the supreme good, the only real good. Virtue for its own sake, not for any fruits which its exercise may yield. Be true to yourself; be not disobedient to the heavenly vision, to the highest vision your mind has sight of. *Respue quod non es*, said Persius, the pure-souled poet of the sect. *Ne te quœsiveris extra.* Seek the ground of your action in yourself.

Among moderns the foremost champion of ideal ethic is also the foremost philosopher of modern time. That title, I think, the vote of experts will assign to Kant. Kant proposes the autonomy of the will as the supreme principle in morals.

" Autonomy of the will is that quality of the will by which, irrespective of the character of all particular objects of its willing, it is a law to itself. The principle of autonomy, accordingly, is to act in such a way that the maxims which govern our choice shall be included in our willing as universal law. . . . When the will seeks the law that shall determine it elsewhere than in the fitness of its maxims to serve for universal legislation ; when, going beyond itself, it seeks its law in the quality of its objects, — we have heteronomy. The will in that case does not give the law to itself, but takes it from its object through the relation which such object bears to its volition. This relation, whether based on inclination or on ideas of reason, admits only of hypothetical imperatives; I am to do this because I desire that; whereas the moral, that is, the categorical, imperative says: 'I must act so or so, whether I desire the object of the action or do not desire it.' . . .

" For example, I must seek to promote others' happiness, not because I care for it, whether in the way of direct inclination or on account of the complacency which Reason may find in it, but because the maxim which should exclude it cannot be included in one and the same willing, as law for all. . . . Love," he remarks, " is a matter of feeling, not of willing. I cannot love because I will, still less because I ought. Consequently, to speak of · the duty of loving is nonsense. But beneficence, as action, may be subject to the law of duty. . . .

" To do good to others according to our ability is duty, whether we love them or not. And this duty loses nothing of its obligatoriness although the sad observation should force itself upon us that our species, alas! is not of such a character that on nearer acquaintance we find them particularly lovable."

Montesquieu says of the Stoic philosophy that it is the only one which has produced great men and great rulers. I would add that it has given us in our own day, in our own country, the most thoughtful essayist and the most commanding moralist of recent time. When we read Emerson's essay on

Heroism, we feel ourselves lifted into a higher atmosphere, we breathe the pure oxygen of the
Porch. The spirit of Antoninus found in him,
after many generations, a kindred soul. It inspires his poetry as well as his prose, and has
given us such choice morsels as we find in some of
his quatrains : —

> " Though love repine, and reason chafe,
>   There came a voice without reply:
> 'T is man's perdition to be safe
>   When for the truth he ought to die."

And this happy versification of Kant's sublime
maxim, " Duty the measure of ability, not ability
the measure of duty : " —

> " So nigh is grandeur to our dust,
>   So near is God to man,
> When Duty whispers low, ' Thou must,'
>   The youth replies, ' I can.' "

I find no valid ground of moral obligation but
the inborn sense of right. To the question, Why
am I bound to act in a certain way ? the final answer is, Because it is right. Prove an act or a
course of action right, and you prove it binding.
There is nothing more to be said about it. To dispute that authority is like disputing the claim to
our preference of beauty over ugliness. Why must
I prefer the bird-of-paradise to the crab ? Why
must I prefer the form of the crescent moon to the

gibbous, the face of Apollo to that of a satyr ? Because the sense of beauty in me requires it.

But now comes the question, What constitutes right ? Here the utilitarian ethic has the merit of supplying most of the tests and the most universal rule of right-doing. Although utility is not the source of moral obligation, it is in most cases the end. When in any case the question how to act presents itself to the conscientious mind, the measurable utility of my action must, in the absence of other tests, decide the question. And in most cases, perhaps, other tests will be wanting. It is always right, and therefore my duty, to act in such a way as to benefit my fellow-men. Bentham's rule, the greatest happiness of the greatest number, is well taken, provided I know what in the long run will be for the greatest happiness of the greatest number. Still, we cannot say categorically that utility is the measure of right; whereas we can say, on the contrary, that right, as discerned by the scrupulous and enlightened conscience, is the measure of utility. There are cases in which the right and the useful appear to conflict. In a presidential or gubernatorial election, we will suppose that the nominee of the party whose general principles and policy, as compared with its opposite, I approve, and which I wish to prevail, is a bad man. He is reckoned available on account of certain popular qualities, and is nominated accordingly. But I know him to be unprincipled, profligate, bad. On the ground of utility I might be tempted to vote for him as helping to defeat the party whose policy I mistrust, whose success I believe would involve much evil to the common weal. But on the ground of right I cannot vote for him, for in so doing I should say by my act that such nominations are justifiable, and that moral qualities are not essential in the head of the nation or the State. In short, I should say : " Do evil that good may come."

And this, it seems to me, is one of the dangers to which utilitarian ethic is liable, — that of doing evil that good may come. It is vain to say that cannot be evil from which good shall spring ; that the only test of an act is its use ; that the tree must be judged by its fruits. I accept the rule, but with a different application. The tree must be judged by its fruits. But who can foresee all the fruit that shall spring from a given act ? Behind the immediate good, who shall say what evil may lurk, slowly ripening to its harvest of death? That act must be evil and a fountain of evil which the unperverted moral instinct condemns. But the moral instinct may be blinded by interest; it may be gagged by casuistry till the oracle turns dumb,

and right seems wrong, and wrong right. I fear
that without something in us deeper and surer
than all calculations of utility, our ethic would
prompt infanticide and putting to death with some
mild quietus the idiots, the misshapen, the hopelessly diseased, the useless members of society.
We know how in time past utility prompted tyran-
nicide, and we know what came of such action.
Brutus thought to do a useful thing by assassina-
ting Cæsar, — he hoped to restore the republic; but
he hastened its final extinction on the field of Phi-
lippi. Charlotte Corday, the beautiful enthusiast,
thought to do a useful thing by killing Marat, — she
would free her country from oppression; but she
caused it to fall into the hands of Robespierre.

Who can measure consequences ? Who, intent
only on use, and knowing no other test, can be sure
of the final balance of good and ill, can cast the
limit of blessing or harm in acts that, prior to all
calculation, have a character impressed upon them
by the deep, prophetic soul, outreaching calculation,
and ordaining, irrespective of seeming use, Thou
shalt, and Thou shalt not ? But this we know : that
the virtues not born of use give birth to uses which
compensate many of the evils that vex the utilitarian mind. Say, rather, they are uses in themselves. Patience is a use ; piety, fortitude are uses.
Of these uses, and the duties we owe to ourselves,

utilitarian ethic makes small account. These it does not especially tend to promote.

But if utilitarianism in morals incurs the danger of doing evil that good may come, the ideal ethic, on the other hand, is liable, when incontinently urged, to the opposite danger of ruthless absolutism. Kant himself, I think, offends in this sort when, in stern consistency with his lofty view of duty, he maintains that no conceivable crisis in human life can excuse the utterance of a falsehood. You must not lie, is the first commandment in his code. You must not lie to spare the nerves of the dying and secure a euthanasia which the truth would defeat; you must not lie to avert the career of a madman; you must not lie to save a nation from ruin. I cannot consent, nor will humanity bend, to this anxious interpretation of the moral law. It seems to me based on a narrow view of truth. Truth is not a question of words alone, not a function of tongue and throat, but of the heart and the life. " Doth not Nature teach you ? " Nature is truth on the cosmic and secular scale; but how Nature will lie, to human perception, with false appearances which deceive even the elect ! Do you say truth is an agreement between word and fact ? Granted ; but truth is a thing of degrees, and the higher may hold the lower in suspense, as one force in Nature suspends another, as the law of gravitation is suspended by the flight of the lark. Truth is agreement of word with fact; but truth is also fitness of means to ends. Let there be truth in the heart and truth in the will, as accordant with mercy and right, and the speech must conform thereto. But is not this precisely a case of doing evil that good may come? And do I not contradict myself, having said that what the moral instinct condemns must needs be evil? I answer that my moral instinct does not, in such cases, condemn the verbal falsehood. My moral instinct does not require me to sacrifice sacred interests to a form of speech. My moral instinct commands me to save life, and not to destroy it.

Fiat justitia, ruat cœlum (let justice be done, though the sky fall), is a favorite maxim of ideal ethic. It is one of those sounding plausibilities which, in some of its applications, the wiser mind will not approve. It depends on what the particular justice is that would get itself done, and what is the sky that is going to fall. The greater must not be sacrificed to the less. The particular justice may mean the cause of a class; the threatened sky may mean the cause of a nation. But the truth is, there can be no real conflict of moral interests, and no real conflict of a moral interest with the common weal. Let justice be done to a class, and the nation will reap the benefit in the end; and, *vice versa*, injustice to a class imperils the welfare of the whole. The truer maxim, therefore, would be, *Fiat justitia ne ruat cœlum.*

It would seem that no one principle of practical ethic can claim unconditional acceptance or admit of universal application. Even the so-called golden rule, " Do unto others as you would that others should do unto you," has its limits. The judge on the bench, the jury in the box, are not doing by the criminal at the bar as they would be done by in like circumstances when they find him guilty and pronounce on him sentence of death. A more comprehensive maxim is that of Kant, " Act according to the rule you would wish to be the universal rule of action."

The right and the beautiful in action, though usually coinciding, are not strictly commensurate. An act is not always beautiful in the measure in which it is right, or *vice versa*. The lie with which Desdemona excuses her murderer is beautiful ; but can we pronounce it right ? An act is not especially beautiful of which the contrary would be base. We bestow that praise only on acts which transcend the bounds of strict obligation and culminate into the heroic. Sydney Smith extols the act of one who, having purchased a lottery-ticket for himself, and another for a friend who was not informed of the number designated for him, when his own number drew a blank and the other a large prize, made over the prize to his friend. He might have changed the destination of the numbers, and no one would have been the wiser; therefore he is said to have acted beautifully. But could he have respected himself had he done otherwise? Would not his conscience have condemned the substitution as false and base? The act, it seems to me, was simply right; it could claim no special beauty.

The act of Damon in offering himself as a hostage for his friend was beautiful; the act of Phintias in rendering himself at the proper time to redeem his pledge and endure the cross was simply right. The beautiful acts which history has preserved to us, the doings of such men as Aristides and Leonidas, of Regulus, of Scipio, of Arnold Winkelried, are the beaming light-points in the annals of humanity. More instructive than all our ethics, they reveal the possibilities of human nature, and teach the utilitarian that the best of all uses are heroic souls. And these are ripened in no utilitarian school, but draw their inspiration from a source which philosophy will never sound. The great man teaches, by his doing and his being, more and better than Plato or Kant, reason they never so wisely. It was said of Cato that he was to Rome the thirteenth Table of Laws. And without the thirteenth how defective the twelve would have been!

The essence of all virtue is disinterestedness, self-abnegation. And of all unbeliefs the most execrable is that which denies the reality and capacity of disinterested goodness, — the vile doctrine, not less blasphemous than it is absurd, that every good deed, every generous effort, if rigorously analyzed, will be found to have its source in self-love. The benevolent, it is said, find satisfaction in the exercise of their benevolence ; it is therefore their own satisfaction which they seek, as the sensualist seeks his in sensual pleasures. They have both the same end in view ; there is no difference between them, except in the methods they have hit upon for the attainment of that end. The one may be more cunning, but morally he is no better than the other. Martyrs, patriots, philanthropists, are all self-seekers ; self-sacrifice is only selfishness in disguise. May such selfishness abound ! In the words of Dr. Brown : " It is a selfishness which for the sake of others can prefer penury to wealth, which can hang for many sleepless nights over the bed of contagion, which can enter the dungeon a voluntary prisoner, . . . or fling itself before the dagger which would pierce another's breast, and rejoice in receiving the stroke. It is the selfishness which thinks not of self, the selfishness of all that is most generous and heroic in man, the selfishness which is most divine in God."

The conclusion is, that utilitarian ethic, however serviceable in complementing the idea and illumining the path of the right, lacks the element of the moral as distinct from the expedient. There is a right and a wrong independent of use. As far as the east is from the west, so far is the right from the wrong, though all the apparent and computable utilities gather round the latter, and only its own sanctity envelop the former.

Well might Kant bow in awe before the sense of right, likening it in grandeur to the starry heaven. For does it not, like that, lay hold on eternity? And is it not precisely the strongest thing in the universe of intelligent being? Lodged in a feeble human frame which a blast may wither, it shall finally compel into its orbit all the powers that be.

GHOST–SEEING.[1]

[*From the North American Review.*]

Wir sind so klug, und dennoch spukt's in Tegel. — *Faust.*

IS there within the bounds of Nature, perceptible
to mortal sense, the reality of what is intended
by the word " ghost " ? Or is all reputed ghost-
seeing pure hallucination on the part of the seer ?

The question, notwithstanding belief in ghosts
is as old as human history, still awaits an authori-
tative answer. It still divides the opinions alike

[1] 1. Zauberbibliothek. 6 Theile. Von Georg Conrad Horst.
Mainz. 1821–26.

2. Artemidori Daldiani et Achmetis Sercimi F. Oneirocritica.
Lutetiæ. 1603.

3. Arthur Schopenhauer. Parerga und Paralipomena. " Geist-
ersehen und was damit zusammenhängt." Berlin. 1862.

4. Hallucinations, etc. By A. Brierre de Boismont. Philadelphia. 1853.

5. The Philosophy of Apparitions. By Samuel Hibbert.
Edinburgh. 1824.

6. The Night-side of Nature ; or, Ghosts and Ghost-seers. By
Catherine Crowe. New York. 1850.

7. Visions : A Study of False Sight. By Edward H. Clarke,
M.D. Boston. 1878.

8. Footfalls on the Boundary of Another World. By Robert
Dale Owen. Philadelphia. 1860.

9. The Seeress of Prevorst. By Justinus Kerner. From the
German. By Mrs. Crowe. New York. 1856.

of the thinking and the unthinking, — some affirming on the ground of experience or credible testimony, others denying on the ground of alleged improbability or impossibility. The one-sided culture of physical science is swift to reject whatever eludes material tests, complacently resolving into temporary suspension of reason the professed experience of witnesses whose mental sanity is otherwise allowed to be unimpeachable.

The aversion of science to this class of phenomena is due to the prevalent assumption of a supernatural origin. Call them "supernatural," and you shut them out from the field of scientific inquiry, whose limits are the bounds of Nature. Let us at once discard this phrase as impertinent and misleading. With what there may be outside of Nature we have nothing to do in this connection. If Nature means anything, it means the all of finite being. The question is : Are ghosts a part of that all, subject to Nature's method and rule ? Grant the affirmative, and you encounter difficulties which seem to the understanding insurmountable. Assume the negative, and you are confronted by a mass of testimony which no sane philosophy can afford to despise, — testimony reaching back to remotest time. When the author of the book of Job makes Eliphaz the Temanite say: "A spirit passed before my face ; the hair of my flesh stood up : . . .

I could not discern the form [that is, the outlines] thereof: an image was before mine eyes,"—he voices the experience of countless ghost-seers from that time to this.   Pliny the younger, writing more than a thousand years later to his friend Sura, asks his opinion about ghosts, and tells a story of a haunted house at Athens which reads precisely like one of the narratives of Jung Stilling or Mrs. Crowe.

However the learned may decide the question, ghosts or no ghosts, *in foro scientiæ*, ghost-*seeing*, explain it as we may, is a fact about which there is no dispute.   It is of this, in some of its phases, that I propose to speak.

I begin with the nearest, the phenomena of dreams.   Dreaming is a kind of ghost-seeing, a beholding of phantoms, personal and impersonal, of forms and faces, human or bestial, animate or inanimate.   "I saw," people say when relating their dreams.   The objects are phantasmal, but the seeing is actual.   We call it seeing with "the mind's eye" when the object seen is not materially present.   But in fact it is only through the mind that we see at all, in the sense of perceiving.   No physiologist can explain the connection between the image on the retina and the act of perception.   In waking vision as well as in dreaming, it is the mind that perceives, constructing from notices furnished by the eye, in accordance with certain cate-

gories of the understanding, the object perceived.
What the eye reports is not the object perceived
by the mind, but only the motive and occasion of
the vision. Images may be painted on the retina
when nothing corresponding with those images is
seen by the mind, because the mind in a fit of abstraction is seeing something else. " Her eyes are
open," says the doctor in " Macbeth." " Ay! but
their sense is shut."

The presence of an external object is not an indispensable condition of seeing; the sensation so
termed may be induced by the independent, spontaneous action of the mind. We see in our dreams
as truly as in our waking experience, or what we
call waking. For, after all, who knows what waking is, except as contrasted with our nightly sleep,
or how far we are really awake when we seem to
be so? Shakspeare may have written more truly
than he knew, or than we interpret him, when he
made the old magician say, " We are such stuff as
dreams are made of." I can imagine a waking out
of this chronic somnambulism of our life which
shall show us the reality of what we now see only
the symbol and the shadow.

Dreaming, like waking, is a thing of degrees.
Our ordinary dreams are a meaningless play of
phantasms for which we see no cause, and care too
little to seek one. A confused rabble of incongru-

ous images drives across the field of our vision like the "wild hunt" of German folk-lore, and leaves no distinct impression on the mind. Dreams of this sort — and they constitute the larger part of our dreaming — are due to imperfect sleep, sleep in which the state of the body, and the action upon us of the world without, prevent the entire seclusion and free action of the soul. The brain is still active, but no longer retains its gubernatorial office; it lets go the helm, and mental life drifts. In perfect sleep the senses are shut to all external impressions, and the soul, which knows no sleep, disencumbered and freed from the thraldom of sense, inhabits and fashions its own world. The dreams which occur in that state have a staid, consequential character; they mean something, had we only the key to their right interpretation. Such dreams are not very common; for although the soul must be supposed to be always active in sleep, yet in order that its action may give us dreams, it must report itself in the brain, and whether, and how distinctly, it shall do so in any case, must depend on the idiosyncrasy of the individual. Then, again, supposing the soul's nocturnal experience to report itself in the brain, there is still another condition of dreaming; to wit, that the record present itself to our consciousness on waking. For a dream which we are not aware of having had, is no dream. And that encounter of our consciousness with the night record depends on the manner of our waking. If the transition from deep sleep to broad waking is gradual, the passage through that antechamber and limbo of the mind is likely to prove a baptism of oblivion. But let a man be suddenly awakened out of a deep sleep, and always, I believe, he will be aware of having dreamed. He will catch the vanishing trail of a vision if he does not recover the whole. That which wakes him will be apt to mingle in some way with the dream, and constitute one of its moments. For, be it observed, no dream is complete, — they are all fragments, episodes to some unknown method and epic of the soul.

The soul has methods of her own, and converses on her own account with the invisible world, — a converse independent of place and time. She has visions not only of what is, but of what is to be. Hence dreams are sometimes prophetic, either in the way of distinct annunciation, as the elder Africanus, in the " Somnium Scipionis," foretells to the younger his coming fortunes; or in the way of allegory, as Pharaoh's dream of the seven fat kine and the seven lean kine foreshadowed, according to Joseph's interpretation, so many years of plenty and so many of famine.

An instance of allegorical dreaming is recorded

by Goethe as happening to his maternal grand-father, Textor, portending his promotion to a seat in the Senate. He saw himself in his customary place in the Common Council, when suddenly one of the aldermen, then in perfect health, rose from his chair on the elevated platform occupied by that board and courteously beckoned to him to take the vacant seat. This man soon after died in a fit of apoplexy; a successor, as usual, was chosen by lot from the lower board, and the lot fell to Textor.

A third class of prophetic dreams are those in which coming events are neither foretold in words, nor allegorically foreshadowed, but seen by the dreamer as actually occurring. Such dreams are styled by Artemidorus [1] "theorematic." Mrs. Crowe, in her "Night-side of Nature," records a dream of this sort relating to Major André, of tragic fame. When André, on a visit to friends in Derbyshire, before his embarkation for America, was introduced to a certain Mr. Cummington, that gentleman recognized in him the original of the countenance of a man whom he had seen, in a dream, arrested in the midst of a forest, and after-wards hung on a gallows.

Schopenhauer relates an instance from his own experience. He had emptied his inkstand by mistake instead of the sand-box on a freshly written

[1] Oneirocritica, lib. i. cap. 2.

page. The ink flowed down upon the floor, and
the chamber-maid was summoned to wipe it up.
While doing so, she remarked that she had dreamed
the night before of wiping up ink from the floor of
that room. When Schopenhauer questioned her
statement, she referred him to the maid who had
slept with her, and to whom she had related the
dream on awaking. He called the other maid, and
before she could communicate with her fellow-
servant, asked her, " What did that girl dream of
last night ? " " I don't know." " Yes, you do ;
she told you her dream in the morning." " Oh, I
remember ! She told me she dreamed of wiping up
ink in your library."

Dreams like this, too trivial to be recorded, and
seldom remembered, are psychologically valuable,
as tending to prove that the soul is essentially
clairvoyant. When not impeded and overpowered
by the action of the senses and the exigencies of
the waking life, it seems to be taken up into union
with the universal spirit, to which there is no here
nor there, no now nor then, and to have sight not
only of what is, but of what has been, and of what
is to be. These categories of past, present, and
future, which determine the action of the finite
mind, have no existence for the infinite. To that
all place is here, and all history now.

This view of prophetic dreaming, familiar to

modern psychologists, is by no means new. Socrates, in the "Phædon," declares that true vision
comes to the soul when detached from the body.
Quintus, in Cicero's "De Divinatione," says: "The
soul[1] flourishes in sleep, freed from the senses and
all impeding cares, while the body lies supine, as if
dead. And because this soul has lived from all
eternity, and has been conversant with innumerable
souls, it sees all things in Nature."[2]

And again: "When the soul in sleep is screened
from companionship and the contagion of the body,
it remembers the past, discerns the present, fore-
sees the future. Much more will it do this after
death, when it shall have altogether departed from
the body. Hence at the approach of death its
divining power is greatly increased."[3] "The dying
behold the images of the dead." Posidonius of
Apamea, he tells us, supposes three ways by which
the soul may have prescience of the future: first,
by its own nature, as related to Godhead; second,
by reading the truth in other immortal souls, of
which the air is full; third, by direct converse of
Deity with the soul in sleep.[4]

The soul, when sleep is perfect, has visions inde-

---

[1] The word is *animus*, which, though usually rendered "mind,"
is evidently, in this connection, equivalent to what we call "soul."

[2] De Divinat., lib. i. 51.

[3] Ib., lib. i. 80.　　　　　　　　　　　　　[4] Ib.

pendent of time and place, seeing as present what
to the waking subject is future. Whether or not
the vision shall be transmitted to the brain, and
there brought to consciousness, depends on organic
conditions which are found in some subjects and
not in others. When thus transmitted it takes the
form of a dream, — it may be allegoric, or it may
be theorematic. And such dreams are prophetic,
fatidic. When, on the other hand, a vision of impending calamity, for want of the requisite conditions, fails to formulate itself as dream in the
brain, it induces, according to Schopenhauer, that
vague, uneasy foreboding of evil which we call
" presentiment." A presentiment, then, is an abor-
tive vision.

Nearly related to the class of dreams which I
have designated as " theorematic " is the kind of
vision which takes the name of " deuteroskopy," or
second-sight, and constitutes a more advanced
stage of ghost-seeing.

Second-sight is dreaming without the accompani-
ment of sleep. The soul involuntarily passes into
the same state of abstraction which it experiences
in deep sleep, and has visions which it communi-
cates to the brain, whereby the seer beholds, as
with his bodily eyes, things distant in space, and it
may be in time, as if they were present realities.

Dion Cassius and Philostratus both relate that Apollonius of Tyana beheld at Ephesus, while talking with his disciples, the assassination of the Emperor Domitian, which was then occurring in Rome. The life of Apollonius contains many incredible things; but this vision has, for those who are not predetermined against everything of the sort, an air of likelihood from the close resemblance which it bears to modern reputed cases of second-sight. It is hard to believe that all the stories, so widely diffused and so strongly vouched, of similar visions are forgeries. But incredulity in seeking to evade a marvel often embraces a greater. Swedenborg, conversing with friends at Gottenburg, is said to have been arrested in his speech, precisely as Apollonius was, by the vision of a fire then raging at Stockholm, — a distance of nearly three hundred miles. No fact in Swedenborg's life is better attested. Such things do not admit of absolute demonstration, and there are minds so constituted as to be incapable of receiving anything of which the understanding cannot detect the method and the law. Incredulity in such matters is commonly regarded as the mark of a strong understanding. If so, a strong understanding is not the highest type of mind. The fact is, it is oftener the will than the understanding which refuses credit to spiritual marvels.

Second-sight, it will be observed, is not vaticination; it is not a foretelling of the future on the ground of the present, not a reading of probabilities, but a vision which *happens* to the seer, — perhaps is forced upon him when not thinking of the subject, but engaged with something else. Dr. Johnson, in his account of a journey to the Hebrides, thus describes it. "The second-sight is an impression made either by the mind upon the eye, or by the eye upon the mind, by which things distant or future are perceived and seen as if they were present. A man on a journey, far from home, falls from his horse; another, who is perhaps at work about the house, sees him bleeding on the ground, commonly with a landscape of the place where the accident befalls him."

The dear Doctor reserves his decision as to the authenticity of these phenomena. "There is against it," he says, "the seeming analogy of things confusedly seen and little understood; and for it the indistinct cry of national persuasion, which, perhaps, may be resolved at last into prejudice and tradition. I could never advance my curiosity to conviction, but came away at last only willing to believe."

A case of second-sight not unlike the visions of the Highland seers occurs in Homer's Odyssey, where Theoklymenos, at a feast of Penelope's suitors, sees them already suffering the vengeance which awaits them, —

εἰδώλων δὲ πλέον πρόθυρον πλείη δὲ καὶ αὐλή,
ἱεμένων Ἐρεβόσδε ὑπὸ ζόφον.

To the same category has been assigned the celebrated vision of Cazotte regarding the Reign of Terror in France, of which he himself was a victim. If authentic, it is certainly the most astounding example of prevision on record. We have it on the authority of La Harpe, who, it seems, did not himself give it to the Press. It was found among his papers, and published after his death. De Boismont says it can only be received with hesitation, though vouched by Madame de Genlis and Madame la Comtesse de Beauharnais. For my own part, I incline to believe that Cazotte did utter in La Harpe's presence the substance of the prophecy ascribed to him, but that La Harpe, writing from recollection, after the events predicted, unintentionally mingled details of what happened with what he heard.

We come now to ghost-seeing, in the narrower and commonly received sense of the term, distinguished from second-sight by greater immediateness of vision in the seer, and a more defined personality in the object. In second-sight the objects are seen as in a picture; but here they are seen as material objects appear to the waking eye.

Foremost in this class are the hallucinations caused by disease, and universally recognized as such, the phantoms evoked by *mania a potu*, and the often-cited spectral affliction of the German Nicolai. Poor Nicolai is pilloried by Goethe in the "Walpurgisnacht," where he figures as "Prokto-phantasmist," with a broad allusion to the leech-cure prescribed by his physician. Scarcely he deserved that punishment, already sufficiently pun-ished by the irony of fate, which doomed the great champion of rationalism, the doughty denier of ghosts, to be visited by troops of ghosts in broad day for successive weeks. The case is important as proving that sight is not dependent on ex-ternal impressions. It is false to say, in such cases, that the subject "imagines" that he sees. He does see, as truly as I see the paper on which I am writing, though not by images painted on the retina. Through the eye alone we see nothing but color and motion. All perception is an act of the understanding; and in the cases we are consider-ing, it is the understanding that distinguishes be-tween phantom and objective reality. The maniac confuses the one with the other. The visual sen-sation is the same; the eye perceives no difference.

The spectre-stricken lady mentioned by Dr. Clarke[1] was obliged to "thrust her fan into the spectre" occupying the chair appointed for her at a dinner-party, to assure herself that a phantom, and not a being of flesh and blood, had usurped her seat.

Speaking of ghosts at a feast, it seems to me a great mistake, in the representations of "Macbeth" on the stage, to make a real body sit for Banquo's ghost in the royal chair. He enters, treads the stage, and takes his seat like an ordinary living person; no power of make-believe can show him other. A good actor, gazing at vacancy, may easily seem to envisage something invisible to the rest of the company. That something vanishes when the usurper resolutely claims his seat.

"Why so — being gone, I am a man again."

We have examples of ghost-hearing, of ghosts that present no visible image, but address themselves to the ear alone.

Captain Rogers, commander of a ship called "The Society," bound to Virginia in 1664, while asleep in his cabin dreamed that some one pulled him by the arm, calling to him to get up and look out for the safety of the ship. He was awakened by the dream, but paid no heed to the summons, and went to sleep again, when the warning was

[1] Visions, p. 24.

repeated. This happened several times, till at last, though aware of no danger, he turned out and went on deck. The wind was fair; a sounding taken a short time previous had shown a hundred fathoms. There seemed to be no ground for alarm, and he was about to turn in again when a voice from an invisible speaker said to him: "Heave the lead!" It was done, and eleven fathoms reported. "Heave again!" said the voice. Now it was seven fathoms. The captain immediately gave the order: "'Bout ship!" and by the time the order was executed the sounding was only four fathoms. Evidently the ship, on her former tack, would have soon run aground.[1]

Robert Dale Owen has recorded an amazing story of the rescue of a wrecked vessel off the Banks of Newfoundland by means of a timely apparition.[2] In 1828 the mate of a bark in that latitude, sitting in his stateroom and working out his observation for the day, espies in the cabin some one whom he supposes to be the captain, writing on a slate. Going nearer, he discovers that it is not the captain, nor any member of the bark's company. The captain is called, but the stranger has vanished. They examine the slate; on it is written, "Steer to the nor'west." The wind permitting, curious to

[1] Ennemoser's History of Magic, appendix. Quoted by Mrs. Howitt from a work entitled "Signs before Death."

[2] Footfalls, etc., The Rescue, p. 833.

know what would come of it, they lay their course in that direction, ordering a sharp lookout from the mast-head. In a short time they come upon a vessel fast bound in ice, threatened with destruction; crew, officers, and passengers nearly famished. These are taken off by the bark, and in one of the passengers is seen the prototype of the writer on the slate, who had been lying in a profound sleep at the time when the stranger appeared in the cabin of the bark. This verifies what Sir John Lubbock says, that in dreaming, the spirit seems to leave the body.

The peculiarity in this case, supposing the narrative authentic, is the want of a previous connection, and attraction arising therefrom, between the ghostly visitor and the mate of the bark. The case is as hard to classify as it is difficult of belief. The strongest argument for its authenticity is precisely its uniqueness in the annals of spectrology. It is simply too strange for fiction.

A careful study of the records of apparitions will show, I think, that such visitations most often occur in the hours of daylight, and not, according to popular superstition, at dead of night. And — what is very important — the best authenticated cases are those of living persons, or persons *in articulo mortis*, or recently departed, and not of persons long deceased.

Of Swedenborg's professed intercourse with the spirits of the departed I have never been able to satisfy myself how much, or whether aught, can be justly regarded as objective converse, as anything more than the seer's dream. The alleged tests, for example, — the reporting of what passed between the Princess Ulrica of Sweden and her brother at their last interview before the death of the latter, — I cannot accept as complete demonstration. The Princess herself, it seems, was not convinced. "How Herr von Swedenborg obtained his information I cannot guess, but I do not believe that he conversed with my departed brother."

Apparitions of the living, on temporary leave of absence from their bodies, present, if not a more credible, a more acceptable phenomenon.

That the soul of a living person possesses this power of disengaging itself for a time from the fleshly body, and appearing at a distance by means of the more ethereal body which is proper to it, and a semblance of apparel with which it invests itself, is confidently assumed by pneumatologists. The theory of these psychical outings explains the supposed fact of spectral apparitions, and was evidently framed for the purpose. Deep mutual sympathy between two widely separated individuals may, it is believed, bring this faculty into play when one of the parties in sore distress craves the other's presence and aid. Captain Meadows Taylor relates a vision which he had in India of a dearly beloved English lady whom he had hoped some time to call his wife : —

"One evening I was at the village of Dewar Kudea, after a long afternoon and evening march from Muktul. I lay down very weary ; but the barking of village dogs, the baying of jackals, and over-fatigue and heat, prevented sleep. I was wide-awake and restless. Suddenly — for my tent-door was wide open — I saw the face and figure so familiar to me, but looking older, and with a sad and troubled expression. The dress was white, and seemed covered with a profusion of lace, and glistened in the bright moonlight. The arms were stretched out, and a low, plaintive cry, 'Do not let me go! Do not let me go!' reached me. I sprang forward, but the figure receded, growing fainter and fainter, till I could see it no longer; but the low, sad tones still sounded. . . . I wrote to my father. I wished to know whether there was any hope for me. He wrote back to me these words: 'Too late, my dear son ; on the very day of the vision you describe to me, ———— was married.'"

Of this *actio in distans*, Schopenhauer claims that the intervening space between the agent and the object, whether full or void, has no influence whatever on the action ; it is all one whether that space be the distance of an inch or of a billion Uranus-orbits. He supposes a nexus of beings which rests on a very different order, —deeper, more original and immediate than that which has the laws of space, time, and causality for its basis; an order in which the first and most universal, because merely formal, laws of Nature are no longer valid; in which time and space no longer separate individuals, and in which, accordingly, the individualization and isolation wrought by those forms no longer oppose impassable bounds to the communication of thought and the immediate influence of the will.

From the ghosts of the living we pass to the ghosts of the dead. If the soul before the cessation of animal life can act on distant objects and present an appearance to distant friends, it would, *a fortiori,* seem to possess this power when animal life is extinct, or on the eve of extinction. The records of apparitions of persons *in articulo mortis* are too numerous and too well vouched to admit of reasonable doubt. Wieland, an inveterate sceptic on all points connected with a future life, admits the possibility of such apparitions, and gives an instance from his own knowledge, which he pronounces " indubitable, but incomprehensible and incredible." [1]

Differing from this in the circumstance that a day had elapsed between the death and the appa-

[1] Euthanasia. Drittes Gespräch.

rition, is the case related by the afore-named Meadows Taylor among his Indian experiences. A soldier enters his captain's tent and begs that the arrears of his pay may be sent to his mother in England. The captain, busy with his writing, takes down the address and promises to fulfil the request. Shortly after, it occurs to him that the soldier had violated the rules of the service in entering the tent without saluting, and in his hospital dress. He summons his sergeant. "Why did you allow —— to come to me in that irregular manner?" The man was thunderstruck. "Sir," he exclaimed, "do not you remember he died yesterday in hospital, and was buried this morning?"

Narrations like this, though not to be received without reserve and careful weighing of the evidence on which they rest, are somewhat relieved of their incredibility by the supposition of an interval, greater or less, between the cessation of animal life and the entrance of the soul on its new career. If any living, thinking principle survives the ruin of the flesh, if there be a "soul," in the popular sense, that soul will be likely to retain for a time the sensibilities and to feel the attractions of its old relations. The desire to benefit surviving friends can hardly be denied it. If this can only be done by a personal apparition, the appearing in familiar form will be simply a question of power to appear.

I can as easily conceive the soul to be endowed with that power as I can conceive of psychical existence at all, dissevered from the animal body. But where the aim of the apparition is merely information,—the communication of some important fact,—it is not necessary to suppose an objective presence. The end may be accomplished by subjective impressions, by action on the mind of the individual to be informed,—in other words, by a vision. And so I can suppose that the captain in the India service, in the anecdote just related, may have had a vision of the soldier, effected by the will of the latter acting on the mind, and through the mind on the senses, of the former. This explanation, it is evident, will not apply to cases in which the reputed apparition leaves a sensible token behind, as in that of the shipwrecked voyager who left his writing on the slate.

Of a different sort, and more difficult of belief, are objective apparitions of the long deceased. The improbability increases with the lapse of time. It would be unphilosophical to deny apodictically the possibility of such apparitions, but one may be pardoned for reserving assent to what, if true, perplexes one's view of the future state with added, insoluble difficulties. The reason for greater slowness of belief in this case than in that of the recently departed is the feeling that souls once thoroughly severed from the flesh, new-bodied and new-sphered, cannot quit their new sphere except by the way of new death. Were it not so, — if, conscious of a former existence and inspirited by its memories, departed friends and departed worthies could " revisit the glimpses of the moon," and make themselves manifest in earthly scenes to earthly sense, — then, assuredly, such visitations would be among the unquestioned and common events of life. But what are the hundreds or the thousands of recorded apparitions to the sumless millions of the dead? Saint Augustine was confident that the dead could not return, for if they could, his sainted mother would have come to him with instruction and counsel and relief. The argument has weight: if one can return, why not others; why not all? If the thing were not impossible, who can doubt that many longing souls would have experienced and established it beyond a question? Were there any sure path or passage, or way of communion with that dumb realm, who can doubt that human affection would have found it out? If the dead could come to us, how often would they not have been forced to come at the call of love? What spirit endowed with human sensibilities could resist that appeal if the way were open to hear and answer? We must either doubt that " quæ cura fuit vivis eadem sequitur tellure repostos," or conclude that the gates of the silent land open but one way.

Says Wordsworth's Margaret : —

> "I look for ghosts, but none will force
> Their way to me; 't is falsely said
> That there was ever intercourse
> Between the living and the dead;
> For surely then I should have sight
> Of him I wait for day and night
> With love and longings infinite."

Modern sorcery, misnamed "spiritualism," professes to have opened the everlasting gates and to maintain free communication with departed souls, — not with former acquaintance merely, but with any and all of the wise and good who figure in human history. The number of those who agree in this profession amounts to many thousands, its votaries say millions. Science has examined their pretensions, and pronounced them groundless; and because, here and there, it detected imposture, has rashly concluded that imposture and delusion are the only factors in the business, — that all who engage in it are either knaves or fools.

Whether any of the phenomena of spiritism necessitate the supposition of unknown, intelligent agents, is a question I do not care to discuss. I will only remark that physical science can hardly be regarded as a trustworthy witness or a compe-

tent judge in a matter where the fundamental positions of the parties are antagonistic, where the
method of the critic conflicts with the postulate
conditions of the advocate, and where a hundred
failures or detected impostures are not decisive
against the whole class of phenomena in question.
But as for pretended communications with defunct
worthies, there is, in my judgment, no sufficient
proof of anything authentic in this kind. The examples which have hitherto been offered confirm
this judgment; and when the necromancers plead,
as excuse for the platitudes of these utterances, that
the communication is qualified by the " medium "
through which it comes, they fail to perceive that
this admission is fatal to their cause. When
Wordsworth and Shakspeare are made to drivel, it
is obvious that we have the mind of the " medium,"
and not the mind he is supposed to represent. For
thirty years and more this sorcery has been in
vogue, and not one ray of unquestionable light has
been shed on that which it most concerns us to
know of the future state. Granting the agency of
spirits in some of its manifestations, the grand
mistake of spiritism is the taking for granted that
disembodied spirits are necessarily wiser and more
knowing than spirits in the flesh. The more rational presumption is that the acting spirits in
these experiments — spirits that have nothing better

to do than to assist at table-tipping and other tricks for the entertainment of gaping marvel-mongers — have lost the little knowledge and the little sense they may have had when clothed with mortal bodies. Justinus Kerner, the most scientific and conscientious of modern pneumatologists, confirms this view. He and others who have studied the subject with serious care agree with Plato that only the souls of the brutal and depraved revisit the earth and approach mortals with objective manifestations.

The question of ghosts, so far as it relates to the sensible manifestation of translated souls, is one which eludes the grasp of science. The negative is indemonstrable on physical grounds; and the affirmative can never, by individual testimony, be established in the common conviction of mankind.

That the spirits of the departed are near us in sympathy and trust, not unconscious of our doings and our fortunes, nor quite unable to help us in our straits with occult influences and unworded suggestions, it is pleasant to believe. That they can be cited and summoned at will, constrained to answer inquiries, brought to the witness-stand in a court of necromancers, cross-questioned by a "medium," pumped to amuse a prurient curiosity, is a notion abhorrent to all my conceptions of a future state, and seems a desecration of the rev-

erend sanctities of the spirit-world. For aught I
know to the contrary, there may be spirits in "the
vasty deep," grovelling, lost creatures, who aid and
abet these fooleries ; but, for my part, I wish to
have nothing to do with these clowns of the pit.

There are mental experiences, mysterious, in-
definable, which suggest the action upon us of
conscious, intelligent powers, — experiences which
answer to the beautiful idea of spiritual guardianship so rife in ages past. Who has not known
them ? Who has not experienced at times those
sudden intuitions, impulses, new determinations of
thought and will, whose advent could not be explained by association of ideas, as links in a chain
of mental sequence, where the preceding involves
the following, but which burst upon us like messages from the Unknown, interposing with a flash
new births of the soul ? Inspirations that shed
exceeding day on the mind, — those inexplicable
warnings that restrained us on the brink of danger,
those swift fulgurations of hope that caught us
tottering on the verge of despair, those sweet con-
solations welling up from the deep in our agony of
grief, — who has not known them ? How natural
to suppose in them a spiritual influence streaming
in upon us from without ! If spirits may not
visit us with those sensible approaches which
make us

" —— fools of nature
So horridly to shake our dispositions
With thoughts beyond the reaches of our souls,"

yet, granting the existence of spirits unfleshed, impalpable, there is nothing in reason that forbids the supposition of their proximity, of their ministering presence, of their quickening influence.

Who can believe that the limits of sense are the bounds of intelligent being? And out of that unseen world where science cannot reach, and which enfolds the visible as space encompasses sun and planet, who knows what strengths may come to feed and refresh this mortal life?

PERSONALITY:

A PAPER READ BEFORE A CLERICAL CONFERENCE.

WORDS exercise a fatal influence on thought and belief. When turned from their original import and fixed in some perverted use, they breed misconception and propagate endless error.

The word *persona* (from which our English "person") meant originally a mask such as ancient actors wore upon the stage. In the Greek and Roman drama all the parts were performed in masks. The mask was called in Greek προσωπεῖον, from πρόσωπον, "face;" in Latin, *persona*, from *persono*, "I sound through." Hence very naturally these words came to signify the part performed, the character represented. We say in English to *personate* a character; that is, to wear the mask of that character.

From the boards of the theatre the phrase was transferred to the scenes of life. *Persona* was used to denote the character which an individual presented to the world, the part he enacted in social life. The part might be genuine or feigned, guise or disguise, nature or art. Livy says, *persona alienam ferre*, " to act a foreign part." Cicero uses the expression, *tantam personam sustinet*, " he acts so important a part." But the fact is, every man in society acts a part. Conscious or unconscious, feigned or true, with or without simulation or dissimulation, every man is an actor; and all that we really know of any man is the part he acts, — his appearance in the eyes of his fellow-men. The real man is never seen, but only his simulacrum. And as that simulacrum is inseparable from the individual, as it represents the individual to his kind, so the word *persona* came to signify the individual himself. *Mea persona*, or *nostra persona*, says Cicero; that is, " I myself."

We use "person" in the same sense; we say indifferently " person " or " individual," making no distinction between the two. For ordinary purposes we are justified in so doing, since all we can know of individuals is their persons, their manifestation of themselves to the eye or ear. Only it behooves us to remember that there is something deeper in man than his person, and that though the person is the outbirth of the individual, is constituted by the individual, it nevertheless is not the individual, is not identical with the innermost being, but something exterior and distinct.

What then is that interior something that underlies the person, — the ultimate ground of our being ? Most men, I suppose, identify it with the *I*, the *ego*, the conscious self. This seems to be the prevailing opinion ; it is a very natural one. When we say " I," we seem to express our innermost being, for the obvious reason that consciousness can no farther go ; the ego is the deepest that consciousness knows. But the application of scientific analysis to the act of consciousness will show that the ego is not the deepest in man, is not the ground of our being.

Observe that consciousness is not a stated condition, but an occasional one. Being is perpetual, consciousness is not. The most inveterate egoist cannot be always aware of himself. Consciousness is the product of occasion ; moreover, it has a physical origin, — it is the result of certain specific motions of the brain. In the case of simple consciousness, — that is, conscious sensation, — what causes the motion is some impression from without. Consciousness is the response of the mind to that impression. The connecting link between the motion in the brain and the consciousness which ensues, is a mystery. That which produces consciousness must of course be antecedent to consciousness, — consequently out of the reach of consciousness.

Still less in the case of compound or self-consciousness can consciousness detect its own origin. All we know is that on some provocation, represented by a motion in the brain, it is born out of the unfathomable abyss of the unconscious which lies behind it. The nearest approach to an explanation of it is to say that it is the product of two factors, — the unconscious spirit, and a human brain.

Such is the genesis and natural history of the ego. And I suppose the ego to be peculiar to man. The brute I suppose to have only simple consciousness, not the reflected consciousness of self. The brute does not think *I.* The action of spirit in that sphere of life is too feeble — or, what is the same thing, the brain is of too coarse a fibre — to produce a conscious self. Neither, at the other end of the scale, can I ascribe self-consciousness to God. Self-consciousness is inconceivable without a body or some kind of framing. Its prime condition is limitation. Self is made self by self-circumscription. In order to be self-conscious God must part with his infinity; that is, cease to be God. When the Scriptures represent him as saying " I," the thought imputed to him is as much an anthropomorphism as the imputation of articulate speech.

From this view of self-consciousness it follows that the human ego, so far from being the real man, our innermost nature, is merely an incidental phenomenon. It is not a being, but an act, a thought, an occasional reflection, of an unknown being in a human organism. I exist only in the act of self-consciousness. Destroy self-consciousness, — and there are lesions of the brain which have that effect, — and I cease to exist. 'T is a fact of vulgar experience that the ego is not, *a parte ante*, conterminous and coeval with our being. There is a time, varying, I suppose, from the second to the fourth year, when a human individual first says to himself, "I." There was a day, an hour, a minute, of my history when, having for some years existed for others as a person, I was born to myself. Sometimes, but rarely, an individual is able to recall the moment of that nativity. Jean Paul, in his autobiography, boasts that experience. "Never," says he, "shall I forget what as yet I have told to no one, a mental transaction whereby I assisted at the birth of my self-consciousness, when all at once 'I am an *I*' rushed before me like a flash of lightning from heaven, and since then has remained luminously persistent. Then for the first time my *I* had seen itself, and forever." What is the psychological import of that experience? We are apt to regard it as the rising into view of the deepest in man, of the whole man. But observe that the act of consciousness which shows us self does not com-

prehend that self, does not fathom it; it only distinguishes it from other selves and the outside
world, our own bodies included. It is a flash
which momentarily defines our individuality, —
defines it laterally, but not vertically; it does not
reach to the root of our being. In the moment of
intensest self-consciousness we bear, not the root,
but the root us.

The question recurs, then, What is the innermost nature in man? What is that interior being
which underlies the person, and which underlies
the conscious self? To that question the only honest answer is a confession of ignorance. "No one,"
says Von Hartmann, "knows directly the unconscious subject of his own consciousness; he knows
of it only as the secret psychical cause of his consciousness." Respecting this unknown being there
are two theories to choose between. The one
coincides with the common belief of a separate
individual soul as the ground and matrix of the
individual consciousness; the other, known in
philosophy as the "monistic" view, supposes that
all individual consciousnesses, all separate egos,
have the one universal Being for their common
ground. The latter view has found its latest and
ablest representative in the author just named.
"The resistance to this view," says Von Hartmann
again, "is only the old prejudice that conscious-

ness is the soul. So long as that prejudice has not been overcome, and every secret remnant of it completely annihilated, the all-oneness of the Unconscious will be veiled. Only when it is understood that consciousness is not essential, but phenomenal, appertains not to the being, but to the appearance; that, accordingly, the multifoldness of consciousness is but a multifold manifestation of the One, — only then will it be possible to emancipate oneself from the dominion of the practical instinct which clamors perpetually, ' I,' ' I,' and to comprehend the beings-unity of all apparent individuals, bodily and spiritual."

The first theory is best represented in Leibniz's Monadology. According to that great thinker, the human organism is an aggregation of indivisible entities, of which the central or regent entity, being capable of self-consciousness, may be called soul *par excellence*, to distinguish it from the others, to which he gives the name of " Monads."

I do not care to undertake the advocacy of either of these views, nor do I feel myself called upon to declare to which of the two I incline. I will only remark, in passing, that if this conference is to be — what, as I understand, the planners of it proposed to themselves — a conference of theologians; if we meet here on scientific ground, and not on the basis of practical religion,

—then current beliefs and theological prepossessions must not be allowed to control our decisions of the subjects discussed.

We have, then, these three constituents of our humanity: 1. The unknown factor which constitutes the ground of our being. 2. The ego, or conscious self. 3. The person. It is the last of these with which I am now especially concerned. The person, I have said, is not the individual proper, but the manifestation of the individual to others, — the image he presents to the world, his character as shown in word and deed, the man as he moves in the scenes of life. Using the word "person" in this sense, what relation does the person bear to the individual? How much of the individual goes into the person? I answer, all that given conditions (in which term I include native endowment, temperament, organization, education, social relations, fortune, worldly position) will allow. We cannot say absolutely that the individual is entirely expressed in his person. We feel in some cases that there are capabilities in a man which are not brought out, which find no scope or demonstration in life. But then, the very feeling which such persons inspire in us is a part of their personality. It belongs to them to create in us this impression of reserved power with which we credit them. On the whole, if we cannot say that the person is all there is *in* a given individual, we can say it is all there is *of* him. It is all, at least, that we know of him. It is all that concerns the world. If we would but see it, it is all that really concerns ourselves.

It is here that I would lay the emphasis of immortality. That the soul, the innermost being, is immortal, requires no proof. It belongs to the nature, to the very definition, of an entity to be indestructible. What most concerns us in this connection is the all-important fact of the immortality of the person, — of the character we present, the part we enact in the scenes of life. That is the true *manes*, — that which remains of us when the fleshly form has vanished out of sight. To live on this earth is not to live while the body lasts, and then no more, it is to live here forever. We are perpetually casting ourselves into our action, and the cast remains; we leave our duplicate behind us when we die. "I am with you always, unto the end of the world," said Jesus to his disciples when about to vanish from their sight. The saying has been verified through all these ages, is still verified in the consciousness of the Christian Church. Christ is still a denizen of earth, — still richly, beneficently, divinely with us in the image of himself which he stamped on the world; he is with us in the faiths and charities which bear his

name, — nearer to us at this moment than he was
to those first disciples who sat with him at the
same board and drank of the same cup.[1] That
divine man is but one instance pre-eminent among
many. We recognize in his case that persistency
of person which is true in all cases. We recognize
it in the men of exceptional genius or piety, —
the prophets, sages, teachers, singers who have
stretched an intellectual firmament over this
work-a-day world, and set their beaming thoughts
in it for sun and stars to light up our life. We do
not recognize it, but nevertheless it is true of all
who have lived and labored in earthly places of
every kind and degree. All who were once here
are still here: their works are they, their words
are they; and though word and work be forgotten, their influence for good or evil survives, — their
person is immortal. In one of the old religions
it was taught that the soul of the deceased on its
way to heaven or hell must traverse a narrow bridge
across a gulf of fire. In that passage it encoun-
ters a spectre, which being interrogated, answers,
"I am the spirit of thy life." Visible or invisible,
recognized or not, in the case of every soul that

---

[1] The bodily presence of a man is not that which best reveals
him, — rather, it is something which intervenes between him and
us. Detached from the body, divested of all that is extrinsic and
accidental, he is seen in his own light, in all his sides and pro-
portions, the immortal person.

has borne the burden of this mortal that spirit survives, — the spirit of the life. Earth teems with such. The world of spirits is all about us, — not in the coarse sense of swarming entities lurking in the air, but in the sense of ideas and influences derived from all the past.

Grandly George Eliot breathes the wish, —

> "Oh may I join the choir invisible
> Of those immortal dead who live again
> In minds made better by their presence, — live
> In thoughts sublime that pierce the night like stars.
> . . . So to live is heaven, —
> To make undying music in the world.
> . . . May I reach
> That purest heaven, — be to other souls
> The cup of strength in some great agony,
> Enkindle generous ardor, feed pure love,
> Be the sweet presence of a good diffused,
> And in diffusion ever more intense.
> So shall I join the choir invisible
> Whose music is the gladness of the world."

The air we breathe is thick with the influences, good and bad, which successive generations have put forth. Every individual in all those generations has contributed something by his character and life to make the world what it is. The humblest and most obscure has contributed something. The humblest and most obscure that has ever lived in this world lives here forever. This is what I understand by personal immortality. It is the only immortality which a wise man need concern himself about; and for him who is careless of this, no other immortality will yield any satisfying fruit.

There is another branch of this subject, "Personality," which perhaps it was expected that I should discuss, — personality as predicated of God.

In what sense can we speak of God as person? Recurring to my fundamental position, that the person is not the being as such, but the being in action, — self-presentment, manifestation, — I answer that all we can know of God is his personality: the manifestation of himself in action. Creation, providence, revelation, moral government, — these constitute the personality of God: his theophanies are his person. Beyond these we cannot penetrate. We must not confuse the manifested God with the transcendental ground of the manifestation, — the revealed with the absolute unrevealable. When asked if I believe in a personal God, I might answer, I believe in no other. But I seem to detect in that question a latent impression of a limiting form, — a God existing in spatial separation from the All.

Mr. Matthew Arnold, the English dogmatist, hugs himself with his definition of God, protruded with wearisome iteration, in his " God and the

Bible," " The Eternal, not ourselves, that makes for righteousness," — surely the thinnest film of Godhead that ever pretended to the honors of theism; scant pattern with which to clothe the spirit of devotion! The moral order of the universe which Mr. Arnold, affecting simplicity, has chosen to designate in this roundabout way, is but one of the modes of deity. It cannot in any proper sense be said to constitute deity; for though practically, for human use, the moral order is ultimate, it can never be ultimate to speculative thought, but refers us at once to an ordering Will as its origin and law. Kant, in the " Critique of Practical Reason," has indicated this connection. The moral law, he argues, commands us to seek the best good of society. The possibility of that good is implied in the law which requires us to seek it. But the highest good is possible only through the adaptation of Nature to that result; that is, through the consent of Nature with the moral law. But the moral law itself affords not the slightest ground for a necessary agreement between well-doing and well-being, between righteousness and blessedness. The subject of that law is himself a part of Nature, and therefore dependent upon it; he cannot force its agreement with the law. " Consequently " (I translate literally), " the existence is postulated of a *Cause* of universal

Nature, distinct from Nature, which shall contain the ground of this connection; to wit, the exact correspondence between blessedness and righteousness," — that is, God is the postulate of practical reason. "The highest good for the world," he continues, "is possible only so far as we assume a supreme Nature which exercises a causality commensurate with moral sentiment."

The phrase "not ourselves," "the Eternal, not ourselves," etc., is peculiarly unfortunate, since it is precisely in ourselves and through ourselves that the eternal moral lives and works. If Mr. Arnold means to say simply that we did not make ourselves, he says what no one will dispute, but what hardly deserved such pompous enunciation, or required to be erected into a "rigorous and vigorous" theory. It was written long ago, "*He* hath made us, and not we ourselves." This venerable saying, of which the latter clause is a fact of consciousness, in one or another sense is accepted by all. The question is what we mean by "He," — whether blind Force, or intelligent Will. It is that which fixes the dividing line between theism and atheism.

Our dogmatist will have no God who thinks and loves. Such a God, he insists, is but "a magnified, non-natural man." "Thinking" and "loving," I admit, are unscientific terms as applied to deity; they are anthropomorphisms. But I maintain that they are necessary anthropomorphisms; religion cannot do without them. Mr. Arnold, though writing professedly in the interest of religion, does not, it seems to me, sufficiently appreciate the exigencies of religion. He would have everything rationalized; he would have scientific statements, abstract formulæ. But abstract formulæ belong not to religion, but to science. Religion is not a realm of philosophic perceptions, but of sentiment and imagination; and the language of religion, derived from the sentiments and imagination, is symbolical. The philosophic mind may be safely trusted to translate such terms as "thinking" and "loving," applied to God, into their philosophic equivalents; but religion reduced to such formulæ as " the Eternal, not ourselves," and religion metamorphosed into this new gospel according to Matthew, would become too volatilized for purposes of worship. Such a religion could never serve the common need of mankind. Sensible of this, impressed with the exigencies of religion as distinguished from science, I cherish the traditional phrases and ritual language of the Church. Whatever Jesus may be historically, ecclesiastically he is Christ the Lord. However my philosophy may formulate its concepts of deity, the God whom I worship is a God who sees and hears, and thinks and loves, and pities and approves. Nor do I at all object to the " magnificd, non-natural man." On the contrary, it seems to me that this is precisely' such a God as religion needs. Not the human form, — although, of course, the vulgar imagination will have that idol, — not the bodily form, but the moral image, the human attributes, the attributes of ideal humanity. The God of religion must be an intelligent and moral nature. No being destitute of those attributes can fill that place ; and of those attributes we can form no idea, except as they are manifest in human subjects. Religion supposes them infinitely extended, and invests its God with their likeness. The God of our devotion, if devotion is to have a definite object, must be in some sense human, — a " magnified, non-natural man : " non-natural, because nature is birth, and God is unborn. I am well aware of the danger of not distinguishing between the moral image and the human form, — or rather, of the tendency to embody in a human form the human attributes of deity. The very use of the personal pronoun in this connection is misleading. It is unavoidable ; we must say *he* and *his* if we speak of God at all. But what subtle idolatries lurk in those pronouns ! How strong the tendency to conceive of God as not only distinct from creation in idea, but as spatially separated from creation, — as an individual in space ! It is a trick of the imagination, of the image-making faculty, to figure the divine presence in a human form. Swedenborg, in whom imagination and reason, the visionary and the thinker, were strangely blended, maintains that the human form is that in which God appears to spiritual vision. I shall not dispute his dictum, for I have no experience which enables me to distinguish between spiritual vision, in Swedenborg's sense, and imagination, — indeed, I can conceive of no concrete theophany other than that of the human form. But spiritual vision does not necessarily imply an objective reality corresponding therewith. To suppose that God exists objectively in that form, is to suppose him materially and spatially bounded, — which conflicts with my conception of the divine nature. If I am asked what form I would substitute, how I suppose the divine nature invested, I answer frankly, I have no substitute. I do not care to idolize God, or to represent him to myself by any mental image. To my conception, nothing less than the material universe can serve us as his embodiment. I follow the analogy of the human microcosm. What the human soul is to the human individual, that I conceive God to be to the universe of things, — its central soul, regent in all and present in all by diffused consciousness, as the soul is present by diffused consciousness in every part of the human organism. The human organism is a world in little, of which the soul is its God; the world in its entireness is a body, of which God is the soul, — not identical with the body in thought, and not separated from it in space. This is the best conception I can form to myself of deity, — conscious, nevertheless, how inadequate all concepts of deity formed by the understanding must be.

The old theology — the Christian theology of the fourth and fifth centuries — took precisely the opposite direction. The idea that the world could be in any sense the embodiment of God, would have shocked the theologians of that day scarcely less than flat denial of his being. The Jewish tradition of the entire separation of Jehovah from all contact with material Nature — a tradition which Gentile converts, disgusted with the grossness of polytheistic Nature-worship, readily . embraced, and which was strongly reinforced by Manichean influences — made the world seem utterly godless and corrupt, given over to the prince of darkness, whom even Luther in later ages recognized as prince of this world. God dwelt, remote from the visible world, in holy seclusion. But " God," says Newton, " is a relative term," — *Deus est vox relativa.*

It was perhaps a dim sense of this truth — discontent with the idea of the insularity of God — which

gave such importance to the doctrine of the Trinity.
I have never seen it suggested, but the thought has
occurred to me, that a powerful agent in establishing the trinitarian theology must have been the
church-feeling of a God-forsaken world. *Deus est
vox relativa.* There must be something to which
God relates, — an object to that subject, or a subject to that object. If the world be excluded from
that relation, what remains but a second God, —
the Word, or the Son ? In the Son, God eternally
generates himself, sees himself, becomes conscious ;
and the Spirit is that in which generator and generated unite, — the ever-proceeding demonstration ;
the end and object of that demonstration being, not
the world, which was wholly ignored in this system, but the Christian Church. Being, Action,
Process, Product, — Father, Son, Spirit, Church :
this was all that theology recognized. Earth and
sun and moon and stars, — the infinite universe
with all its forces and systems, of which those
brooding, wrangling churchmen were the momentary products, did not come into their calculation.
All that was the Devil's domain, — brute background
to the ghostly All. The author of the " Theologia
Germanica" says : " The Evil Spirit and Nature are
one." The All, as these Fathers interpreted the
scheme of God, was complete without Nature. The
Mother was left out in the cold, expelled with a

three-pronged fork, so great was the reaction against the Nature-worship of the Græco-Roman world. You know the proverb, *Naturam furca.* Do you know who it was that emancipated the modern mind from the narrowness, the one-sidedness, the spiritual thraldom, of trinitarian theology? You will name to me perhaps the recognized fathers of Unitarianism, — Servetus, Cellarius, the Sozzini, and certain English worthies, who knocked away the Biblical supports of the Trinity and ruled it out of their creed. They did a good work: far be it from me to undervalue their labors. But I greatly doubt if exegesis alone, if improved Biblical criticism, would ever have wrought that deliverance which is now going on in the popular mind, by which, in spite of conventional symbols, of formal confessions, of labored expositions, and agonizing efforts of here and there a disputant to reinforce and rehabilitate the obsolete dogma, is gradually pushing it aside, and, without denying or caring to controvert, is dismissing it from the habitable chambers of consciousness to the limbo and chancery of things indifferent; so that whereas to impugn it once was a monstrous exception, to contend for it now with much earnestness is almost as exceptional. This change is due to Spinoza. He, by his doctrine of the One Substance and the immanence of God in creation, shifted the balance of divinity from the realm of ghostly abstraction to the visible All. He re-established the sacredness of Nature, — that Nature which the author of the "Theologia Germanica" expressly identified with the Evil Spirit; he restored the natural world to its rightful place in the reverent love of human kind. Natural science succeeded to the vacant chair of scholastic philosophy. Newton and Leibniz and Haller and Harvey succeeded to Saint Thomas and Duns Scotus and Occam and Hugh Saint Victoire. They thought it worth the while to study a world which God had set in their hearts, and in studying which they became acquainted with him. Spinoza turned the Devil out of doors of the *rerum natura;* and with that extrusion the old theologic world recedes more and more into dim and spectral distance and forgottenness. It sounds strange to say that trinitarian doctrine needs the support of the Devil; but it is so far true that the fancied domination of the Devil, and the consequent profaneness and accursedness of the sensible world, excluded Nature from that place in the interest and intellect of earnest, studious men which it now occupies, and which trinitarian theology occupied then.

I use the word "trinitarian" by way of *pars pro toto.* I have no quarrel with that particular dogma on account of any falsity in it, but only on account of its inadequacy, compared with its claims and the place it has usurped in the scheme of things. The dogma is true enough as far as it goes. Father, Son, and Spirit, — unquestionably these three are in God, and they are one God; but they do not comprise, or do not express, the whole of deity. I can hardly imagine a trinitarian formula that would. In any such statement the categories must either be too comprehensive to serve the purpose of exact classification, — that is, to prevent the unlawful confounding of the persons, — or else they must be too rigid to prevent the forbidden dividing of the substance. My God is not tri-personal, but multi-personal. But out of this multitude of divine personalities I distinguish with special note two persons, not indicated, or very imperfectly indicated, in the ecclesiastical Trinity, — Providence, and Moral Rule. Independently of all ecclesiastical teaching, led by my own observation and reflection, I think I should have recognized a divine Providence in human things, shaping, guiding, controlling, and causing all things in the final result to work for good to human subjects. If there be such a Providence, its motive must be benevolent design, — what theologians call "the goodness of God." And yet the so-called goodness of God is precisely the weakest point in natural theology; it is there that the *a posteriori* proof of the being of God — the proof from Nature and life — is most difficult and most assailable; it is there that pessimism and atheism find their advantage and deal their most telling blows. The goodness of God consists with a great deal of misery and helplessness and want and distress; it consists with extreme suffering; with the existence of myriads who are born diseased and maimed and crippled, and drag their life through years of pain, without apparently one full draught of the joy of being; it consists with the perishing of hundreds of thousands by Indian famines in the absence of rain; it consists with tempest and earthquake and blight; it consists with the fears and fightings of the animal kingdom, brute preying on brute, and with all the conflicts and agonies of irrational Nature which constitutes so large a portion of the life of the world. The answer to all this, so far as man is concerned, is given in the one word, " Progress." Misery abounds; but life is stronger than all its ills, and statistics show that, taking large periods into view, the human condition, on the whole, improves. The moral forces of the universe, unlike the material, are a constantly increasing quantity; and with increase of moral force the miseries and woes of human life are gradually abating. The reign of reason is slowly, but surely, gaining on the reign of passion, the reign of love on the wrath of man, the dominion of science on brute nature. A better understanding of the laws of health, as well in the social as in the physical economy, will more and more triumph over pauperism, intemperance, and disease, — the three main sources of mortal woe. The goodness of God, impugned by the ails and sorrows of life, is vindicated by its vast possibilities and the ever-new-blossoming hope ineradicably planted in the human soul. The sufferings of the brute-world present a more difficult problem. Here our theodicy has to assume that existence to every creature is, on the whole, a blessing. If the contrary could be proved, then I confess my theodicy would be hopelessly at fault; for brutes I consider have an equal claim with human kind on the author of their being for a balance of joy in the dispensation of life, and a God of whom goodness and omnipotence can be predicated is bound to secure that balance to the meanest of his creatures. But excess of suffering in the brute creation can never be proved or made probable to any but a pessimistic interpreter.

The other person in the Godhead to be distinguished with special emphasis is the moral governor and judge. There is nothing more definitive in deity than the moral jurisdiction which the Ruler of all exercises over rational natures.

The demonstration of this rule is given in each man's consciousness in that principle — inborn, I think we may call it — which distinguishes between right and wrong; in fact, creates that distinction which commands the right and forbids the wrong, and which punishes disobedience with internal suffering more or less acute, according to moral development. These three, — moral perception, moral obligation, moral retribution, — which for want of a better designation we call " conscience," constitute the Eternal *in ourselves* that makes for righteousness. They are a part of ourselves, — no other satisfactory account can be given of their origin, — and they are our surest witness and proof of deity. Let no one think to find complete demonstration of a moral government of the universe out of the realm of conscience, to find the Eternal that makes, etc., in human society, in the external fortunes of men. Some indications there are of the operation of a moral law in the fortunes of individuals and of states sufficient to illustrate, but not sufficient of themselves to establish, the moral government of God. A close observation of the facts of life reveals but a very imperfect correspondence between character and fortune, between destiny and desert. Obviously the best men are not the most prosperous. The virtues that bring the amplest and surest rewards in the way of

worldly success are the little virtues, virtues of
the lowest class; the great virtues do not "pay,"
in the worldly sense. And when we observe in the
administration of social justice how the little rogues
are caught in the meshes of the law, while the
great rogues escape; how the wretch who commits
an act of petty larceny to save his children from
starvation is sent to prison, while the financier,
who impoverishes thousands by dishonest speculations, flourishes in impunity; when we note how
the girl who sins through momentary weakness
becomes an outcast, while her guilty seducer maintains his place in society,—there would seem to be
as much in the "not ourselves" that makes for un-
righteousness as there is that "makes for righteousness." It is not there, not, at least, within the
horizon of individual experience, that the moral
governor of the universe can be found. In the
large historic courses "which the brooding soul
surveys," it may be true that the wrongs of life
are transmuted into means and motives of moral
growth. An atoning Providence will macadamize
the stony injustices of passing time into smoother
roads for the feet of advancing Humanity; but
within the sphere of the visible present these
roughnesses are stones of offence to seekers of
the right which almost justify the pessimism that
swears by them and at them. Tragic enough, if

we look for manifestations of the moral order in earthly fortunes, is the fate of many who have blessed the world with their words and deeds. What reward have they who have given the strength of their days and hours of bloody sweat to lift mankind a little out of darkness and bondage into liberty and light? Our imagination perhaps opens for them the gates of heaven, and sees them crowned in the long hereafter with a diadem of praise. But do you think that any divine soul was ever actuated by hope of such a heaven? What reward have they? An approving conscience? A doubtful good. An approving conscience implies a consciousness of virtue; but conscious virtue is tainted with something that is not virtue. To say that virtue is its own reward is false if it means that moral heroes find satisfaction in the contemplation of their worth. What reward have they? I know of but one,—they increase in themselves the amount of being; that is, of Godhead. The end of all right doing is to greaten the sum of being. To be heroic and strong and good is the true and only compensation for earthly loss and pain. This is eternal life, which is not a thing to come, but a thing that is. In fulness of being we have the unknown quantity in the dark equation of character and fortune which has puzzled the wit and tried so sorely the faith of mankind.

Life has two prizes which it offers to man's choice, — having, and being; having part in the goods of life, and being part of the absolute Good. Both are desirable, but not always compatible the one with the other. Heroic souls, when driven into straits where both will not go, where one or the other must be sacrificed, give up having and the hope of having, and find their reward in new measures of being. Blame not those who believe greatly in having; it is impossible to deny the advantage of possession, the hold it gives on this mortal world. But "I have overcome the world" was the saying of one who had nothing, and yet had all. Possession is good, but, after all, the best thing is to possess one's self.

THE THEISM OF REASON AND THE THEISM OF FAITH.

SIR HUMPHRY DAVY, the foremost genius among Englishmen of science in the early part of this century, declared toward the close of his life that he envied no man's talents, wit, or learning; but that if he were to choose what to him would be the most delightful, and he believed the most salutary, it would be a firm religious faith. Such a choice indicates a certain measure of faith already existing. It is the cry of the heart asserting itself against the doubts of the understanding: "I believe; Lord, help thou mine unbelief."

On the other hand, Michael Faraday, pupil and successor of Sir Humphry, and next to him on the honor-roll of science, seems to have experienced no such conflict between faith and understanding; was troubled apparently with no religious doubts; as much at home in the conventicle as in the laboratory; never turning on the deeper questions of the soul — questions of spiritual import —

the light which he shed so effectively on chlorine and carbon ; coolly ignoring his identity ; erecting a barrier of non-intercourse between Faraday professor of chemistry, and Faraday the Sandemanian devotee ; accepting in the one character the invitation of the Queen to dinner on a Sunday, and in the other submitting without a murmur to the rigid discipline of the most intolerant of sects for so doing.

There can hardly be a question as to which of the two positions is the nobler, the more worthy a rational soul, — that of the master, who hesitated before the mystery he could not fathom, or that of the pupil, who shut his eyes and swallowed the creed, ignoring any mystery involved in it ; that of Davy, in whom inquiry bred doubt, or that of Faraday, who obstinately refused to inquire. In all belief there is choice, either active election or passive consent. In the even balance of reasons for and against, if decision is taken it is an act of volition, conscious or unconscious, that turns the scale. But faith which is merely a creature of the will, repelling investigation or predetermining the result, has no enlightening influence and no value as a minister of truth ; it is not inspiration, but arrest, — not a perception, but a grab in the dark.

A third position as to religion assumed by men

of science is that of Mr. Tyndall and others, who, without affirmation or denial, simply wash their hands of all that, rule it out of the domain of philosophic inquiry, and complacently relegate spiritual truths to the region of the emotions.

From these examples, which are typical, and from other examples of scientific renown, it appears that science, which has so illumined the material world and conquered such vast tracts from the realms of space, which has changed the face of the earth, affords no aid to the soul in her deepest need, and sheds no gleam of light on those interests without which all that science can achieve is just to amuse and to ease this creature life. It is amusing to know that the sun is ninety odd millions of miles distant from our earth, and is made of sodium, calcium, iron, carbon, manganese, and other substances identical with earthly elements. It amuses us to know that four hundred and sixty millions of millions of light-waves hitting the eye in a second make red, and that there are stars so distant that if suddenly struck out of existence, dwellers on the earth would continue to see them for thousands of years by the light which they emitted thousands of years ago. Then again it is an easing of our creature life to be able to accomplish in a few hours a journey which formerly required as many days, to get messages in less than no time from the other side of the globe, and have one's leg cut off, when necessary, without a sensation of pain. But I cannot see that man's estate as a moral and immortal being is essentially benefited, or spiritual progress furthered, by these comforts and curiosities. Conquests of time and space have no-wise facilitated the conquest of self. It is nearer to Japan than it was seventy years ago, but as far as ever to the peace of God. The scientist himself, if not a mere fingering and ogling busybody, must sometimes be visited by questionings to which laboratory and observatory furnish no answer. The world which Science occupies with her lenses and crucibles, is ringed and washed by a sea of wonder, navigable only to Faith. The former, science, is the sum of those views which are verifiable by sense; the latter is the sum of those views which are not verifiable by sense. Which of the two is the larger domain? Science has no knowledge of the future. If things remain as they are, then such and such things will happen. But will things remain as they are? Science is dumb. Yet how much of life depends on things remaining as they are! We betake ourselves to nightly rest, not doubting that a morrow will dawn and the old world move in its accustomed grooves, as all our yesterdays have known it to do. For this assurance we are indebted, not to Science, but to Faith.

Astronomy predicts an eclipse of the sun which, some time hence, shall be visible in certain localities. We entertain no doubt of the accuracy of that prediction. Competent observers of such phenomena make their preparations accordingly. The prediction is based on the supposition that sun and earth will continue in being until the term assigned. That supposition rests wholly on Faith. Science furnishes no guarantee that sun and earth may not explode before that term arrives, or that some distant body, unknown to astronomy, some fiery traveller from the confines of being, may not invade our skies and dash our system into chaos.

Again, Science knows nothing of causes or causation. She knows only certain habits of matter which she dignifies with the name of laws. She can give no account of the origin of things. She finds the beginnings of the solar system in a cloud of fire-mist. Whence that fire-mist she does not say ; for all she knows or cares, it may have existed from eternity. She derives the vegetable and animal world by progressive evolution from certain primordial cells, — what she calls protoplasm, — rejoicing in the thought of a genesis independent of any creative fiat. To the question, how came protoplasm and the life proceeding thence, Science has no answer. She knows only things, and the evolutions of things from things.

Intelligent Will and a moral government of the universe, implied in our sense of moral obligation, are the only God that reason knows; they constitute the substance of philosophic theism. But the God of reason is not commensurate with the God of faith, and does not satisfy the demands of religion. Religion leans to anthropomorphism; it craves a personal God, a being not only ideally distinct, but essentially secerned from the world. God and the world, — religion demands the antithesis. Indeed, the world, until a comparatively recent period, was held by Christian theologians to be utterly godless. The author of the "Theologia Germanica" expressly declares that material Nature and the Devil are one. Christendom — thanks in part to Spinoza, whose fundamental thought has had its influence even with those who repudiate his pantheism; and thanks still more to natural science, which has taken the place of the old scholastic philosophy, Bacon, Newton, and Leibniz succeeding to Duns Scotus, Occam, and Saint Thomas — Christendom no longer entertains the notion of a God-forsaken world. But religion still craves the separate God, — a God who has his dwelling outside the world; in popular phrase, above the skies.[1] Here reason is at fault, and wants to know where and how.

[1] "Infinite lengths beyond the bounds
Where stars revolve their little rounds."

Swedenborg asserts that the human form is that in which God appears to spiritual vision. Who shall dispute his saying? Who can practically distinguish between spiritual vision and imagination? No doubt, if I am to conceive of God at all as taking a definite shape, it will be the human form, since that is the most perfect that I can conceive. But the mental concept does not necessarily imply a corresponding object. To suppose that God exists thus objectively concluded in a human form, is to suppose him spatially bounded, — an idea which reason refuses to entertain. Reason is satisfied with nothing less than the universe of being as embodied in the Infinite Presence.

Essential to religion is belief in prayer, in the hearing and granting of prayer by the Ruler of the universe. The belief is one of the dearest convictions of the human heart. If philosophy condemns it, better, one would say, to let go philosophy than be without it.

Here again reason is at fault. The notion of a sovereign who hears and considers the petition of a subject, and grants or denies as may be most expedient for him, is one whose leading, reason cannot follow. It supposes the All-knowing, the Unerring, to act upon an impulse from without. The finite mind is liable to be so actuated.

Moved from without, swayed by foreign impulse, it is forced back upon itself. It considers, questions, deliberates; in a word, reflects. If man were infallible, all-knowing, there would be no arrest in his mental activity, no reflection. Can we impute reflex action, the result of arrest, to Infinite Intelligence? Can there be in God any arrest of continuous action, any backing of the current, any deliberation, where the will itself is clairvoyant, and seeing and doing are one? To reason such reflex action in deity seems incongruous. In the view of reason, the divine mind acts without deliberation, without reflection, — not blindly, of course, but knowingly, infallibly, comprehending the consciousnesses of finite beings in its own super-conscious action.

Prayer, accordingly, in the view of reason, cannot be a suggestion to the Infinite Mind of something to be considered and granted if expedient. Rather, it is a part of the system of things, a power which takes effect when not overborne by contrary forces, or frustrated by the necessities of Nature. No one claims that prayers, even of devout souls, are always answered in the sense of the suppliant. The theological statement of the cause of the failure is that God, having heard, for wise though inscrutable reasons sees fit to deny. The philosophic statement, identical in substance, is that the force exerted in the prayer collides with contrary forces, or breaks against the necessities of the common weal. Where the prayer *is* answered in the sense of the suppliant, it is not necessary — as Science assumes, and therefore rejects the theory of prayer — to suppose a change in the order of Nature; rather, that the prayer itself is a part of the order of Nature, embraced in the great world-scheme of which all the parts and agencies work together as factors, latent or apparent, in every event that occurs. It will naturally be objected to this view that prayer is spontaneous in the consciousness of the suppliant, that the feeling which prompts it originates in the urgency of the moment, that it takes for granted a present hearing, and that no one would pray who supposed his prayer to be, as it were, a foregone determination. I might reply to this objection that the word "foregone" misstates the case by attributing to God, with whom there is no before or after, the limitations of human nature, which knows things only in the order of time. But I withhold the reply. I frankly admit the force of the objection, and content myself with saying that this is a case where reason cannot follow, — where reason must yield to faith. Fortunately our ratiocinations do not of necessity influence our conduct. The intellectual and the emotional life may pursue their parallels in one and the same subject, never converging in one operation, and never conflicting in their separate courses. A man may theorize freely, and yet, when emotion prompts, pray fervently, although the implied expectation of the prayer can find no warrant in his theories.

So much as to prayers for external good. The question of prayer for internal aid and blessing, — prayer whose objects lie within the domain of the moral life, to which it is insisted by some that prayer should be confined, — admits of an easier solution. We may suppose, beyond the limits of the fleshly life, an invisible community of finite, conscious intelligences, whose action is not determined by any world-scheme or natural necessity, but free to obey impulsions which come to them from kindred spirits, whether in the flesh or out of the flesh, and to club their forces for moral ends. Such a community, a society of spirits united by spiritual affinities, cognizant of human on-goings, and banded together under moral leadership for moral ends, may be conceived as one being, a divine man in Swedenborg's sense, the Lord of the moral world. Upon such a being human prayers — so they be prayers of the inner man — would act with *compulsory* force, engaging all the powers of Heaven to combine in rendering the desired help. I say of the inner man. Prayer does not always represent the interior will. It may be sincere so far as the consciousness of the suppliant is concerned. The slave of lawless passion in a fit of remorse may pray with fervor to be delivered from the bondage he loathes. But underneath the superficial repentance the will may still be held captive and withhold its consent. It is only when the will prays that the prayer is effectual.

In this hypothesis of a spirit-world distinct from the material, having its own leader and head, I am confronted with a question which reaches to the very foundations of theism. Is the ruler of the moral or spirit world identical with the Power that reigns in the natural, with the Author and Governor of the material universe? If so, what proof have we of that identity? I have never been satisfied with the logic of Natural Theology, so called, when from the marks of almighty power and skill apparent in Nature it stretches its argument to prove from Nature the moral attributes of justice, love, and holiness. In the world of sense the clear adaptation of means to ends, the compensations of celestial mechanics, the miracles of vegetable and animal life, declare a superhuman Intelligence; they reveal the divine artist, the geometrizing God. On the other hand, in the world of spirit, in the conscious human world, the moral sense and moral experience declare with equal distinctness a moral government, an authority independent of the human, a supreme order which man did not invent, of which he feels himself the subject, and whose jurisdiction he cannot escape. Here are two distinct powers: are they one and the same God? The old theology, as we saw, evaded the problem by consigning the material world to the Devil. The tendency of modern science is to resolve the moral world with its law and Lord into a process of nature. The theory of evolution pronounces what we call the moral law and receive as divine authority to be the result of the accumulated experience of the human race, demonstrating, and therefore commanding, what is most conducive to human well-being. The demonstration I grant, but not the command. Perception of expediency does not exhaust the idea of right, nor explain its origin. Cases are conceivable in which expediency, except in the reflex sense of satisfaction of conscience, shall conflict with the right. The very idea of right implies an aboriginal sense of moral obligation entirely independent of expediency, a moral law within, which prescribes in some cases a course of conduct not at all, so far as human foresight can measure, conducive to our own or others' well-being. Nothing can account for this sense of right but the supposition of some authority prior to all experience and independent of the

fleshly will. Have we any sufficient ground for
identifying that authority with the author and
governor of the material universe ?

Kant, as we saw,[1] finds a bond of unity between
the two ; he reasons from the moral law to a God
of nature. The existence of a God, he argues, is a
postulate of practical reason, as being the only security for the realization of that good for which the
moral law commands us to strive, the only ground
of the supposed connection between goodness and
blessedness. A postulate is not a demonstration.
But what is the good for which the moral law commands us to strive ? Only such as under known
conditions we are conscious of a power to promote.
And what is the supposed connection between
goodness and blessedness ? It is purely moral ; a
moral blessedness, goodness is supposed to insure,
not a material good. No one claims that virtue is
a negotiable draft on Nature for physical satisfactions. It is only, then, a God of the moral world,
not a God in nature, identical with that moral ruler
which Kant's argument goes to prove. It assumes
a connection between the natural and the moral,
which is the very point in question. The question
is still unsolved.

Is the ruler of the moral world identical with
the author of the material ? — identical with the

_____
[1] See the previous Essay, page 290.

Power that rounded the suns and flung them into place, that peopled the earth with her various kinds, that in one mood feathered the cockatoo and painted the butterfly's wing, and in another mood fashioned the milleped and the mud-turtle, and in still another the cobra and the scorpion? If so, should we not expect to find in the one the antitype of the other, or at least a marked consent between the two? But in vain do I seek in Nature for any confirmation of the moral law, in vain for any intimation, for any faintest recognition, of the sense of right. On the contrary, what most impresses me in Nature is the absence of moral bonds. I see violence, rapacity, cruelty, murderous cunning everywhere rampant, subject to no retribution, sure of equal satisfactions with meekness and innocence. The moral law forbids its subjects to harm one another, it bids them do unto others as they would be done by. But the tribes of earth are organized and intended to prey on each other. Universal internecine war is the order of Nature. It is nonsense to say that "all Nature's difference keeps all Nature's peace." What kind of peace is that where one half of the brute creation are perpetually lying in wait for their prey, and the other half living in perpetual dread of their enemies? What the poet really meant was that all Nature's difference keeps all Nature's balance, prevents the excess of any one kind. But who will pretend that such excess might not have been prevented, had it pleased creative power, in other less murderous ways? I see in Nature the will to perpetuate her kinds, but not to secure their happiness, except so far as may be necessary for their preservation. I see what seems to be, from a human point of view, a malicious multiplication of noxious vermin, — Colorado-beetles, buffalo-moths, canker-worms, cimex lectularius, pulex irritans, phylloxera, aphides, and no end. I suppose these creatures have some satisfaction in being; some immunities they certainly enjoy, — absence of moral responsibility, exemption from the rancors of ambition and the stings of remorse. But I question if the satisfaction of life to them compensates the annoyance they cause to us. If dowered with reason, these creatures might complain of the existence of man, so detrimental to insect life. But the gift of reason would seem to confer on man a prior right to the ground; and, reasoning from a human point of view, I must think that the business of parasitic life is overdone.

Can we exonerate Nature from the charge of moral indifference by any evidence of moral qualities in the animal kingdom? Is there anything that can be strictly termed *moral* in brute Nature? The love of the brute mother for her offspring, which might seem to partake of this character, admits of another interpretation. These instinctive affections of bird and beast may be viewed as simply the cheapest expedient by which Nature could secure the protection of her several kinds in the dangerous period of their infancy. They accordingly cease when the creature arrives at maturity. They are beautiful to witness, but not distinctively moral. The fidelity of the dog to his master is a better instance; but in the case of animals tamed and domesticated by man, the question is transferred from original Nature to another sphere, where human influence has grafted new qualities on the primitive stock. In the realm of Nature proper, of wild Nature, I find no proofs of moral life, no conscience, no sense of wrong distinct from fear, no just retribution, nor any pity for human woe. On the contrary, I am affronted with the injustices, the cruelties which everywhere prevail,—the animosities, the conflicts, the struggle for existence, the parasitic invasions, the inhospitalities, the rigors of climate, the ferocity of tempests, the unsparing devastations, the rages and the ruin. Unfeeling is Nature; mortal agony calls upon her in vain in its supreme hour for sympathy or aid. Nations perishing with famine can extort with all their prayers no rain from her skies, and no food from her clods.

Theologians, seeking in creation the reflection

of their own idea, find marks of divine benevolence
in the animal kingdom. They point to the large
provision made for the satisfaction of animal wants,
they praise the manifest joy of living things, the
sports of young creatures, the merry gambols, the
song of birds, the aimless ecstasy of insects waltz-
ing in the sun. I am not insensible to these feli-
cities ; but here again I discern the same policy of
self-preservation which Nature exhibits in all her
works. The brute creation could not be denied
some modicum of satisfaction if the brute creation
is to hold its place in the scheme of things. Some
joy of being, some tracts of contentment there
must be in order that animal life may endure. If
the life were all, and only pain, it would long since
have failed from the earth. The question is not
whether brutes have pleasure, but whether their
pleasures exceed, or even equal, their devastations
and their pains. Who knows ? What we *do* know
is that " the whole creation groaneth and travaileth
in pain together until now."

Unfeeling is Nature, and yet how fair ! With
how bland a smile the enchantress conceals her
atrocities ! She lures with the ravishing blue of
summer seas, and hides the devil-fish and the
shark that lurk in their depths. She charms us
with " meadow, grove, and stream," and seems unconscious of the pests and the poisons which she

harbors in her bosom,—the nightshade in the glen, the rattlesnake beneath the rock. Pregnant with mischief, yet serenely fair. That surface-beauty who will deny? Whom has it not beguiled? I know it well,—the peace which steals into the soul with the contemplation of the outspread land-scape, the pensiveness, the mysterious witchery, the sense of a near and loving presence which takes us captive when the great Mother spreads her lure in sun and shade and invites us to her breast. I feel the fascination; it has constituted a large part of my enjoyment of life. But it is not there that I find any logical proof of the God of my faith. That sense of a comforting presence which we feel in our commerce with Nature, is it anything more than the soothing influence which contemplation of natural beauty exercises by drawing away the soul from itself, by hushing for a little the mordant cares, the vain desires and vain regrets, by checking the importunity of the will, and putting self-consciousness to sleep? Perhaps that enjoyment of Nature so character-istic of the modern as contrasted with the ancient world, is due to the fact that modern life is more subjective than the ancient, and finds in objective contemplation its needful complement.

Many attempts have been made to reconcile the evils of life with the belief in an omnipotent, all-wise, and beneficent God. I find no difficulty in such adjustment so far as the evils arising from the operation of natural and moral laws are concerned. Sickness, pestilence, famine, disasters by sea and land, even sin and its consequences, — social disorders, hereditary taint, — all these I see to be liabilities inherent in such a constitution of things as on the whole shall make for good and not for evil. The difficulty arrives when I detect in Nature what seems to be a malicious intent, — a quality in things animate or inanimate which must of necessity cause more pain than pleasure, and the possible good accruing from which I must believe, could have been secured by other, safer means. It is there that my theism wavers, and I see very clearly why Christian theologians have assigned the dominion of Nature to the Devil, and why all the ante-Christian religions have assumed along with their good deities an opposition dynasty of evil ones, — it was so natural to believe in an aboriginal Evil from which somehow all subsequent evil has sprung.

Must I then renounce the view without which Nature would cease to charm? Shall I refuse to see God where Spinoza saw nothing else? Something in me more persuasive than logic, in spite of the moral blank and in spite of the malignities which affront me in Nature, forces me to believe

that one Power reigns in Nature and the soul!
There must be some atoning word which recon-
ciles the holy and the hateful, the known divine
and the seeming undivine, which resolves this
dualism of nature and spirit in that deeper unity
which piety craves.

That word is *man*. The microcosm of the human world comprehends the moral and immoral,
the divine and the undivine, the holy and the
hateful, in one. In man are the heights and the
depths, the horrors and the graces; the cobra
and the scorpion are in him along with the lover
and the saint. The blessedest and the damnedest,
Satan and Christ, heaven and hell, define the
scope and measure the compass of his being.
But a true philosophy teaches that pure, unqualified malignity is not found in him; that in
man, at the vilest, the seed of God is not wholly
extinct; that, as Emerson says, "Love never
relaxes its effort;" that the Spirit will finally
prevail. And so we may believe with Paul that
the creation itself will yet be "delivered from
the bondage of corruption into the glorious liberty of the sons of God." And so we may see
reflected in that wondrous synthesis, man, the
unity of God and Nature pervading the macro-
cosm of the universe, the identity of the Holy
that inhabits eternity with the Power that works

in earth and time. But reason alone does not suffice to establish that identity, does not suffice to prove the God whom religion craves.

From the nature of the case the existence of such a God must be undemonstrable; for only that can be demonstrated which can be succinctly defined, and only that can be defined which is finite. Transcending the reach of the understanding, eluding the grasp of Science, this supreme truth will be likely, in an age in which Science is more active than Faith, to encounter opposition of the understanding, which distastes what it cannot comprehend. The atheism of Science belongs to the method of Science, and should not discredit the idea of God, which, if held at all, must be held by Faith. And let it be understood that Faith is not the resort of weakness, but a master faculty which has its rights in philosophy as well as religion; not the vassal of Tradition, but a peer of the intellectual realm, co-ordinate with Reason, and equally essential to the health and growth of the human mind.

Faith, it is true, requires the qualifying check of Science, without which she would lapse into monstrous superstition. But Science requires no less the counterpoise of Faith, without which she would soon deplete the mind of all those aspirations and hopes which sweeten and ennoble the gift of life.